FREEFALL

OTHER BOOKS AND AUDIO BOOKS
BY TRACI HUNTER ABRAMSON:

Ripple Effect

Undercurrents

The Deep End

FREEFALL

a novel

Traci Hunter Abramson

Covenant Communications, Inc.

For the dedicated individuals who protect the freedom we enjoy

ACKNOWLEDGMENTS

A special thanks to Nikki Abramson and Rebecca Cummings for your invaluable advice while this book was still in its infancy. Thank you to Kirsti Kirkland and Katie Stirling for seeing what this book could become and encouraging me to strive to make it better. Thank you to Kat Gille for shepherding this book through the publication process so efficiently and for seeing what everyone else missed. And thank you to the other wonderful people at Covenant, especially Angela Eschler and Kathryn Jenkins, for your continued support.

Finally, my continued appreciation goes to my husband and children for sharing me with the computer even when it means eating cereal for dinner, and to my extended family members, friends, and readers who continue to provide me with much needed encouragement. Without you this book wouldn't exist.

CHAPTER 1

My father is going to kill me, Amy Whitmore thought to herself. Of course that was assuming that the terrorists across the room didn't decide to take care of the job for him. Amy looked up at the two men guarding the penthouse door, automatic weapons in hand. When one glanced at her, she averted her eyes, looking back to the two-toned beige carpet, and prayed that help would arrive soon.

Why hadn't she listened? Her parents, her brothers—everyone had told her that travel in this part of the world was too risky right now. Of course that was part of the problem. They had told her. With an inward sigh, Amy wondered why she kept falling into the same trap. Ask her nicely to do something and she was bound to agree in a heart-beat. *Tell* her to do something and she would refuse twice as fast.

Still, when the job offer to work in the Diplomatic Corps had come her way, she had jumped at it. Politics had been part of her life for as long as she could remember, and working for the State Department finally gave her something that wasn't directly in her father's control.

Senator James Whitmore had been in politics since before Amy was born. The honorable senator from Virginia was well known for his honesty, his integrity, and his ability to get things done. He knew how to play the game, and he knew how often the rules changed. When he saw something he could do to make his country better, he moved forward with an intensity that was unequaled in the senate chamber.

When Amy had graduated from college, he had offered her a job working on his staff. She could admit now that she had been tempted and probably would have even accepted the job had it not been for Jared. Their brief engagement during her senior year of college had started on Christmas Eve and ended before the new year even began.

Amy had been excited about getting married, but as she prayed each night about her decision, she continued to feel uneasy. Three days after agreeing to marry Jared, she had walked into her kitchen to find her parents standing at the stove, her dad's arms wrapped around her mom's waist. The unity of their stance, the humor in their voices, and the love that flowed from them struck her, making her realize that she wanted what her parents had—which was something she couldn't find with Jared.

Jared hadn't really taken her seriously when she broke off their engagement. Instead he thought she just needed some time before she would be ready to settle down. Despite her insistence that they had no future together, Jared had simply chosen not to believe her. Not sure what else to do, Amy had let him believe whatever he wanted.

When she had turned down her dad's job offer, she had told him that she needed to live outside of the shadow of the Whitmore name for a while. To some extent, she had been telling him the truth. She needed to find an identity separate from the rest of the family. After all, it wasn't always easy being the senator's daughter. Both of her older brothers cast pretty long shadows as well. Charlie, who was two years older than she was, had just graduated from college at the top of his class, and Matt, the oldest, was playing his fourth season of major league baseball for the Florida Marlins.

At one point, Amy had planned to utilize her artistic abilities full time. After working a few summers with her dad, however, she'd decided to pursue a career in the political arena instead of developing her natural drawing ability. What she wouldn't give for a chance to go back and rethink that decision!

Taking an overseas assignment a few weeks after her college graduation had seemed exciting and ambitious. Now it just seemed dangerous.

She had barely even heard of Abolstan, the little country tucked along the Mediterranean coast between Turkey and Syria. As soon as she'd accepted the assignment, she had read everything she could get her hands on about Abolstan, including its culture, climate, and politics.

The research she had done in the weeks before her arrival had suggested that terrorist activity was inconsequential in the capital city. Obviously the person who had written that article had never stared down a man holding an AK-47.

A total of seven hostages were seated around the hotel room—five Americans and two Brits. This hotel typically housed the new arrivals for both the American and British embassies. Newly transferred employees often lived at the hotel for the first month or two until permanent apartments became available. Though the hotel was equipped with a high-end security system, it apparently wasn't good enough to withstand last night's assault, when a bomb of some sort had gone off. Seconds after the explosion, Amy and the others had been dragged out of their rooms and brought to the penthouse. Once inside the penthouse, the terrorists had separated them, making them sit far enough apart so that communication wasn't possible. One of the men guarding the door spoke English well, and Amy guessed that he had been educated in the United States.

The two armed men in the room were the latest shift of those sent to guard the hostages. She studied their faces, thinking that they would look normal if it weren't for the guns they held. She had counted at least fifteen terrorists when they had been abducted, and many of their faces were already etched into her mind. All she had to do was close her eyes and she could replay the moment her door had been kicked in.

She had originally mistaken the bomb for an earthquake and was standing in the doorway between the living area and the bedroom when her door simply fell into the room. Naively, she had thought that the two men staring at her from the hallway were part of the hotel's security staff and had come to make sure that she was okay. Then she'd seen their weapons. Eyes wide, she had just gaped at them as one trained his weapon on her. When the other man swiftly came toward her, she instinctively backed up, but she quickly realized she had nowhere to go but through the door her abductors had come through. Terrified, she had dug her heels into the carpet as the man grabbed her by the arm and dragged her into the hallway.

Any lingering hope that someone would help her disappeared when she saw six other hostages being pulled from their rooms at the same time. She considered trying to fight her way free until she saw the man next to her do just that. He took the butt of a gun to the side of his head and crumpled to the floor in pain. Amy leaned toward him to help, but the two men holding her by the arms didn't give her the opportunity. Instead, she could only watch in horror as several other hostages were brutalized for resisting. Below them, other hotel guests were screaming as they fled from the hotel.

Amy now thought the hostages had been individually targeted. Like her, all of them were new employees of their respective embassies, each of them in the process of securing a more permanent home in Abolstan. Amy was the newest arrival in the group, having landed just two weeks earlier. She had no doubt that the terrorists knew who they were and who they worked for. Specifically, they knew who her father was.

She shifted her willowy frame, leaning back against the wall. Her auburn hair was still in a ponytail from her workout on the treadmill in the hotel's gym right before their unexpected guests had arrived. Thankfully, she was still dressed comfortably in the T-shirt and sweat-pants she had worked out in.

She turned her head to the left and studied the other misfortunate souls who were sharing this misery. Each of the five men had been beaten when they had tried to resist, and she could tell that if they didn't get help soon, some of them might not last through negotiations. Frank, her new supervisor at the embassy, adjusted the bandage on his leg where he had been shot. His injury provided an example of what would happen if they didn't cooperate. For now, they had little choice.

As darkness fell outside, Amy closed her eyes against the tears that threatened. She bowed her head and once more began her silent prayers.

* * *

This isn't going to be pretty, Brent Miller thought to himself as he continued through the dark shadows into the alley behind the hotel. The back of the building was charred black from the explosion nearly twenty-four hours earlier. The doors leading to the kitchen were gone, their remnants scattered on the pavement along with fragments of broken glass from the windows on the first three floors.

Brent took a moment to consider his target. The building was twelve stories high, but light was only visible from the windows on the top floor. He scanned the fire escape on the far side of the building and the wrought-iron balconies above him. He didn't sense any movement on the first several floors, leading him to believe that he could simply enter the building and make his way upstairs.

But Brent had never been fond of obvious choices, and his training as a Navy SEAL reinforced his natural instincts. Ignoring the fire escape and the back doorway, he ran a hand over the brick and found his first handhold. Slowly, meticulously, he started his climb up the side of the building. Soot covered his fingertips as he silently stepped onto the first floor balcony and proceeded to make his way up to the next floor.

Through his headset, he heard Tristan Crowther's western drawl. "Time frame?"

"Twenty minutes," Brent answered, his voice low.

The elite five-man team was well-trained for situations like this. As a Navy SEAL, Brent knew where his teammates were and how dependent they all were on perfect timing as they worked through this operation. His job was simple enough: neutralize any terrorists with the hostages. As he approached from this side of the building, two of his teammates were moving into position from other locations to help attain their objective. All were anxious to complete this part of their assignment so they could move on to the difficult task of transporting the hostages to safety.

All of them knew what they were up against. Namir Dagan, a radical who had long been challenging for power in Abolstan, had claimed responsibility. His list of demands had been long, including the removal of all American forces from the region. Unfortunately, no one believed that he would ever release the hostages alive. Whether he got what he wanted or not, none of the hostages would survive negotiations unless Brent and his team successfully recovered them by force.

Brent edged his way past the seventh floor, sensing movement inside the dark room to the left. He worked his way farther up the building before speaking once more into the microphone. "Activity on seven, southwest corner."

"Got it." This time it was Quinn Lambert's voice that came over the mike. "I'm showing eleven heat spots on the top floor. Looks like two are in the hallway."

Brent nodded to himself, grateful that it wasn't him sitting across the street staring at the building with infrared goggles. "Give me five more minutes and I'll have a visual," Brent told him, finally climbing onto the top floor balcony. He moved to the edge of the nearest window and peered inside to count the hostages who were sitting on the floor. From his angle he could see six of the seven—one woman and five men. Two terrorists flanked the door, weapons in hand.

"I've got two guns by the door, and I've got a visual on six of the hostages." Brent relayed the information, recalling the files on the hostages. Two women had been identified as missing, one a thirty-six-year-old from London and the other a twenty-two-year-old from Virginia. The woman in his view was the older one, making the missing hostage Amy Whitmore, the senator's daughter.

He'd known who she was even before he had seen her picture. After growing up in Virginia, it would have been tough not to remember the vibrant daughter of Senator Whitmore.

Sliding down onto the balcony, Brent crawled past several windows so that he could look at the room from the other direction. A sigh of relief escaped him when he saw the younger woman sitting on the floor across the room. He knew he was only a few of years older than she was, but he couldn't help thinking how young and fragile she looked sitting there with her knees pulled up to her chest, her face pale.

A need to protect her surged through him as he studied her. She was beautiful, even in these less-than-perfect circumstances. In her photo, her gorgeous blue eyes had been alive with humor, combined with a smile that was full of fun. He hoped this experience wouldn't erase that part of her—the fun-loving manner he suspected was an integral part of her personality.

He took a moment to gauge the situation. The hostages all had their backs to him, but he had enough of an angle to recognize each of them from the pictures he had been shown during their mid-flight briefing.

One of the men was badly bruised on one side of his face, and Brent could only guess that he had tried to resist capture. A quick scan indicated that he hadn't been the only one. All five of the men appeared to need medical attention. The most visibly wounded was the man who had ripped off part of his shirt to bandage his leg. Unfortunately, the man next to him labored with each breath and appeared to be in shock.

Brent indicated to his teammates that he was in position, drew his weapon, and waited for the signal.

* * *

Amy felt the tension in the room increase as one of the gunmen spoke into his walkie-talkie in some language she couldn't identify. He scanned the room and focused in on her. She saw the intent in his eyes even before he turned his weapon on her. *I'm going to die,* she thought to herself. Terrified, she pushed back against the wall, as if those few inches might make a difference.

A moment later gunshots sounded, and then he was lying motionless at her feet. Her scream pierced the air as the window shattered and she watched wide-eyed as two men dressed completely in black jumped into the room, one from the balcony and the other through the door. The man who had come through the window stepped on the gunman's hand, which still held the weapon, and checked for a pulse. Amy didn't have to be told that the man was dead.

A helicopter echoed in the distance, but she didn't recognize the sound. Shock paralyzed her and her breath came in shallow bursts.

"Are you okay, miss?" The voice was all-American, the face smeared with something dark.

She knew he was talking to her, but her brain wasn't functioning well enough for her to think to respond. Nervously, Amy looked around the room again. The other gunman was also sprawled out lifeless on the floor. She couldn't catch her breath, and suddenly the rapid shallow breaths weren't enough. She gasped for air, her chest tightening as she struggled for another breath.

"Take it easy." The black-clad American pushed her head between her knees and spoke in a calm voice despite the gunshots that were still sounding somewhere downstairs. "We're here to take you home. You're hyperventilating. I need you to relax."

His voice was soothing, but still she struggled.

"Come on now. In, out. In, out." He put a hand on her back, rubbing it back and forth. "That's it."

His hand stilled on her back and Amy lifted her head, finally able to get some air. She noticed for the first time the communications headset he wore as he made a comment into the little microphone by his mouth. He turned his attention back to her and gave her shoulder a squeeze. "I'm going to check on the others. Just wait right here."

Amy watched him move effortlessly from one hostage to another as his partner started at the other end and worked toward him. They gave each of the hostages whatever emergency medical treatment was necessary to transport them. Finally, he moved back to where she was still sitting.

"Can you walk?"

Amy nodded, chastising herself for falling apart. Still shaking, she pointed across the room. "Is Frank okay? He was shot in the leg."

The man nodded. "He'll be fine. The members of my team are going to move the wounded into the helicopter, and then we'll get you out of here."

He took up a position by the door, weapon in hand, as two other men came in and helped move the wounded out of the room. He appeared completely in tune with everything around him, but his stance was relaxed.

Amy watched him, wondering what it must be like to work in the armed forces. He probably didn't have any idea where he would be next month, or even next week, but would just be going where his superiors sent him. She shook her head, surprised that her mind was wandering at a time such as this. Still, she was grateful that there were people like him in the world—people who were willing to sacrifice their personal freedoms to protect her safety.

When the last of the wounded had finally been escorted out along with the other female hostage, the man returned to Amy and reached out a hand. "Come on. Let's get you out of here."

Amy let him pull her to her feet and was surprised when she had to tilt her head back to look at him. At six feet tall, she was used to looking most men in the eye. "Can I ask you a question?" she asked. When he nodded, she continued. "What's your name?"

He smiled at that as though they had just met at the grocery store instead of in the middle of a rescue operation. "Lieutenant Brent Miller, U.S. Navy SEAL."

"Well, Lieutenant." Amy brushed off her sweatpants and turned her gaze back to Brent. "Thanks for dropping by."

"Anytime."

CHAPTER 2

Brent pushed open the door to the roof, where Tristan was helping the British woman onto the helicopter. The hostages needing medical attention were already settled in the back of the 72-foot-long helicopter along with Quinn. The rest of the team had already taken their seats as well, except for Kel, who was waiting for Brent by the door.

Brent took Amy's hand in his and pulled her to a ducking position as he escorted her to the waiting chopper. They were barely inside when his commanding officer yelled to the pilot.

"All bodies in!" Kel shouted, motioning for them to strap in as he took his own seat. "Let's get outta here!"

Still holding onto her arm, Brent helped Amy into a seat as they took off. A moment later a bright light flashed and the helicopter rocked violently. Sparks flew from the door next to Amy, and flames licked along the bottom of the doorway. A split second later, the door latch sparked and the door crashed open. Tristan grabbed a fire extinguisher and doused the flames in the now-open doorway.

"Where's it coming from?" Quinn shouted over the cries of the hostages.

"Looks like another terrorist cell in that building. There's an anti-aircraft gun on the roof," Kel answered, pulling his microphone in front of his mouth to communicate with the pilot as they increased altitude. "How bad are we hit?"

"We're okay as long as we get out of range fast," the pilot told him, already turning the helicopter away from the threat. "We just got word that the insurgence is spreading. Everyone is pulling out."

Kel turned his attention to Tristan, who had abandoned the fire extinguisher and now had both gloved hands on what was left of the door handle. "Get that door closed."

"It's jammed. I can't close it."

"Then get strapped in."

Tristan reclaimed his seat and glanced at Amy, who was staring wide-eyed at the charred black edges that surrounded the open doorway next to her. Tristan pointed to the seat belt that was not yet fastened around her. "Get buckled in!"

Before Amy could comply, the helicopter rocked violently onto its side to avoid another attack. Brent heard Amy's scream and turned just in time to see her tumble out of her seat and grasp for something to hold onto. Another evasive maneuver by the pilot sent her sliding toward the hole where the door should have been. Brent tore off his seat belt and lunged after her, sprawling out on the floor of the helicopter that was currently at a forty-five degree angle. He grabbed Amy's wrist just as her body slid through the doorway into open space.

Brent felt someone grab his feet to keep him from tumbling out right after her, but his eyes stayed on Amy. Her body was dangling in the air, her blue eyes wide with shock and fear. The angle of the helicopter made it impossible for her to reach the landing skid to stop her fall or use it to help herself climb back in.

His own upper body was hanging halfway out of the helicopter, and he could feel at least two of his teammates struggling to support his weight along with Amy's. The pilot's voice came over his headset. "The horizontal stabilizer must be damaged. Get everything secured. It's going to be a bumpy ride."

Brent reached down with his other arm to grasp her wrist, hoping to pull her in, but gravity was an opponent he wasn't able to overcome. He saw her awareness. She knew that the only thing keeping her from plummeting more than thirty feet to the ground was the slippery grip Brent had on her arm. She was a hanging target as the pilot tried to move out of the city with gunfire sounding in the streets below.

She was slipping, and Brent knew that it was only a matter of time before his grip faltered. He could hear one of his teammates trying to edge in beside him, but the angle of the helicopter was still tilted dangerously to one side. Another minute hanging and one of the antiaircraft guns was bound to get a clean shot.

A split second was all it took for Brent to make his decision. He wasn't going to let this woman die like this, and he knew all of the hostages were at risk until they cleared the border. Brent called out to Kel.

"Have the pilot head for the biggest roof he can find." Brent kept his eyes on Amy's. "Preferably in a nice dark corner of the city."

"We're losing fuel." Kel's voice came over the headset Brent wore. "If you can't bring her in now, we may not get another chance."

"I'm going with her," Brent said, instantly hearing scrambling going on behind him. He knew the risks, but sometimes the only way to save something was to let it go. If they were losing fuel, they might not be able to take off again if they landed. Since his grip wasn't solid enough to pull her in at this angle, he had no other choice.

The helicopter dropped altitude, and Brent prayed that he could hold on long enough. Amy's eyes were huge as she realized there was no way she could get back into the helicopter.

The rooftops below them grew closer and closer to Amy's feet as they dropped altitude, but Amy didn't look down. Her eyes were locked on Brent's as he fought to hold onto her. Brent felt himself slide another inch out the door, the sweat of his hands on Amy's arm making it nearly impossible to maintain his grip. He felt her slipping, his heart pounding as her arm slid through his hands. She screamed. Brent leaned a little farther out of the helicopter, trying to reclaim his grip.

Just as her fingers started to slip free, Kel's voice came over Brent's earpiece. "Now!"

Brent didn't hesitate. He felt the hands on his ankles release, and he let go of Amy and allowed his body to fall forward out of the helicopter. He tucked his head and a split second later rolled onto an unforgiving hard surface a few feet from where Amy had landed.

Brent turned to see a package drop onto the far side of the roof as Amy shifted beside him. He crawled over to her to check for injuries. "Are you okay?"

Amy shook her head and looked at him like he was crazy. Stunned, she pointed above them. "We just fell out of a helicopter."

"Are you injured?" Brent corrected.

She considered for a moment before answering. "I don't think so."

As soon as the words were out of her mouth, Brent's attention shifted to the helicopter above them. He could see the fuel spraying out into the air, and he spoke into his microphone.

"You're losing fuel fast. Get out of here." Even as Amy started to protest beside him, he held up a hand to silence her. "We'll get our feet wet and see you in a few days."

Kel's voice came back. "I'm going to drop Quinn first."

"Negative. You have the wounded. If you land early, you're going to need all the hands you've got," Brent replied. A second later the helicopter elevated and moved off into the dark sky.

"Are you nuts?" Amy sat up, her eyes wide as she looked from Brent to the helicopter and back to Brent again. "You sent them away?"

"At the rate they're losing fuel, I'm not sure they'll make it past the border as it is." Brent scanned the rooftops nearby as he spoke. "If they take the time to pick us up, and add the additional weight, all of us would be on foot long before we reached the border. The others need medical attention. You don't."

The shock faded and was replaced by concern. "Do you think they'll make it?"

"They have a good chance." Brent studied her, pleased that she was already working through her shock. "If not, they'll land and have to carry the wounded out or hide until it's safe to send another chopper in after them."

Amy took a deep breath. "What about us? Are we waiting for another helicopter?"

Brent shook his head. "The city is too dangerous to risk sending in another crew to look for us. We're going to have to take care of ourselves."

"And you're okay with this?" Disbelief filled her voice, and again she questioned his sanity.

"Just part of the job." Brent motioned for her to stay where she was while he went to the far side of the roof and retrieved the pack his teammates had dropped. As soon as he was beside her once more, he opened the black backpack and started pulling out pieces of clothing.

"Here, put these on."

Amy started to question why, but reconsidered. She pulled the black pants over her sweats, noticing for the first time that her pant leg was torn. She then proceeded to do the same with the matching hooded poncho. When she finished, she turned to find Brent staring at her. She felt her cheeks flushing under the intensity of his gaze.

"Look, before we start out, you need to understand what we're up against," Brent started. "Insurgents are taking over sections of the city, and we have no idea how hostile it's going to get. If I tell you to do something, you can't take the time to ask questions. You just have to do it."

Amy sighed with resignation. "This will be a lot easier for me if I understand what we're about to do."

"Fair enough." Brent motioned to the escape ladder on the far side of the roof. "We're going to start by going down that ladder. If the street is quiet, we'll try to move out of the city. If not, we're going to find someplace to hide out for tonight. Either way, we're going to make our way to the nearest port, where we'll secure transportation out of here."

"Please tell me it's going to be as easy as you make it sound."

Brent shrugged. He needed her trust, but he wasn't going to lie. "I'm afraid this job doesn't come with guarantees."

* * *

Amy saw Brent's hand go up, signaling for her to stop. She pressed her body against the building they were passing and froze. He had explained that in their dark clothing, if they could stay in the buildings' shadows, they would be invisible to anyone passing by. The trick was staying perfectly still and not looking at them.

She heard footsteps approaching and concentrated on keeping her breathing steady. Not looking up when she heard voices took considerable effort, but thankfully they faded into the distance instead of moving closer. Without a word, Brent tapped her shoulder and started quietly down the alleyway once more.

Amy followed Brent silently, perfectly aware that he held her life and her future in his hands. Without him, she would remain lost in this country that was now on the brink of civil war. Finally, after what seemed like hours of slipping through shadows, they reached the edge of the city.

Something rumbled in the distance as they emerged onto an empty street. In front of them was nothing but darkness. In the distance, the black sky was beginning to turn a deep blue, indicating that the sun would be up in less than an hour.

Brent turned to her and spoke in a low voice. "How are you doing?"

"Okay, I guess." Amy shrugged. "Why?"

"That noise in the distance is enemy tanks coming in to occupy the city. We need to put some miles between us and them." Brent pointed at the still-dark eastern sky. "There's nothing but open desert for the next five miles. We have to get past that before the sun comes up."

"Just point me in the right direction." Amy shook out her arms and ignored the pounding of her heart.

"Let's go." Brent started out at a brisk pace, following the paved road. Less than a mile later, he left the main road and veered off into the sandy desert.

Amy kept up with him, ignoring the way her calves were tightening as she continued to push herself. The lack of sleep was starting to wear on her as the adrenaline that came from fear began to subside. In the distance the sky was lightening, and she could only wonder how far they had already gone.

They came over a rise just as the sun started to break through. Below was a cluster of buildings, a dilapidated car parked next to one of them. Brent crouched down behind an outcropping of rocks and motioned for Amy to do the same. He just stared for a moment, his body motionless. Then he eased himself down onto the ground and pulled out his canteen.

Amy sat down beside him, reaching her hand out when he passed the canteen to her. She took a sip, concerned that the canteen only appeared half full, and the desert and rocky terrain in front of them stretched on as far as she could see. Though it was still spring, Amy knew how hot days in Abolstan could get.

Glancing over at Brent, she started to ask what came next but suddenly was wary of making any sound. He had his binoculars out and was scanning the nearby hills. He then turned his gaze back to the buildings below.

As the horizon lightened, Amy looked around, realizing how vulnerable they were. If anyone flew overhead, they would stand out in their dark clothes against the desert sand. The night chill was also quickly dissipating, making her wish for somewhere to change so she could shed her extra pair of pants.

Wearily, she settled against a rock and let her eyes droop closed. She couldn't remember the last time she had slept, and her arms and legs felt like lead. The noise of an engine startled her awake, and Brent put a hand on her shoulder to hold her down so she wouldn't reveal their position. Fully aware of the danger, she nodded, unsure how long she had dozed.

She heard a vehicle driving away and wondered how long they were going to just sit there. Five minutes passed before Brent moved once more. "Stay here. I'll be right back."

Without any further explanation, he moved down to the buildings below. The minutes stretched out as Amy struggled with her current reality. What would she do if something happened to Brent? How could she possibly find her way out of this country by herself? She didn't have any identification or money. In fact, the only things she did have were the clothes on her back.

At least thirty minutes passed before Brent finally reappeared at her side. Over his shoulder was a canteen fashioned out of leather, and his dark hair was now covered in some sort of cloth head-covering similar to what she had seen many of the locals wear. He held a similar headpiece out to her.

"Put this on. We're going to move into the hills and find some shade so we can get some sleep." Brent offered her a drink from the water bag. "When it cools down again tonight, we'll try to put some distance between us and the city."

"Exactly how far do we have to go?"

"It's not too far," Brent assured her with a quick grin that belied the seriousness of their situation. "We should be able to make it to the coast in two or three days."

"Days?" Amy's eyes widened. "How many miles are we talking about here?"

"Less than a hundred." Brent started toward the hills. "The faster we get into the hills, the sooner you can get some sleep. Trust me, you'll feel better once you get some rest."

"I'll feel better when I'm back in Virginia," Amy muttered, but she stood and obediently followed.

CHAPTER 3

"Have you heard anything yet?" Senator James "Jim" Whitmore cradled the phone next to his ear, his arm around his wife, Katherine.

FBI agent Doug Valdez's voice came over the line from his office in Miami. "Let me check and see if any more news has come through in the past hour or so. It will just take a minute." His close friendship with the senator's eldest son, Matt, had made him practically part of the Whitmore family, and he just prayed that any news he found would be good news.

Jim held back a sigh as he looked down at his wife's normally serene face. Anguish and worry showed in her eyes as they continued to wait for news about their only daughter. Jim supposed it should be easier getting information about Amy from Doug Valdez than from someone they didn't know, but right now all he wanted was to hear that Amy was safe and on her way home.

Across the room, Charlie, the younger of their two sons, paced back and forth. He had the look of his father, standing a few inches over six feet, with short blond hair and piercing blue eyes. At twenty-four years old, Charlie's only cares had been earning money for law school and balancing an active social life until he had received the phone call about his sister. His easy-going manner had disappeared in an instant, and he had immediately joined his family in focusing on one goal: seeing Amy safely home.

After an interminably long minute, Doug's voice came over the line again. "It looks like we do have some new developments." He took a deep breath before speaking once more. "We have every reason to believe that Amy is still okay," he started. "The special unit we sent in crossed the border early this morning with the hostages. Unfortunately, Amy wasn't with them."

Jim's heartbeat accelerated and his hold on his wife tightened. He forced himself to ask the obvious question, "Then where is she?"

"She's still in Abolstan. There was a problem with the helicopter. One of the team members stayed behind and will bring her home. Unfortunately, because the insurgents have taken over the capital city and some of the surrounding countryside, we expect it to take a few days for them to make their way to where they can secure transportation."

"This can't be happening," Jim muttered even as he turned to his wife and mouthed that Amy was okay. "Do we have any communication with the man escorting her?"

"He does have communication equipment with him, but he likely won't risk using it for fear that it might be traced," Doug informed him. "We expect that he'll make contact with us as soon as they're out of the country."

Jim closed his eyes for a moment. His baby girl was somewhere behind enemy lines and he couldn't do anything about it but trust some man he had never met to bring her safely home. He glanced over at Charlie, who was waiting with anticipation for any news, and then asked about his oldest son. "How is Matt holding up?"

"He's worried," Doug admitted. "He's here in Miami for his game tonight, but he has tomorrow off, so he's going to head up to Virginia after his game ends."

"It will be good to have him home."

"There's one more thing, Senator . . ." Doug hesitated. "You and your family have to proceed as though Amy is with the other hostages. If the press realizes she isn't with them, they'll start announcing to the terrorists that she's still in Abolstan. We're going to try to keep the story quiet until she's safely home, which shouldn't be too difficult since most of the hostages will be in the hospital for at least several days."

Jim closed his eyes as reality overwhelmed him. "I understand."

As soon as he hung up, he relayed the information to Katherine and Charlie. Then he did the only thing he could do: he knelt down with his wife and son and prayed for his missing daughter.

* * *

Brent bowed his head in prayer, silently running the words through his head for fear that if he said them out loud they might be heard by more than just Amy Whitmore. His five-man unit was the only one he knew of that was made up entirely of Latter-day Saints, and they had long ago established the practice of opening each day with a prayer. He wasn't about to change that habit now, especially knowing that he still had to go eighty miles with a civilian in tow before he could secure transportation to safety.

He ended his silent prayer and turned to look at Amy sleeping just a few yards away. Her color was better than it had been the night before, her hair falling loosely over the hard ground. In more ways than one, she wasn't what he expected. From her photo, he already knew that she was beautiful and vibrant. He hadn't realized, however, that she was six feet tall. That fact was actually helpful at this point, since she could pass for a man as long as her hair was hidden and she was wearing baggy clothes.

Still, as the daughter of a U.S. senator, Brent had expected her to be more trouble. She hadn't made the common complaints yet about fatigue, their sleeping arrangements, or the food. She had instinctively rationed her water intake as though she, too, was aware that what little they had would have to last. Throughout the night, despite her exhaustion, she had kept up without too much trouble. And she didn't speak unless she was spoken to, allowing him to concentrate on their mission of getting out of here rather than worrying that she might start jabbering at an inopportune moment.

He imagined she had spent a few weeks of her teenage years "roughing it" in girls' camp, though he doubted she had ever expected to use any of her basic survival skills in the middle of the desert. Just about everyone in Virginia knew that the Whitmore family was LDS, and Brent hoped that Amy had a deep well of faith to rely on over the next couple of days.

He pulled his gaze away from her and looked out over the horizon. The sun had already dropped behind the hills in the distance, and he hoped to set out in less than an hour. As the heat started to dissipate, he thought of how different this assignment was from the experience that had started him on this path.

He had only been seventeen when he and three teammates had been on their way back from the state high school swimming championships.

Suddenly a blizzard hit in southeastern Virginia. His coach, who also happened to be his mother, made the decision to stop for the night when they were at least twenty miles from any towns. Still she had managed to find them shelter, even though it ended up being the top-secret variety.

One of her friends had been a chief of something-or-other at "The Farm," the training facility for the Central Intelligence Agency. He hadn't been happy to see five civilians on the doorstep of the secure location, but he had made arrangements to house them until the storm passed and the roads were cleared.

Brent had always known that his mother had worked for the CIA before he was born, but spending those few days snowed in at the CIA's training facility and seeing the level of security had brought home a reality he had never before considered. His mom, in her own small way, had helped keep their country safe for a time. From that point on, Brent had been headed in this direction. He wanted a chance to help protect the freedoms he had always enjoyed and often taken for granted.

He sensed movement behind him and turned to see Amy move to the cave opening. "Did you sleep okay?" he asked.

He expected her to complain about sleeping on solid rock, but instead she just nodded. Her eyes were somber. He sensed that she knew he was her only way out of here and it scared her. If he had to guess, he doubted Amy Whitmore was accustomed to relying on anyone but herself. She was clearly in uncharted waters and didn't look too happy about it.

"Are you ready to set out?"

Amy nodded again. "Yeah."

Brent passed her the water bag, watching her take a drink as he dug an energy bar out of his pack. "Eat this. Just make sure you put all of the wrappers into your bag. We don't want anyone to be able to track us."

"What about footprints?" She pointed down at her running shoes.

"The wind will take care of most of that for us," Brent told her. "Besides, we don't know if anyone even realizes that we're here. The terrorists that were holding you probably think we made it out on the chopper with everyone else."

"I would think someone would notice two people falling out of a helicopter."

"Not when they're more concerned about the shooting going on right outside their windows." He motioned to the open terrain in front of them. "Come on. The farther we get from the city, the less likely it is that anyone will be looking for us."

* * *

Amy moved forward, concentrating only on following Brent. She wasn't sure how long they had been walking, but her body told her they had traveled a good distance from where they had started. The darkness was broken up only by the stars in the sky and a sliver of the moon.

Brent had continued at a steady pace, stopping only once for a few minutes to drink some water and eat another portion of his energy bar. Amy couldn't say she liked the taste of hers, but it was better than nothing. Their water supply was holding so far, thanks to the water bag Brent had commandeered the day before. At the same time he had filled the water bag, he had also refilled his canteen and the water bottle that was in his backpack.

The muscles in her legs were screaming with fatigue, but Amy had stopped listening to their complaints a few hours earlier. She couldn't imagine how she would have been able to make this trek had she not already been in shape. As she watched Brent walk in front of her, she realized that maybe she wasn't in as good of shape as she thought. He didn't look like he was even winded, and they had been walking for hours.

Shadows of what looked like mountain ranges stretched out on either side of the flat, open area they had been traveling through. They were nearing one of them as she saw the glow of lights in the distance and Brent signaled for her to stop. She wondered if he even realized that he was using hand signals to communicate with her despite the fact that she had never been told what they meant. Still, somehow she had adapted, and when the signal came to take cover, she moved silently with him against a large boulder.

She didn't even have to watch for the signal to stay, already anticipating that he was about to go exploring once more without her. He slipped off his backpack and set it beside her before moving off into the night. Quietly, she settled down in the sand. Ignoring the tension that was settling in her shoulders, she stretched her feet out in front of her and pulled up on her toes to stretch out the muscles in her calves.

Already Brent was out of sight, and she wished he had told her exactly where he was going and how long he was going to be. Her next thought was that in his business he probably didn't know the answers to those kinds of questions. What must it be like, she wondered, to try to have a relationship with someone who could simply vanish right in front of your eyes?

She pushed away that thought, instead leaning back and looking up at the stars. Without the lights of the city to compete with, they dominated the sky. She couldn't ever remember seeing so many before, and she thought of those summer nights when she would ride her horse down to the park near her house and camp by the river. It was the only time she could remember just lying on the ground and staring up into the sky. What she wouldn't give right now to be out for a leisurely ride, galloping through the trees with her hair blowing behind her.

When Amy heard horses in the distance, she thought perhaps she had imagined it. As the sound grew closer, she stood and settled Brent's pack on her back. She pressed back against the rock, remembering what Brent had told her about staying still and controlling her breathing. She kept her eyes on the ground and struggled not to gasp when half a dozen horses and their riders passed within five yards of where she was standing.

A moment later, at least ten more horses pounded over the rise, apparently in pursuit of the first group that had passed. The gunshots didn't register at first, but the cry in the distance made them reality.

She was afraid to move, and equally afraid not to. What if Brent had been caught in the crossfire? And what would happen if she was still here when the sun came up? There was no way she could survive the day out in the desert without some sort of shelter. Besides the obvious threat of the armed men nearby, the heat from the desert could be deadly.

"Please let him be okay," Amy whispered, praying Brent back to her. She tried to think positive thoughts, wondering what he would look like without his face painted with camouflage. His eyes were dark and serious, and his rugged features made her think he would look just a little dangerous, even if he wasn't carrying a gun.

She wondered what he did for fun when he wasn't flying all over the world rescuing hostages. They had been together for over thirty hours straight, and she realized she knew nothing about him. She didn't know where he was from or if he had family. Did he have a wife or a girlfriend back home worrying about him the way her family was surely worrying about her? Or would his family even know that there was something to worry about?

Amy's mind raced with questions as shots continued to ring out in the distance. Minutes passed slowly, and she finally took a seat once more as silence replaced chaos. Her body was shaking with fear and tension, and she was beginning to think she had no other choice but to move forward alone.

Another fifteen minutes, she promised herself. She would wait that long before heading for the distant hills that would hopefully offer her some shelter during the day and also give her a bird's-eye view of the terrain below. Fifteen minutes passed, and then five more. Panicked that Brent must have been one of the victims in the skirmish over an hour before, Amy stood and prepared to set out. Somehow she had to find a way to send for help.

She heard her name whispered softly. Whirling around, she saw Brent standing behind her.

"I was so worried!" Not thinking, she moved into his arms and held on. Warmth washed through her as one of his arms came around her waist. She shifted to look up at him, sliding her hand down onto his arm. It was only then she noticed the slick wetness on her fingers. Her eyes widened, and she tried to stem the panic attempting to surface. "You're bleeding!"

"We have to get you out of here," Brent told her, leaning against the boulder for support.

"Can you make it up to those rocks?" Amy asked warily. "I thought there might be some caves where we could hide."

Brent nodded. He didn't release her, instead allowing Amy to keep her arm around him and support some of his weight. They moved slowly, barely making it to the protection of some caves as the sun rose in the east.

Amy helped Brent sit down at the mouth of a shallow cave and immediately shed her pack to take a look at the damage. "Take off your shirt," she told him, reaching to help him undo the buttons. He winced in pain as he shifted and let Amy help him remove his combat vest and his shirt to reveal his bulletproof vest. Beneath the vest was a T-shirt, the right sleeve red with blood.

Brent looked down at his arm. "I can't tell if the bullet passed through."

Amy took a deep breath. She moved to examine the wound, finding the small hole where the bullet had entered the fleshy part of his arm just below his sleeve. Gently, she then lifted his arm to study the underside, where a larger wound was still bleeding. "It looks like it passed through, but the exit wound doesn't look good."

Brent leaned back against the wall of the cave. "Look in my combat vest. There's a med kit in one of the pockets."

Amy started riffling through the pockets. That's when she saw a hole in his vest, this one without an accompanying bloodstain.

"Were you shot more than once?"

"I got hit once in the vest. It just bruised a couple of ribs."

"I'm afraid it did more than that." Amy held up the remains of his communications headset.

Brent closed his eyes in frustration.

Amy opened another pocket, this time coming across a pocket-sized Book of Mormon. "You're Mormon?" she asked, surprised.

"Yeah." Brent nodded. "The med kit should be in the next pocket over."

Still absorbing this new information, she opened the next pocket and found the medical supplies. She pulled out a plastic bag that contained an assortment of items, including bandages. She found some antiseptic and applied it to both wounds. Brent winced in pain but said nothing as she went about cleaning the wound.

"There's a syringe with a local anesthetic in there. I'm going to need you to give me a shot of that, and then try to stitch up the wound," Brent told her. She glanced up at him quickly, her eyes wide with surprise. "I'll lose too much blood otherwise," he explained. "And we don't want anyone to be able to track us."

Amy's heart lodged in her throat as she considered actually using a needle and thread on human skin. Skeptically, she asked, "Are you sure you trust me to do this?"

"I'll walk you through it," Brent assured her. "Just give me the shot and wait a few minutes. Then you can start sewing me up."

"You make it sound like I'm in home ec class."

His eyebrows lifted. "Did you ever take home ec?"

"Would you feel better if I lied and said yes?"

The corner of his mouth quirked up. "Probably, but either way, you're all I've got. I can't do it myself."

Amy nodded, wincing as she inserted the syringe into his arm. Brent told her what she needed to do. When his arm was numb, Amy tried to imagine that she was dealing with fabric instead of human flesh. She took a deep breath, fighting back the wave of nausea that washed over her. Slowly, meticulously, she inserted the needle and started on the entry wound. It only took four stitches, though she probably could have done it in three larger ones.

She tied off the sutures the way Brent told her to, and then she turned to the more difficult task of stitching up the exit wound. Unlike the first one, the skin was torn apart and not easy to repair. She took another deep breath and started once more. Again, she kept her stitches small, hoping that she was performing the task correctly. In the back of her mind, she wondered if he would really be able to recover enough to travel.

When she was finally done, her fingers were cramping and her back was knotted with tension. She let out the breath she didn't realize she had been holding, concerned that the exit wound still looked pretty ragged. "I think I'm done."

Brent looked down at her handiwork and then looked back at her, his eyebrows raised. "I thought you said you didn't take home ec."

"I didn't, but I do have a mother who insisted on teaching me how to sew." Amy shrugged. "Somehow I don't think this is quite what she had in mind."

"I'll have to make sure I thank her when we get home."

"Where is home for you?"

"Same as you. Virginia."

CHAPTER 4

The throbbing in his arm woke him while the sun was still high in the sky. Brent closed his eyes against the pain, willing it to go away. Realizing that willpower alone wasn't going to work, he shifted so that he could reach for his shirt where Amy had put his med kit after she finished with it.

"I'll get it." Amy moved forward and picked up his shirt. "What do you need?"

"There should be some painkillers in there."

Nodding, Amy unzipped a pocket and held out his choices for him. "Maybe you should consider the prescription stuff."

Brent shook his head. "If I do that, we won't be able to travel tonight."

"That might be the wisest decision we can make right now," Amy told him. "It isn't going to do us any good if you don't heal a bit before we set out again."

"The longer we stay here, the more likely it is that we'll be found." Brent nodded at the terrain leading up to where they were. "I probably left a blood trail that just about anyone could find."

"I already took care of that," Amy told him.

Brent's voice turned sharp. "What do you mean you took care of it?"

"I went back down and covered up all of the bloodstains so that no one would notice it." Amy looked at him apologetically. "I had to use up some of our water to get rid of the blood on the boulder though."

"You went down there? By yourself?" Brent's eyes widened with disbelief. "You could have been seen."

"It had to be done." Amy pulled out his canteen and handed it to him, along with a dose of medicine. "Besides, now we can stay here for the night and let you rest."

The throbbing was making it impossible to think straight. If the blood trail was really gone, they would be better off taking a day to rest. Frustrated that they were even in this position, Brent accepted the canteen and the pills she offered him. After downing the medicine, he turned back to look at her.

"Why haven't you gotten any sleep?" Brent asked. "You have to be exhausted."

"I took a nap a while ago." Amy hesitated a moment. "Can you tell me what happened last night?"

Brent shifted, closing his eyes for a moment while he waited for the medicine to take effect. When he opened his eyes, Amy was still staring at him.

"With the exception of a few of the militant groups, this area is mostly uninhabited. I had hoped we could pass by without being seen, but when I saw that light, I wanted to see what we were up against." Brent took another sip of water. "I found a good-sized base right in our path, probably one of the local tribes that keeps challenging the government for power."

"How can you tell?"

"Regular military would have equipment, Jeeps, that sort of thing. These guys have horses and are as ragtag as they come." Brent took a deep breath as the pain started to ease. "I was circling back to you when another group came out of the hills. It sounded like they were warring factions from the same group. Anyway, a couple of stray shots caught me when I was trying to take cover."

"I was so worried about you," Amy admitted.

"I was worried about you too." Brent reached out and took her hand. He hadn't even realized he had done it until Amy shifted to sit closer to him. Then it seemed silly to take his hand back. "I saw those men come right past you and I couldn't tell if . . ." His voice trailed off.

"I'm fine, thanks to you." Amy gave his hand a squeeze. "I did what you told me and faded into the shadows."

Brent felt himself drifting, Amy's hand still warm in his. He looked at her, for the first time noticing the bloodstain on her sleeve from when she had hugged him hours before. He wondered if he would have a chance to hold her again under different circumstances. With that thought on his mind, he drifted off to sleep.

* * *

"I can't believe they haven't heard anything." Matt Whitmore paced across his parents' living room, nearly colliding with Charlie. For the past five years, Matt had enjoyed a successful career in major league baseball along with the financial benefits that went with it. Even more importantly, he and his wife, CJ, were grateful that they could live together safely.

CJ had been even younger than Amy when she had entered the Witness Protection Program after witnessing a friend's murder. Of course, CJ had only been hiding from the men involved in the smuggling operation she had helped expose. Amy was hiding from an entire country.

Frustrated, Matt ran a hand over his face. More than once he and CJ had faced men with guns aimed in their direction, but he never expected that any of his family would confront that kind of terror again. He could feel his perspective shifting as he thought of his sister. Up until a couple of days ago, his only real problem had been finding time to spend with his family during baseball season. Now, all he could think about was how his sister was going to get home.

"Doug said we probably wouldn't hear anything before tomorrow," CJ reminded her husband, even though she was just as impatient and worried as he was.

"Mama!" A little voice sounded from the kitchen. "Horsies!"

CJ turned to see her eighteen-month-old daughter in her mother-in-law's arms. Katherine forced a smile. "Kailey wants to go up to the barn."

"I'll take her." CJ stood up, her stomach just starting to show the signs of her pregnancy.

"No, honey." Matt stopped his pacing and turned to his wife. He laid a hand on her arm and kissed her cheek. "I'll do it. I need something to take my mind off of this." He crossed to his mother and took his daughter into his arms. "Besides, it's not often enough I get to spend time with my little girl."

"Daddy!" Kailey grinned as she shifted into Matt's arms.

"I'll come with you," Jim told his son.

Together they went through the kitchen and out the back door toward the narrow path leading through the thick trees behind the house. They walked up the path together in silence, Kailey squealing in delight when they reached the opening where the stable was located. Two horses were in the pasture, standing in the shade of the barn.

Matt moved closer so that his daughter could pet one of the horses. He set her down, taking her by the hand to keep her safe.

"You know, it seems like just yesterday that you were this age," Jim said. "I don't know where the time goes."

"I know. I just can't stop thinking about Amy. It wasn't that long ago that she was sixteen and Charlie and I were taking turns intimidating her boyfriends." Matt shook his head. "Now she's all grown up and we have no idea when she's coming home."

"I never should have let her go." Jim's voice was filled with anguish. "I should have stopped her."

"Nothing any of us said would have stopped her," Matt told him. Then, as though reading his father's thoughts, he added, "And if you had pulled strings to keep her from going, she never would have forgiven you."

"Logically, I know you're right." Jim watched his granddaughter petting the horse. "But emotionally, I feel like I failed by letting her go somewhere where I couldn't protect her."

They stood there for a moment in silence. Kailey moved closer to the corral, and Jim scooped her up in his arms before Matt had the chance.

"How about giving your grandpa a big hug?" Jim asked, running a hand over her blond curls.

"Kiss!" She puckered her little lips and leaned forward to kiss her grandpa on the cheek.

Jim turned to Matt with tears in his eyes. "Enjoy your kids while they're little. They grow up too fast."

Matt nodded, his own eyes moist. "I will, Dad."

* * *

"Is there anything I can do?" CJ asked her mother-in-law.

"I'm just glad you and Matt were able to come up for the day." Katherine stood in the kitchen peeling potatoes.

"Actually, if you don't mind, I thought I might stay a little longer," CJ said casually. "Most of Matt's games are on the road this week."

Katherine looked up, hope filling her eyes. "I would love it if you could stay."

"Thank you." CJ smiled. She didn't have to explain to Katherine that she didn't want to be home alone while Matt was on the road with his baseball team, or that she didn't want to have to drag Kailey on a road trip where she would be stuck inside a hotel room all day. She thought of Amy, afraid to mention her, and equally afraid not to. "Maybe we can have a big family dinner on Sunday night. If I remember correctly, Matt's game is in the afternoon. By then, we should have Amy home."

"I hope so." Katherine set a potato aside and looked up at her. CJ looked like a typical young wife and mother, but her life had been in jeopardy more than once after witnessing a friend's murder. "I just can't believe that after all we went through with you and Matt we have to go through something like this again."

"Yes, but I was in the Witness Protection Program for three years. Hopefully Amy will be home in three days." CJ knew what it was like to face danger, but she had never before played this waiting game. "Was this what it was like for you when I was in hiding?"

Katherine shrugged. "In some ways. There were days when everything seemed so normal, and then I would see something on the news about a shooting or a car bomb and I would realize that it could be you." She hesitated a moment. "Now I'm afraid to watch the news. I'm afraid of what I might see."

"You know, when you're in these kinds of situations, you just react," CJ told her, thinking of the numerous times she had heard gunshots fired in her direction. "You do whatever it takes to survive. Amy is young, and she's strong. She's not going to just give up over there. She's doing everything she can to get back here so that we can all yell at her for not listening to us."

Katherine laughed despite herself. "She has always been stubborn."

"That could be a good thing right now."

CHAPTER 5

"Why are you being so stubborn?" Amy stood with her hands on her hips as Brent continued to argue with her. "I just want to see if I can find some water."

"With hundreds of insurgents in the valley right below us," Brent pointed out.

"Insurgents with horses," Amy reminded him. "Horses can't travel through these rocks, and I have to imagine that there is some kind of natural water source around here or those men down there wouldn't have horses."

"Are you always this difficult?"

Amy stopped a moment and considered his question. Finally she nodded. "Yes. I think I am." She poured the remaining water from the water bag into Brent's canteen and then stood once more. "The sun is already starting to set. I'm just going to look around for a few minutes. If I don't find anything, I'll be right back."

Brent sighed in frustration. She had clearly gotten over her initial shock about their situation, moved past the realization that she couldn't get home without him, and jumped right into an equal partnership he wasn't so sure he wanted. Whatever tender moment they had shared as he had drifted off to sleep earlier was now lost in the battle. Resigned, he pulled up his pant leg, revealing a pistol. "At least take this with you."

Amy stared at him for a moment before reluctantly moving forward to accept the weapon he held out to her.

"Do you know how to use it?"

Amy nodded. "Yes." Her father had taken her to the shooting range to teach her how to use a gun when she was a teenager. She checked the weapon, made sure the safety was on, and then slipped it into the pocket of the backpack she now thought of as her own. "I'll see you in a few minutes."

"If you're gone over thirty minutes, I'm coming after you."

"I'll be back before dark." With that, Amy stepped out of the cave and started farther up into the rock formation. She tried to imagine she was spelunking in the caves of West Virginia with her dad and brothers, but she couldn't quite pull it off. She found two caves, but she estimated that both of them were too shallow to provide any kind of water source. She was headed for another cave when she noticed an opening in a rock face that was more of a crack. It was only about five feet high and barely wide enough to squeeze through. Following instinct rather than logic, she moved to the cave opening and peered inside. She put her hand on the rock, then immediately pulled it back and rubbed her fingers together. Moisture.

She ran her fingers along the inside of the opening once more, again wetting her fingers. Then, ducking, she squeezed through the opening and took a moment to let her eyes adjust to the darkness. A few feet inside, the cave ceiling expanded so that she could stand up straight. She only had to move a few yards farther to find the spring inside the cave.

With a grin, she leaned down and filled up the water bag. She glanced down at her wrist where her watch should have been and remembered that it was still in her hotel room. Estimating that she had only been gone for fifteen minutes, she set her pack down and pulled out the toiletries kit she had found when she had surveyed the contents earlier that day. She moved several feet away from the spring to preserve the freshness of the water, removed her clothes and carefully set them on a rock. She dumped some of the water from the water bag over her head. After washing off, she then used the rest of the water to rinse off. Though she wanted to wash her clothes also, she realized that the chill that would accompany nighttime made that idea impractical. Instead, she hoped Brent wouldn't have too much of a fit if she came to wash her clothes tomorrow when the sun would dry them quickly.

After drying off with the little camp towel she had in her backpack, she got dressed and refilled the water bag. Amy then moved back to the opening of the cave. She waited for a moment, listening for anything that didn't belong. She then moved through the mouth of the cave and back down to where she had left Brent. Her return trip took less than ten minutes, and she found Brent sitting with his weapon in his hand.

He looked up at her, surprise lighting his eyes. "Why is your hair wet?"

"I took a shower." Amy handed him the water bag. "There's a spring in one of the caves up there."

"How did you manage a shower?"

"I used the water bag." Amy sat down beside him and pulled out one of the energy bars from her pack before she continued. "The opening is so small I almost missed it. I thought tomorrow I could go back up to top off our water and wash our clothes."

"I wouldn't mind heading up for a shower myself," Brent admitted.

Amy broke her energy bar in half and handed the larger portion to Brent. "How many more of these do you have?"

"Just one."

"I have three more in my pack. That means we have two days worth of food, right?"

Brent nodded.

"That's not enough," Amy stated matter-of-factly, hiding her concern. "You said it would take us a couple of days to get to the coast, and that was before you got shot and we made this detour."

"If we ration, we can probably stretch the energy bars to last for an extra day," Brent told her. "I was studying the maps earlier. It looks like we might be able to work our way through these rocks and avoid the insurgents down below."

"How far out of our way will it take us?"

"About six miles," Brent told her. "And it isn't an easy six miles."

"There's a cave right next to the one with the spring," Amy said, unfazed. "Why don't we move up there for the night and then tomorrow we can wash up and rest. That is, if you think you can move."

"I can move." Brent nodded, but instead of standing up, he motioned for her to sit down with him. "But why don't we say an evening prayer before we start out."

Surprise lighted Amy's eyes, followed by a smile. "I'd like that." She knelt down next to him as he moved to kneel as well.

"Do you mind if I offer it?"

Amy shook her head, bowing her head as he began. She felt such a warmth come over her as Brent expressed his appreciation for their safety and the Lord's guidance during their travels. Then he asked that they would be blessed with protection and guidance as they made their way home. When he closed his prayer, Amy felt tears sting her eyes. She blinked several times before looking up at him.

"Let's get going." Brent stood up, reaching out a hand to help her stand as well.

Amy stared at him for a minute before asking, "Is it hard being LDS and being a Navy SEAL?"

Brent shook his head. "Not really, especially since my whole unit is LDS."

"Everyone? How did that happen?"

Brent gave her a quick grin. "You have to realize my unit is only five people. It started out being just me and Kelan Bennett. Kel got promoted about the same time Tristan Crowther and Quinn Lambert finished their training. The commander of our SEAL team was reorganizing and he decided he might as well throw the Mormon boys together."

Amy looked at him, questioning. "That's only four. What about the fifth?"

"Seth Johnson." Brent's grin widened. "He was the odd man out who got stuck with the Mormon boys. The funny thing is that he's the one who suggested we start each day with a prayer. He converted to the Church about a year ago."

"That's amazing," Amy said as they packed up and started toward their temporary home. Brent moved slowly, but they had just enough light for him to be able to see the rough terrain. They reached the cave just outside of the one where the spring was located and settled in for the night.

"Let me check out your arm," Amy said as soon as Brent had sat down against the smoothest of the cave walls.

"It's fine."

"Good." Amy retrieved a flashlight from her pack. "Let me check it anyway."

Reluctantly, Brent took off his shirt and let her examine the stitches. The antibiotics he had taken right after Amy had stitched up his arm seemed to be working and there wasn't any sign of infection. The new supply of water would help him get the fluids he needed to help counteract the blood he had lost.

"I'm no expert," Amy said after she unwrapped the bandage. "But it looks like it's starting to heal."

"Since you insisted on seeing that for yourself, are you going to bandage it up again for me?" Humor laced his voice and he saw the beginnings of a smile on her face.

"I suppose." Amy took the med kit he handed her and pulled out a package of clean gauze pads. After giving him the flashlight to hold, she then went about the task of placing the pads over the wounds and wrapping his arm once more. "Is that okay?"

Brent moved his arm, wincing in pain. "Yeah, that's fine."

"If it's bothering you, why don't you take some more painkillers?"

"I'll take some Tylenol before I go to sleep." He turned off the flashlight. "I just need something to take my mind off of it. Tell me about your family."

She blinked in surprise, but she settled down on the ground next to him. Darkness enveloped them, with only a bit of moonlight coming through the cave opening. "Well, I'm sure you know my father's a senator." When he nodded, she continued. "I have two older brothers. Charlie is two years older than me. He'll start law school in the fall. Matt's the oldest. He plays baseball for the Florida Marlins."

"Are they married?"

"Matt is. His wife, CJ, was an Olympic swimmer before they started having kids. Their second baby is due this winter."

"I remember reading about her," Brent commented. "She's the one who was a government witness against that huge smuggling ring right before competing in the Olympics."

Amy nodded. "Her best friend was a cop, and she was there when he was killed by a couple of men he was investigating. CJ helped figure out who was heading up the drug ring."

"Pretty impressive." Brent shifted to get more comfortable. "What about your mom?"

"Mom is a senator's wife, and she's good at it." Amy smiled when she thought of her mother. "I think she's behind all the success the rest of the family has had. She's just always there, you know? If you do something wrong, you know she'll find out about it. When you do something right, she's always there to congratulate you."

Brent returned her smile. "She sounds like my mom. She quit working before I was born to stay home full-time. She coached the high school swim teams as kind of a hobby, but it was amazing how much information she picked up. We couldn't get anything past her."

"What about your dad?"

"We didn't see him much during the daylight hours, but Mom made sure he knew everything that was going on. Until he retired, he worked for a government contractor. He had to commute into DC every day, but he spent most of his time on the weekends with us kids. Every time I drive from Stafford into Washington I realize how much he sacrificed so that Mom could stay at home. It must have taken him at least an hour each way."

Amy grinned. "Yet you chose a job where you have to commute across the world at a moment's notice."

"That's different," Brent told her, amused by her observation. "I live on base when I'm not on assignment, so I don't even have a commute. When something comes up, my team is so focused on what needs to be done, we don't really think about how far we have to travel."

"Still, it must be hard on your family." Amy dropped the bait.

"They worry some, but they know that traveling on I-95 is usually more dangerous than my job is." Brent studied her a moment before he offered the information he hoped she wanted. "And there isn't anyone else back home to worry about me."

"I should say I'm surprised, but I don't imagine it's easy to date with your job."

"I don't know." Brent reached for her hand, lacing his fingers with hers. "I can't say that I ever gave it much of a chance."

Nerves fluttered in her stomach, and for a moment she thought he might just lean down and kiss her. His hand was warm in hers, and he was staring down at her in a way that made her wonder if her heart was designed to beat quite this fast.

Brent stared at her for a long moment, lost in his own thoughts. Finally, he pulled her hand to his lips and kissed the back of it. "We had better get some sleep."

Amy saw something flicker in his eyes as he released her hand and tried to get comfortable. Confused by her feelings, she watched him for a moment longer before lying down in the darkness.

CHAPTER 6

Amy sat just inside the cave, scissors in hand. She had gone up to the spring first thing that morning, first washing her own clothes so that she could let them dry while wearing the poncho and pants Brent had given her. Once they were dry enough to wear, she had taken a shower and washed the rest of her clothes.

As soon as she returned, Brent went up to the spring so that he too could shower and wash his clothes. He was moving much better this morning, and he had suggested that she try to get a nap before they set out that evening.

For now she had other plans. To battle the midday heat, she was dressed simply in her T-shirt and her sweatpants that she had cut off at the knees. Though the small scissors made the task difficult, she was currently turning the extra fabric that had once covered the lower part of her legs into bandages. After analyzing their supplies that morning, Amy realized exactly why Brent was so slow to take the painkillers. They were running out, and she had to assume he wanted to save them for when he would really need them. The roll of gauze bandages was also nearly depleted.

They had already started rationing their food, deciding to share one of the energy bars for the day since they would have access to as much water as they wanted for the time being. Amy imagined they would need their full portions once they started traveling again, but hopefully they could make it through tonight on a little less.

As she continued to make bandages, she let her mind drift back to her conversation with Brent the night before. Until he had gotten shot, he had seemed almost invincible, but last night he had seemed just like any other guy. Well, maybe not like any other guy, but for the first time she could almost envision him outside of a hostile environment. The way he talked about his family revealed a lot about him, and Amy was realizing that she would like him even if he hadn't saved her life.

She wondered what he would be like when he wasn't behind enemy lines, but her imagination didn't stretch quite that far. Setting down the scissors, she rubbed at the cramps in her fingers. Methodically, she began to pack the scissors and the new bandages into her backpack.

She didn't hear Brent approach, but suddenly there he was in front of her. She hardly recognized him. His face was free of the paint he had smeared on it at the beginning of this ordeal, and he had shaved. He looked younger and yet somehow more formidable at the same time.

He didn't notice her staring as he settled down next to her. "Can you bandage this up again for me?"

"Sure." Amy took out one of her newly fashioned bandages and scooted closer. He smelled like shaving cream and toothpaste, and nerves danced in her stomach as she retrieved the antibiotic cream and began spreading it over his wounds. She took a deep breath and told herself to think about something besides the way the muscles rippled in Brent's arms.

"Did you go to college or on a mission before joining the military?"

Brent nodded. "Both. I went to Moscow for my mission, and I graduated from George Mason University." He glanced down at his arm as she finished bandaging it. "And let me guess. You graduated from BYU, right?"

Amy smiled. "Good guess. I got my degree in international relations." Now finished with his arm, she put the medical supplies back into her pack. "Obviously, there were a few practical lessons they didn't teach me."

Brent laughed, appreciating the sarcastic tone. "For someone who has literally been dropped into a combat zone, I think you're holding up pretty well."

"Believe me, falling out of helicopters was never mentioned in any of my orientation classes at the State Department."

"But hostage situations were," Brent pointed out.

She nodded. "I was naive enough to think it couldn't happen to me."

The vulnerability was back, and Brent bit back on his frustration. Had he not been wounded, they would be within a night's journey of safety. He marveled that Amy didn't complain about the setback and that, despite her situation, she continued to be optimistic that he could get her home.

She shifted beside him, and her hair curtained her face. Without thinking, he reached over and tucked it behind her ear as she turned to face him. Embarrassed, he told himself to keep his distance, but he struggled to keep his body from moving closer anyway.

She stared up at him as he settled against the cave wall beside her. She was quiet for a moment before asking, "Is this the first time you've been shot?"

Brent nodded. "Believe it or not, Navy SEALs usually don't get into fire fights. Typically our operations are covert. If everything goes well, we're in and out before anyone even knows we're there."

"I guess that wouldn't have worked this time."

"The guys who took you hostage were expecting us," Brent said.

"What do you mean?"

"They set traps, making it look like we could enter the building safely when I'm sure they were just waiting for us."

Amy studied him for a minute and then asked, "How did you get onto the balcony?"

"I climbed."

"You climbed up the building?"

He gave a casual shrug. "It was a better alternative than getting shot." Before Amy could point out that he ended up getting shot anyway, he added, "This injury was from being in the wrong place at the wrong time, not because I fell for a lame ambush attempt."

Amy considered his words for a moment before speaking. "Personally, I'm glad you and your friends are good at your job."

"Thanks." Brent leaned his head back against the cave wall and resisted the urge to put an arm around her. "We should get some sleep before we head out tonight."

Amy nodded and settled down beside him. Moments later she closed her eyes and let the sound of his breathing lull her to sleep.

* * *

When Brent had said that the six miles of hiking through the rock formation weren't going to be easy, he hadn't been kidding. They had set out three hours before dusk hoping to reach the desert by dark, but it had already taken nearly four hours to make it those six miles.

"Do you need a rest?" Brent asked Amy as they approached the sandy terrain ahead, the darkness of the night now complete. Only the moonlight illuminated the empty space ahead of them.

"I just want a quick drink." She pulled her water bottle from her pack. "How are you doing?"

"I'm holding up." Brent motioned for her to sit down, and he pulled out his canteen and took a sip. He then opened up his map and clicked on a penlight to study it.

"How far is it to the nearest shelter?"

"It's hard to say." He shifted closer so that she could look at the map also. "The nearest port is this way, but there's nothing but desert between here and there."

"Which means we would be out in the open during the day," Amy finished for him. "What other alternatives do we have?"

"We can head north toward this village on the river. We might be able to pick up a boat. If not, we can follow the river out to the ocean." He turned to her. "Unfortunately, our latest intelligence said that the town just upriver from the village is where the rebels have one of their command centers. In fact, we think that's where Namir Dagan is holed up."

"Isn't Dagan the one who tried to overthrow the government three years ago?"

Brent nodded. "We have to assume they have troops there, but we can avoid the main thoroughfares."

"Sounds like a better bet than risking dehydration. And like you said, no one realizes we're even here," Amy pointed out. "How far is it to the village?"

"About fifteen miles. We can make it before morning," Brent said as he folded up his map once more.

"Let's go then." Amy stood up, preparing for the next workout. Thankfully, her shoes were holding up so far except for a little hole in the toe where she'd stubbed it on a sharp rock a couple of miles back.

Brent wasn't moving quite as fast as he had the first two nights, but his stride was long and he didn't appear to be struggling. The minutes passed by in silence. Amy recognized that he had clicked back into work mode and his senses were working overtime as he scanned the area for any perceivable threats.

The trees in the distance told her they were getting close to the river. She could even smell the water from almost a mile away. Brent slowed down and took her hand in his for a moment. "If anyone sees us, just keep your eyes on the ground. Let me handle it, okay?"

Amy nodded, oddly disappointed when he released her hand. Her mind turned to Jared, the man she had briefly considered marrying. She expected the next time she saw him he would pull the I-told-you-so routine. Repeatedly he had told her that she shouldn't take this assignment, that it was too dangerous. Little did he know that she had taken the job as much to get away from him as to satisfy her own sense of adventure.

She could admit now that she also needed to put some distance between her and her friends back home for a while. After she broke things off with Jared, she had watched many of them move into marriage while she remained firmly in single adulthood.

Maybe that was why she had been so eager to get out on her own. She didn't want to be part of the singles scene, and the few times she had attended the singles ward at home she had felt like everyone expected she was just there to find a husband. She glanced over at Brent and wondered if he had the same problem. Perhaps he just wasn't interested in a relationship at this point in his life. His life was certainly exciting enough without adding any other elements to it.

Still lost in her thoughts, she barely noticed Brent slow his pace. He reached out and touched her shoulder to get her attention as he approached the riverbank. He then signaled for her to be quiet as they moved slowly forward.

She expected that he would find a spot to leave her so that he could scout out the village, but instead he motioned for her to follow behind him. The village was primitive, made of simple huts. Even though the sun was now visible, they couldn't see any sign of life in the village except for some livestock near the river. A goat stood on the bank drinking water and a few chickens were pecking the ground outside the nearest hut. Three horses were grazing just beyond it.

The dock that gave the village access to the river was void of boats, an oddity in itself. From where they stood, sheltered by a few trees, Amy could see a watchtower that was twice as tall as the huts surrounding it, but it too appeared empty.

Brent studied the village for several minutes before finally turning to Amy. He signaled for her to be quiet and then drew his gun and motioned for her to follow him. He moved to the first hut, peered inside, and then led the way to the next one. Slowly, meticulously, he checked out each of the huts, over twenty of them, before moving to the watchtower in the center of the village.

"Stay here," Brent whispered before starting up the ladder. He reached the top, staying low so that he couldn't be seen by anyone in the distance. With his binoculars he scrutinized the countryside before descending the ladder to where Amy was waiting.

"Did you see anything?"

Brent nodded. "There are signs of a battle in the town a couple of miles upriver. The villagers must have deserted their homes and fled for safety."

"They can't have been gone long since they still have animals grazing here."

"The boats are all gone, but those horses look domesticated." Brent stared down at her a moment. "You can ride a horse, can't you?"

"Yeah, I can ride." Amy looked around the eerily quiet village. "Are we staying here for the day?"

"Actually, if you're up for it, I'd rather start for the coast. If anyone comes along today, those horses will be long gone before we would be able to set out tonight."

"Isn't that pretty risky?" Amy asked hesitantly.

"I think it's riskier to stay here." Brent pushed open the door to the hut where he had seen some of the locals' clothing left behind. "If it was safe, the villagers would have already returned."

Amy took the robe Brent handed her. "I don't suppose you saw any bridles anywhere."

"There's some rope beneath the watchtower." Brent moved to look beneath the two-story platform. Suddenly he jumped back and aimed his weapon at the dark space in the corner.

Instinctively, Amy moved back. Fumbling, she retrieved the pistol from her bag just as Brent kicked another weapon out into the dirt in front of her. She didn't know much about weapons but she recognized the gun in front of her. It was the same kind her captors had used.

A moment later, Brent pulled a motionless man out from beneath the tower. He wasn't dressed like a local but instead wore some kind of uniform.

"Is he—?" Amy left her question dangling as Brent checked the man's pockets.

"Yeah, he's dead, but he hasn't been for long." Brent stared down at the face for a moment. Surprise crossed his face, followed by disbelief. "I think this is Rashidi Re. He's Namir Dagan's chief military advisor."

"What would he be doing here?"

Brent shrugged. "He probably tried to escape the battle and got shot in the process." He checked the man's pockets, tossing various items onto the ground: a handful of coins, a torn photograph, a cigarette lighter. The last item he fished out was a Palm Pilot. Brent studied it for a minute, punching various buttons. He let out a sigh when his first attempt to bypass the security failed.

Amy averted her gaze from the man sprawled on the ground, instead looking at Brent. "What are you doing?"

"Trying to bypass the security codes," he said. "My Arabic is a little rusty. This may take a few minutes."

"You speak Arabic?"

"Enough to get by." Brent glanced up long enough to see her confusion. "All SEALs have to learn at least one foreign language, but the more we know the easier it is to do our job."

With a shrug, Brent turned his attention back to the computer. He continued to punch buttons as the sun rose higher in the sky. Finally, he hacked his way through the computer's security systems. His eyes widened as he scanned through emails and notes.

Amy felt Brent's tension level rise. "What's wrong?"

"I'm not sure." Brent continued reading. "There are schematics and photos in this email. It looks like an assassination attempt, but I can't tell who or where." He glanced down at his watch to check the date and then scrolled through to where a date was listed along with the photo of a building. "Whatever is going on is supposed to happen two days from now."

"Can I see?" Amy let him come to her rather than moving closer to the body. She looked at the building photograph and recognized it immediately. "That's a picture of the hotel in Cairo I stayed at on my way here."

"Are you sure?"

Amy nodded. "It was only a few weeks ago. In fact, that's probably where the U.S. embassy staff was evacuated to until it's safe to return to this country again." She turned to look at him. "Do you think the ambassador could be the target?"

"Not the ambassador. The DCI."

"What?"

"The Director of Central Intelligence was supposed to be coming here for a meeting with the ambassador. The hostage situation might have been part of a bigger plan to get the ambassador out of the country. Here in Abolstan the DCI would have been invisible, arriving by helicopter at the embassy and leaving the same way." He shook his head, turning back to retrieve the rope he had started to get a few minutes earlier. "I don't know why the DCI was coming, but it must have been pretty important for him to decide to come here instead of just having the ambassador come to Washington."

"Oh my gosh." Amy dropped onto the ground, tears swimming in her eyes.

Brent leaned down beside her, tentatively laying a hand on her shoulder. "What?"

"When I told my dad I was taking the assignment here, he just about came unglued. One of the things he said was that Abolstan has been trying to develop biological weapons. The day we were taken hostage, the intelligence officers and the ambassador were in meetings all day. Something big was going on, but no one knew what. When I was dropping some papers off for the ambassador at his office, I heard one of the intelligence officers tell him that there was no way to get the proof to Washington safely."

"You think they had proof that Abolstan was developing biological weapons?" Brent's eyes widened.

Amy nodded and took a deep breath. "That's not all. The ambassador had a map on his desk of the Washington DC subway system."

"Right before we shipped out, the alert status in DC went up to red. That might be why." Brent shook his head.

"If someone released a biological weapon in DC . . ." Amy trailed off. "I can't even imagine what kind of chaos that would cause."

"Especially if someone managed to assassinate the DCI right before a terrorist attack. It would be cutting off the right arm of the intelligence community." Brent nodded toward the river. "We've got to go catch those horses, and then we have to find a way to get a message out."

"How are we going to do that?" Amy asked skeptically.

"We have to get to the port city tonight," Brent decided. "An aircraft or a boat would have some kind of communication device we can use." He dropped the Palm Pilot into one of the pockets of his combat vest and reached out his hand to pull Amy to her feet.

"Let's go then."

CHAPTER 7

"Why haven't we heard anything?" Charlie raked his fingers through his hair.

"Charlie, any number of things could have happened to slow them down," CJ told him, knowing from experience just how true her words were.

"I hate not being able to do something." He turned to face CJ, who was calmly rocking her little girl to sleep. "Do you realize I'm always the one in this position?"

"What do you mean?" She ran a hand over her daughter's soft curls before looking up at her brother-in-law.

"The two times you disappeared, I got a message that something was wrong and then all I could do was wait around for the phone call." Charlie leaned against the arm of the sofa. "Now here I am again, waiting for a phone call."

"Would you rather be the person we were all worrying about?"

"I don't know." He glanced over at the television, where the news was on mute. The other hostages were recovering, and already the situation that had taken his sister from him was old news. No one even knew that she was still caught somewhere behind enemy lines. "I just know I'm sick of waiting."

"That makes two of us," CJ agreed. She shifted the toddler in her lap, hoping she could put her down for the night. "As strange as it sounds, maybe we should get out of the house tomorrow and do something."

"Wake me up when you go swim in the morning," Charlie told her as she stood up. "Maybe I'll go pump some iron and see if I can work out some of this frustration."

"It can't hurt."

* * *

Brent followed Amy along the riverside. After circling around an occupied village a few miles back, he had her take the lead in case anyone followed after them. So far they had made good use of the daylight hours, but in front of him he could see Amy beginning to tire. She rolled her shoulders as though that might erase the aches and pains from riding for the past eleven hours. He didn't have the heart to break it to her that they still had at least six more hours to go, most of which they would have to travel at night.

Their horses were both Arabians, and while they were clearly domesticated, they were also high-strung. Without the aid of bridles, Brent and Amy had struggled to keep their horses in check during the first several miles. Now that the horses were tiring, they had settled down and were much more cooperative.

Though they could have made better time by riding along the nearby road, they had stayed in the trees by the riverbank, partially to remain out of sight and partially to help them battle the desert heat. They had already stopped once midday and had taken the opportunity to go for a quick swim to cool themselves down. Their clothes had dried within an hour, but it had helped them survive the worst of the heat.

As they approached a sandy spot along the riverbank, Brent rode up beside Amy. "Let's stop for a few minutes and water the horses."

Amy nodded in agreement and guided her horse to the river. She dismounted, and her legs nearly buckled underneath her when her feet hit the ground.

"Are you okay?" Brent slid off of his own horse, his legs not in much better shape than Amy's, but still he moved to her side.

"I'm fine. Just a bit tired." She took a tentative step forward, and her knee gave way. Before she could regain her balance, Brent caught her by the waist.

"You need to sit down," he said, but instead of moving he just stood there staring down at her. The weariness in his own body dissipated as he felt the warmth of emotions rush through him. Amy's hair was hidden beneath the headpiece she wore, and her robe was at least a size too big, nearly managing to hide her feminine curves. Yet as he looked down into her piercing blue eyes, he knew he would never mistake her for a man, even from a distance.

He sensed her confusion, followed by her awareness as he moved closer. A warning rang in the back of his mind that his feelings for her were probably just caused by the intensity of their situation, but for once he ignored reason. He pulled her into his arms, a myriad of emotions rushing through him. Psychologically, he knew he should keep a professional distance between them, but when she leaned her head against him, all logic disappeared.

She was frail at that moment, and his instinct to protect her took on an unaccustomed urgency. A light breeze whispered around them, chasing away the desert heat. Brent closed his eyes, lost in the sweetness and simplicity of the moment. When he pulled back, he chastised himself for not keeping a professional distance. He looked down at her, frustrated that she could make him forget why he was here and block out everything around them. Quickly, he looked away.

"We should water the horses and eat something before we start out again," he said, grateful that she was steady on her feet when he released her.

Slowly, Amy led her horse to the water and then looked over at Brent. Her voice was tentative when she asked, "Am I going to see you after we get back to the States?"

He looked up at her, unsure of how to answer her. Did he want to see her after they got back? Yes. Could he afford the emotions she evoked in him? He wasn't sure. The only married member of his unit was his commander, Kel Bennett. Despite the fact that Kel and his wife had a temple marriage, from what he had seen of their relationship, he wasn't sure marriage and his profession were compatible.

Though they had only been together a few days, Brent already knew that Amy wasn't the type he would be able to just forget the minute he left for an assignment. Instead, she would make him anxious to get back home.

Rather than answer her question, he asked one of his own. "Are you going to stay in the States, or will you go back out on assignment?"

"I don't know," Amy admitted, running a hand over her horse's neck as it drank. "I love to travel, but I don't think this is an experience I'll want to repeat."

"Maybe you should ask to go someplace like London or Stockholm," Brent suggested. As soon as the words were out of his mouth, he realized that many of the safe assignments would put half a world between them.

Amy felt his words and the implication of them. She watched him for a minute, hoping she had misunderstood. She knew that he wanted her to be safe, but surely he realized that those assignments would put thousands of miles between them. How could he hold her one minute like she was the center of his world, and then the next minute suggest she live on a different continent from him? She dropped her eyes to the ground, realizing that at this moment she was the center of his world, but only because it was his job to protect her.

Disappointment shot through her, followed by a wave of irritation. Perhaps the closeness they shared was no more than a result of being together constantly for the past few days. She looked out over the river, annoyed that she would let herself feel anything of a romantic nature for this man who was being paid to keep her safe. If Brent wanted to see her tucked away in some safe post where she would never see him again, she had to assume that he wanted to reestablish a professional distance between them.

In the west the sun was sinking behind a mountain range, and fingers of pink, red, and orange streaked across the sky. Water rippled over a fallen tree, creating a mini-waterfall. Under different circumstances the sandy beach would have made an ideal picnic spot. She took a bite of her energy bar and decided that even though they were eating here, energy bars and spring water definitely didn't count as a picnic dinner.

After a few more minutes, Brent led his horse away from the water and swung himself onto the horse's back. "We had better get going," he said. He winced as pain shot through his arm, but he was grateful that the constant throbbing hadn't returned even though his painkillers had worn off.

Amy mounted her horse and followed as Brent took the lead. Her mind raced as they moved forward, and she was forced to ask herself if she would really want to see Brent again after they made it out of Abolstan. As much as she enjoyed his company, she wasn't sure she would want to be involved with someone who would have to fly halfway around the world at any given time. She watched Brent ride through the trees, telling herself that he didn't appear to want to see her again anyway. With a shake of her head, she reminded herself that she was just tired. Maybe the fact that they hadn't slept in almost twenty-four hours was further confusing matters that were confusing enough already.

She counted up the number of days since they had fallen out of the helicopter together, surprised that she had only met Brent four days earlier. In fact, this whole ordeal had only started five days ago, but as they pressed forward, she could barely remember what it was like to sleep indoors or not have to worry about the gunshots and tanks that sometimes sounded in the distance.

Could they really have met only four days ago? she asked herself as she struggled to stay alert. Rolling her shoulders again, she decided it didn't matter how long they had been on this journey. The important thing was to get out of here in time to warn the right people that their country was about to come under attack. In two more days, her family could end up in a far worse situation than she was in now.

* * *

"Four days." Jim Whitmore paced across his office, a cordless phone up to his ear. He nodded at Jared Elliott, who was manning the desk outside of his office, and then shut the door between them. "Doug, how can we not have heard anything by now?"

"I don't know, sir." Doug's voice came over the line. He hated dealing with the unknown, but for the past several days the only news he'd had was that they had no news. "The unit commander said that Lieutenant Miller only had one communications device. If that was somehow broken when he and Amy were separated from the rest of the group, it's possible that they have already left the country and just haven't been able to get word out."

"That's the optimistic possibility." Jim's voice took on an edge. "What's on the other side of the coin?"

"Senator, I think it's too soon to consider any negative outcomes," Doug said carefully. "The press has not yet discovered that your daughter is missing, and none of the warring factions in Abolstan is making any demands. If they had been captured, someone would have contacted us by now."

Jim closed his eyes and pressed his fingers to his temple, refusing to consider that his baby girl might already be dead. He couldn't give up, and for now he chose to believe that a successful outcome was not only possible, but inevitable. "I understand that the DCI is leaving for Cairo this morning to meet with the ambassador to Abolstan. I think perhaps a trip would do me some good."

"Do you really think that's a good idea?"

"I don't know if it's a good idea or not, but I don't think I can sit around here much longer and pretend that everything is okay."

"What will the press think?"

"After we leave, I'll have my staff issue a press release saying that I'm going to meet Amy there so that I can escort her home," Jim told him. "Charlie is already working on the arrangements."

"Charlie's going too?"

"It was actually his idea," Jim explained. "CJ and Kailey have helped distract Katherine, but Charlie and I just can't wait around anymore."

"Is your wife okay with this?"

"If she didn't feel like CJ needed her here, I think she would come with us, but yes, she understands why we need to go." Jim thought of their long talk the night before. Katherine had been torn between wanting to go and wanting them to stay. After a lot of discussion and prayer, they had finally decided that Katherine would stay behind with CJ and Kailey while Matt finished up his road trip. Meanwhile Charlie and Jim would fly to Cairo in hopes of bringing Amy home.

"I assume you will want me to speak with your wife if I hear anything further," Doug said.

"Yes, but they're actually headed down to Florida later today. They thought it would be easier on Kailey to be in her own home, and they wanted to see Matt tonight before he leaves on his next trip." Jim checked his watch before continuing. "I'll make sure CJ and Katherine know how to reach me."

"Good luck, Senator," Doug said. "Give Amy my love when you see her."

"I will." Jim closed his eyes and prayed it would be just that easy.

CHAPTER 8

"Matt! Katherine! Come quick!" CJ stood in the doorway leading from the backyard into the spacious living room, where the television was playing behind her.

Matt scooped his daughter up in his arms and ran into the house with his mother just a step behind him. "What's wrong?"

CJ simply pointed as the newscaster continued.

"Our sources suggest that one of the hostages never made it out of Abolstan. So far, no one has been able to confirm that Amy Whitmore has been seen since she was taken hostage nearly a week ago."

"Oh, no." Katherine sank down onto a chair, both of her hands covering her mouth as the newscaster went on. Next to her, Matt set Kailey down and stood riveted to the television.

"Despite the assurances from Senator Whitmore's staff that he is on his way to Cairo to escort his daughter home, one eyewitness said that Amy Whitmore fell from the rescue helicopter along with one of her rescuers when the helicopter came under fire. We have been unable to confirm whether or not they survived the fall."

CJ wrapped her arms around Matt's waist, her eyes tearing as her husband drew her closer. Their prayers couldn't have all been in vain, but how could someone make up such a story? Could Amy really have died during the rescue? And if so, why hadn't anyone passed along that information?

Taking a deep breath, CJ looked up at Matt. His jaw was set and she could tell that he too was struggling with the possibilities. "It can't be true, Matt."

Matt looked down at her, his eyes moist.

Realizing that he was afraid to speak, CJ continued, "If she had died during the rescue, we would have been told."

Matt swallowed hard. "How could she possibly survive falling out of a helicopter?"

"People in the military jump out of helicopters all the time," CJ pointed out. "Let me call Doug and we'll see if he can find out where this story is coming from."

Her hand was shaking when she picked up the phone and dialed Doug's number. She hadn't even finished dialing when the doorbell rang.

"I can't deal with anyone right now," Matt told her, sitting down next to his mother and reaching an arm around her shoulders.

Nodding in understanding, CJ walked to the front door and opened it to find Doug on the doorstep. Desperation was in CJ's voice when she spoke. "Please tell me that the story on the news isn't true."

"It's misleading," Doug said, and he walked through the door.

CJ motioned to the living room. "Why don't you come tell all of us what's going on so that you don't have to explain twice." She led the way down the hall, and Doug took a seat across from Matt and Katherine.

Doug waited for Matt and Katherine to look up before he spoke. "First of all, we have every reason to believe that Amy is alive and well. The story about her falling out of a helicopter is somewhat exaggerated."

"How exaggerated?" Matt asked.

"We didn't give you this information because we didn't want to worry you, but when the rescue helicopter was leaving with the hostages, it came under fire. The door next to Amy was hit, and during evasive maneuvers she slid through the door. One of her rescuers caught her before she dropped, but they weren't able to bring her back in safely." Doug took a deep breath. "Afraid that someone was going to get a clean shot at either her or the helicopter, Lieutenant Miller opted for a controlled fall with her onto a roof. He then instructed the helicopter to leave them behind when he noticed how quickly they were losing fuel."

"They could have picked her up and didn't?" Matt asked incredulously.

"Matt, the lieutenant made the right decision," Doug said gently. "The helicopter made it within four miles of the border before it went down. Had they stopped to pick up Amy and Lieutenant Miller, they probably wouldn't have cleared the mountain range near the border. A couple of the other hostages wouldn't have lived long enough to receive the medical attention they needed."

"But she was okay when they left her?" Katherine asked softly.

"Yes." Doug nodded. "The team leader said that Lieutenant Miller had already checked her for injuries before they left and that she was fine."

"Now that the story is out, will she stay fine?" Anger tinted Matt's voice. "If they haven't already left the country, every terrorist in Abolstan is going to be looking for them. It's going to be impossible for them to get out."

"From what I hear, 'impossible' has never been in Brent Miller's vocabulary."

* * *

"Take cover," Brent whispered at the approach of a vehicle. Darkness was falling quickly, but he knew they were still visible in the fading twilight if someone looked into the trees along the road.

He slid off his horse, using the animal and the trees to shield him from the road. Amy followed suit. She let her horse have its head so it could graze and pressed herself up against a tree to hide. They had several yards of wooded area between them and the road, but Brent didn't want to take any chance of someone seeing the movement by the river.

The first of the headlights came into view, and Brent identified the vehicle as a Jeep. A convoy of at least a half dozen vehicles followed behind it, and in the distance he could hear tanks. Something was happening, and he wasn't sure he wanted to know what. The vehicles he saw all appeared to be heading in the same direction they were.

They stayed in the shadows for several minutes after the convoy passed. Finally, Brent turned to Amy and motioned for her to mount up as he did the same. He started forward, estimating they should be within an hour's ride from the port city.

After a few minutes they came over a rise and saw the first evidence that they were on the right path. The lights in the distance brought both relief and a sense of trepidation. Finally, the end of their long journey was in sight, but at that end was danger beyond any they had faced so far. Those tanks in the distance had been headed straight for the city.

Brent didn't know how they could secure transportation if the city was under attack, or whether there would even be any transportation available. For all he knew, the residents of the city could have vacated the same way the villagers several miles back had when the battles came too close.

Suddenly the trees were behind them, and the river opened up into the ocean. Realizing that the horses were about to become more of a hindrance than a help, Brent stopped and dismounted. He looked back to see Amy also dismounting.

They were both exhausted, but neither of them even considered stopping. Just a little farther and they might be able to get word out.

"Did you want to water the horses again?" Amy asked as she rolled her shoulders.

"We'll be too noticeable on horseback from here on," Brent explained. "It's only about three or four more miles."

Reluctantly, Amy nodded in agreement. She helped Brent remove the makeshift bridles so the horses would look like strays and then watched him bury the rope in the sand.

Brent dusted off his hands and turned to Amy. Surprising them both, he reached out and took Amy's hand in his, leading her down the stretch of beach. Everything was eerily quiet, but then Brent didn't imagine that many towns generated much sound at two in the morning.

They easily crossed the first mile and most of the second. Then they came upon a grouping of huts overlooking the beach. Using hand signals, Brent told Amy to stop. He listened for a moment before motioning her forward again. Together, they crept along the water's edge for over a half mile until they passed the cluster of huts.

They were barely clear of them when something rumbled in the distance. Grabbing her arm, Brent pulled Amy down to the sand. He ignored the pain shooting through his arm.

With Amy lying right beside him, Brent held a finger to his lips as the rumbling continued in the distance. Amy nodded in response, lying silently on the sand except for the pounding of her heart and her slow, deep breaths. Minutes passed by and still the rumbling continued. A moment later, the ground shook, followed by a flame shooting up into the sky.

Brent shifted to gauge the distance of the artillery. He knew instantly that it was now or never. "Stay close to me."

Amy nodded, rolling onto her knees and then standing when she saw Brent stand up. He started out at a slow jog and then increased his speed when he realized that Amy was keeping up. They reached a pier five minutes later, and Brent led the way beneath it. He motioned for her to stay quiet, but he needn't have bothered.

He scanned the water for a boat that would serve their needs. Not finding any viable options, he continued down the last of the beach to where a rocky pass shielded them from whatever lay beyond. Slowly, they climbed the slippery rocks, reaching another stretch of beach just as another explosion rocked the ground.

Amy looked up at Brent to see him grinning.

She turned to see what he was looking at but was unable to make anything out in the darkness. She followed him another mile before she was able to identify the shadows in the distance as a small dock just outside of a beachside hotel. At the dock were several small motorboats.

They crept along the beach slowly, for once grateful for the lack of moonlight. They reached the dock, but instead of climbing onto it, Brent motioned for Amy to hide beside it.

Her eyes widened when he moved into the water toward the nearest boat. The sound of the waves masked any sound he might have made, and he quickly disappeared into the darkness. Another burst of fire shot into the air as the ground shook beneath them. Amy took a deep breath, not allowing herself to think of what might happen if they weren't successful now.

In the distance she heard screams followed by a burst of gunfire. She closed her eyes against what was happening in this country, knowing that she was powerless to stop the fighting. She had to focus instead on the war she could battle—the terrorism attempt on her own country.

She thought of her family and knew that no matter what, they had to get out of the DC area tonight. The subway in Washington was used by everyone, rich and poor alike. If these terrorists succeeded in their plan, the devastation could equal or even exceed that of 9/11. She remembered too vividly the day that airliners had crashed into the Twin Towers, the Pentagon, and that field in Pennsylvania. With her father, she had attended many of the funerals that had resulted from that day. If there was any way she could prevent it, she wasn't about to stand by while it happened again, no matter what the weapon was.

A wave crashed in front of her and suddenly Brent emerged from the water. He reached out and took her pack from her. He settled it onto his back and then motioned for her to enter the water with him.

The water was freezing and the weight of her clothes made it difficult to move, but she followed him along the side of one of the boats and then to the ladder that led up the back. Brent climbed up first, then dropped the pack on the floor before reaching down to help Amy climb in.

"Lie down," Brent whispered as soon as she was in the boat.

Already shivering from the cold, Amy simply nodded and curled up on the floor as Brent moved to the steering wheel. A few seconds later the engine roared to life and Brent quickly headed straight out to sea.

A shout echoed from the beach, followed by a spray of gunfire. Brent increased his speed, staying low as they moved out of range of whoever was shooting from the beach.

Curious to know if they had a working radio, Amy crawled along the floor until she was beside Brent. "Can we send a message now?"

He shook his head. "We need to get into international waters," he said as he checked the instruments. "As soon as we pass the twelve-mile mark, we'll radio in our position and pass on the information."

"Why do we have to wait?"

"Abolstan has several naval vessels in this region. We'll be easy to find once we get on the radio, and I want to make sure our military can get someone to us before we get intercepted."

"Do you think someone will be ready to come get us?"

"Don't worry," Brent assured her. "My team will be waiting for us."

CHAPTER 9

Kel Bennett watched the latest news broadcast, his anger rising with each word that came out of the perky newscaster's mouth. His team had been on board the USS *Enterprise* for the past three days waiting for their chance to go in and get their missing man and the last hostage. With each day, his frustration had grown and doubts had begun to creep in.

He knew his decision to let Brent stay behind with the Whitmore girl was the right one, but that didn't mean he had to like it. Now that the whole world knew about it, the potential consequences of his decision took a drastic turn for the worse. "So help me, if I find out who leaked this information, I'm going to kill him."

"Now, Commander," Tristan drawled. "You know you wouldn't be able to do that."

Kel turned and glared at Tristan. "You think I don't have the guts to kill whoever put this operation in jeopardy?"

Tristan grinned. "I know you've got the guts. I just don't think you'd be able to beat me to him."

"Get back to work," Kel growled, but not before the corner of his lips quirked up. He turned to Quinn, who was studying the map of the area. "What's the status of our rescue chopper?"

"It's standing by on deck." Quinn tapped his finger on the map. "All of their destroyers are staying inside their territorial waters, but it looks like they're trying to make it hard for Miller to get out of there."

"You know, we've all been assuming that he's heading for Khalar," Tristan said, shifting the map so that they could look at the terrain.

He pointed to the desert surrounding the capital city. "We know there's been heavy fighting in this area. If Brent had to detour, he may have changed plans."

"But Khalar is closer."

"Yeah, but if they couldn't get into these hills over here, they'd be looking at a two-day walk through the middle of the desert," Tristan pointed out. "They don't even have a tent with them. There's no way Brent would want to try that with a civilian, especially with a limited water supply. But that might explain why we haven't heard from him yet."

"That's true," Quinn agreed. "But if he comes through one of these smaller ports, we're completely out of position to pick them up."

"Yeah, but so are the terrorists," Kel noted.

Tristan nodded. "Do you want me to have the captain shift to the north just in case?"

"Yeah, and double-check to make sure our chopper is ready to go," Kel ordered. "I don't want them to have another rough ride."

"Yes, sir."

* * *

Brent studied his map using his penlight while Amy was at the wheel. He could see her shivering, but she had insisted that she could take over while he figured out which direction they should head. His unit would assume that he had headed for Khalar, which meant there would be a helicopter standing by somewhere within a few minutes of there, but since they had diverted to Bharat instead, they were off by more than thirty miles. That thirty miles could cause problems if their signal was picked up, but Brent didn't know whether they could afford to wait the extra time it would take to move to where their ride was likely waiting for them. If he was alone, he would just send the signal and take his chances, but with Amy—well, he just didn't think he could risk it.

"Turn a little more to the left," Brent told her as he folded the map back up and stuck it in his pocket.

"What's wrong?" Amy asked, trying to hide the fact that her teeth were chattering.

"My unit is going to assume we're thirty miles to the south. If we signal as soon as we get to international waters, I'm not sure who will get to us first, our side or theirs." Brent hesitated, finally opting for the truth. She had the right to know. "But if we wait to send a signal, we can't be sure our military can stop the assassin in time."

"What would you do if I wasn't here?" Amy asked him.

"I'd send the message now," Brent admitted.

"Then that's what we need to do."

"It's only five more miles until we hit international waters. We'll send it then."

* * *

"We've got them," Kel announced as he shoved the phone back into place. "Let's roll."

His team didn't have to be told twice. In less than three minutes, they were over the ocean scanning the darkness below. In the air, Kel briefed the rest of their team. Brent's communication gear wasn't functioning, so he had used an unsecured channel to send his location. There was little doubt that they hadn't been the only ones listening in on the conversation.

"ETA?" Kel asked the pilot.

"Six minutes."

"Is there anything on the radar?"

"Yes, sir. It looks like a destroyer heading this way. Estimated time to intercept, eleven minutes."

"We've only got a five minute window, tops," Kel informed the rest of his team. "Check the harnesses. Let's get this done right."

A few minutes later, they found what they were looking for. They flashed a signal and, in the darkness below, a boat's running lights switched on.

They lowered the harness and Brent helped Amy get strapped in. They brought her up slowly, all of them remembering how her last helicopter ride had ended. As soon as she reached the open doorway, Quinn and Tristan each grabbed one of her arms and pulled her securely inside as Kel unhooked her and sent down another harness.

"Get her strapped in," Kel ordered, turning his attention to the destroyer that was closing in fast.

Quinn guided her to a seat and helped her buckle in. He recognized the early signs of hypothermia and shouted out to Tristan, "Get me a blanket back here."

A light shot through the air, and Amy screamed as the helicopter rocked to the left. The helicopter then swung to the right and dropped altitude for a moment.

Kel kept his eye on the second harness and the man in it, who now dangled fifteen feet below the helicopter. "Let's get him in!"

Seth moved to Kel's side and together they steadily reeled Brent in despite the helicopter's drastic movements. Brent stretched out his hands and helped pull himself in as soon as he was in reach. He crawled into the helicopter and Seth immediately slammed the door.

Kel spoke into his mouthpiece. "All bodies in!"

The helicopter rose rapidly as they all strapped in. Brent claimed the seat between Amy and Quinn.

"Welcome back," Quinn shouted to Brent. "Did you have a nice vacation?"

Ignoring him, Brent reached over and touched Amy's hand. She was still shivering and her hands felt like ice. Tristan passed him a blanket, but rather than use it for himself, he wrapped it around Amy's head and shoulders.

Turning his attention back to the problem at hand, Brent motioned to Quinn to give him his headset. Quinn handed it over, and Brent pulled it on, setting it so he could communicate with his team.

"We've got an assassination attempt on the DCI in Cairo. It's probably going to happen within the next day or two."

"What?" Kel turned back to look at him even though Brent's voice was transmitting clearly. "Where did you get your intel?"

"We picked it up along the way," Brent explained. "We've got to pull the DCI out of there."

"We'll get the word to him," Kel agreed. "What about the senator?"

"Which senator?"

"Senator Whitmore arrived in Cairo this morning."

Brent looked over at Amy, grateful that she couldn't hear what was being said. "Clear everyone out of the hotel. We can't be sure the DCI's the target, but we know that whatever is going down is going to happen at that hotel." Brent paused for a fraction of a second. "We also need to alert the DC subway. We suspect a potential attack using biological weapons within the week."

"You've got to be kidding me." Kel's eyes widened, but his voice held concern rather than disbelief. He turned to Seth Johnson, their communications expert. "Johnson, get the word out."

"Consider it done."

CHAPTER 10

Charlie walked through the crowded lobby of the Cairo hotel, exhausted from travel. He wasn't sure what time it was, but he was surprised that the sun was shining outside. To Charlie it still felt like the middle of the night. Glancing around, he noticed that most of the people in the lobby were businessmen. Annoyed that everyone else looked refreshed from a good night's sleep, he glanced over at his father.

They had both dozed during their flight, but that still hadn't made up for the days that they had barely slept since Amy was taken hostage. His father had put on a convincing front for the press and those he came in contact with through his job, but now Charlie could see what a toll the pretense had taken on him. Wearily, they approached the front desk.

Thankfully the desk clerk spoke English, which helped expedite the otherwise slow process of checking in. As they turned to follow a porter to their room, the DCI, Sam Palmer, approached with his entourage. Standing only 5'10", Director Palmer was barely visible behind his bodyguards. Still, a combination of power and tension radiated from him as he moved through the lobby.

Charlie recognized the four security men for what they were, each of them wearing an earpiece so they could communicate with one another. Each of them also had a subtle bulge beneath their suit jackets where their weapons were holstered.

The DCI spotted Jim Whitmore and moved to greet him. The two men shook hands and then Jim turned to introduce Charlie. Though he would have preferred to go straight to his room, Charlie forced a smile and reached out to shake hands. He looked into the man's face just as a tiny red light illuminated the DCI's forehead. Charlie didn't think—he reacted.

Rather than take Director Palmer's hand, he lunged forward, wrapping one arm around the DCI and the other around his father. When the three men fell to the ground, the security men reacted by moving toward them. The shot that rang out a split second later diverted their attention from Charlie to the real threat.

Weapons drawn, two of the Secret Service agents moved through the scattering crowd in search of the gunman, while the other two crouched down in front of where the DCI was sprawled on the ground along with Jim and Charlie. One called back to him, his eyes staying on the room. "Are you okay, sir?"

Shaken but clearly unharmed, the DCI nodded. "Yeah."

The other agent communicated with their driver and they all started toward the front door. Someone turned to Charlie and asked, "Where was the shooter?"

"I don't know. I saw one of those red targeting beams and I just reacted."

"That's odd," one agent said as they stepped outside. "Most snipers don't use that kind of scope for that reason. They don't want their target to have any warning."

"Unless he wasn't the only one," Charlie commented.

Awareness dawned in the agent's eyes and he turned and pushed the DCI back into the hotel just as another shot rang out. The agent's body jerked from the impact, and Charlie instinctively grabbed the wounded man by the jacket and dragged him back inside.

Across the lobby, the other gunman had blended into the crowd of people rushing for the exits. He might have stayed hidden from the Secret Service agents had he not tried to take another shot. He raised his gun, but he never managed to squeeze the trigger. Instead he was hit by both bullets as the agents eliminated that threat once and for all.

"There's no way to tell how many shooters may be outside," one agent said, turning to his wounded partner. "How are you doing?"

Winded, but not bleeding, the downed agent said, "It got me in my vest."

"How are we going to get out of here?" Jim asked.

"Through the kitchen," one agent suggested. "I'll have our driver leave and then circle back."

"Let's go then." Charlie helped the wounded agent to his feet.

Together, they made their way through the restaurant, into the kitchen, past the staff who looked on curiously, and then to the service entrance at the back of the building. As soon as they got the message that their vehicles were in position, two agents stepped out and checked the area before letting the others file out into the waiting SUVs.

As soon as they were under way, the driver of their car turned back to the senator. "Senator Whitmore?"

"Yes?" Jim asked, surprised to be called by name since they hadn't arrived with the DCI.

"We just got a message for you, sir," the driver said, then hesitated a moment as he made a left turn. "Your daughter is safe. She is on her way to our naval base in Italy."

The relief was immediate, as were the tears that filled his eyes.

* * *

Brent sat silently as the doctor examined the gunshot wound. He had gone through several hours of meetings at the naval base in Italy before he mentioned the gunshot wound that had landed him at the base hospital. The X-ray had told him what Brent already knew: the bullet had missed the bone completely, entering and exiting through the fleshy part of his arm.

While waiting for the X-ray to be developed, he had spent nearly an hour hooked up to an IV to combat any possible infection and dehydration. The doctor had been kind enough to have the nurse take the IV needle out when he came into the treatment room, clearly aware that Brent intended to do it himself otherwise.

The door opened and Kel walked in. He leaned against the doorjamb and waited for the doctor to finish.

The doctor barely glanced at Kel before turning his attention back to Brent. "The stitches have been in too long to redo them. It's going to leave a nasty scar, but overall the gal that stitched you up did okay for her first time around." He smiled. "I'll have the nurse come in and apply a fresh dressing, and we'll plan to take the stitches out in a couple more days."

Kel raised an eyebrow but didn't say anything until the doctor left. "I guess your civilian did okay by you."

Brent's stomach pitched at Kel's comment. He had been chastising himself for the past two hours for getting emotionally involved with "his civilian," as Kel called her. Determined to change the subject, he asked, "Have they cleared the hotel yet?"

"We didn't get the message to the hotel in time. The assassination attempt went down this morning," Kel stated.

"What?" Brent looked at him, confused. "You said 'attempt.' Is everyone okay?"

"Yeah, we got lucky." Kel grinned when he added, "Actually, the attempt was broken up by the senator's son."

Brent shook his head. "I still don't understand. The date on the Palm Pilot I picked up was tomorrow's date."

"Could they have known that their information was compromised?"

"I doubt it. It was pure luck that we happened to come across the information."

"What if the date wasn't for the assassination, but rather for the subway attack?"

Brent's face paled. "That doesn't give us enough time."

"Meet me in our briefing room as soon as the nurse finishes patching you up," Kel ordered. "Everyone else is already in there waiting for us."

"I've got a better idea." Brent jumped off the examining table and grabbed his shirt. He had just finished buttoning it up when the nurse walked in with the bandages.

"I'll take that," Kel said, swiping the bandages off of the tray she held and then stepping past her.

"Wait, I have to bandage his arm," she protested. Her eyes widened when Brent followed behind Kel.

"He'll take care of it for me," Brent assured her and then promptly left without giving the nurse a second glance.

Kel and Brent walked outside to where Kel had a Jeep waiting. A few minutes later they pulled into the parking lot of a nearby building.

They entered the briefing room that the rest of the team had already converted into a temporary command center. Tristan was staring at a computer screen listing details about various biological weapons. Next to him, Quinn was on the phone. Across the room Seth had two computers set up, one displaying a map of the Washington DC subway system and the other showing someone's email correspondence.

Kel threw the roll of bandages at Tristan. "Here, patch up Miller."

Tristan snagged the roll right before it hit him between the eyes. "Thanks, boss." He stood up and let Brent take his seat.

"Someone in the CIA knows what we're dealing with," Brent said as he glanced at the list of known biological agents. "Amy said that the intel officer at the embassy met with the ambassador the day she was taken hostage."

"Anyone know who the CIA folks were at the embassy?"

"Quinn's working on that now," Seth said as Quinn started scribbling notes on a pad of paper.

"How come I have to play nursemaid?" Tristan muttered as Brent pulled his arm free of his shirt to expose the wound.

"Just lucky, I guess," Brent told him without sparing him a glance.

"What have we got so far?" Kel asked as Quinn hung up the phone.

"I talked to the CIA agent that was in Abolstan. He says the biological agent we're dealing with is airborne, has an estimated range of a few hundred cubic yards, and remains effective for up to six hours," Quinn informed them. He paused before adding, "He also said that there isn't a counteragent."

"That means either we're dealing with the suicide types, or someone is going to set up some kind of delayed release." Brent started to stand, but Tristan held him in place.

"Hold still for a minute. I'm almost done here." Tristan tied off the bandage and then released Brent.

Quinn spoke up once more. "The CIA is sending over the report from the Center for Disease Control, but from what they said, this is nasty stuff. Death is within minutes of contact."

"What kind of support do we have in Washington?" Brent asked as he moved to look over Seth's shoulder.

"They're activating two reserve units, and we're asking the various police departments to pull some overtime hours to help us conduct searches," Quinn said. "The problem is, even with the extra help, we don't have the manpower to conduct thorough searches at all of these metro stations."

Tristan spoke up. "Since the DCI was targeted, I think we need to concentrate the manpower on the Pentagon station. If someone managed to take out the Director of Central Intelligence and then wipe out a portion of our employees at the Pentagon, our intelligence system would be crippled."

Kel nodded in agreement. "Quinn, call Admiral Mantiquez and tell him we need him to task some of the Pentagon units to cover the searches at the Pentagon and Pentagon City stops."

"If they can drum up enough manpower, we should have them take care of National Airport too," Brent suggested.

Kel nodded and signaled for Quinn to make the call. He then turned back to Brent. "If you were a terrorist, what other stations would you go for?"

"Metro Center has high traffic, as do most of the stations in DC," Brent suggested. "I think we should concentrate most of the manpower there."

"What about us? Are we shipping out?" Tristan asked. "If we leave now, we can make it there before tomorrow."

"We're on intel for this one. We'll do what we can to help from here, but for now we need to see what else we can retrieve from that Palm Pilot." Kel motioned to Seth. "Johnson is already trying to trace this guy's communications to see who he was talking to."

"How are we going to monitor the subway stations in Washington?" Brent asked.

"We have computers being delivered any time, and we're going to set up a secure link with the closed-circuit security cameras for the metro," Kel explained. "The transit authority is already working with our computer guys in DC to set it up for us."

"Where do you want me to start?"

"For now, why don't you go down and pay a visit to Amy Whitmore?" Kel suggested. "You can check on how she's doing while you ask if she can remember anything else the ambassador said."

Brent stood, ignoring the flutter of anticipation that shot through him. He told himself he was just anxious to see for himself that Amy was all right. He took two steps before he thought to ask, "Why don't we just talk to the ambassador directly?"

"We would if we could."

"Wasn't he at the hotel in Cairo?"

Kel nodded. "Oh, he was there. Apparently all of the excitement of being evacuated last week and the assassination attempt today resulted in some kind of nervous breakdown. He is currently under sedation."

Tristan rolled his eyes. "How in the world did he get posted to this part of the world?"

Kel ended the speculation with a look. "It doesn't matter. Either way, most of the intel we have is from what Brent and Amy have pieced together. We can't afford to turn away whatever sources we still have."

"This is so not fair," Quinn complained. "We get to sit around and stare at computers for the next who knows how long, and you're sending him on a date."

"Don't wait up, Mommy." Brent grinned and headed for the door.

"At least send us some pizza!" Quinn called after him as laughter echoed out into the hallway.

CHAPTER 11

"Can you please take this needle out of my arm?" Amy asked for the third time in less than an hour.

"I'll have to ask the doctor, miss," the nurse said as she breezed out of the room.

Amy sighed, frustrated that she had been confined to this hospital bed for the past eight hours. Within an hour of getting into dry clothes, her shivering had finally ceased, but the doctor had insisted on hooking her up to an IV as a precaution. She had refused the flimsy hospital gown the nurse offered her and was now dressed in a pair of army fatigues that someone had managed to scrounge up.

After she had finally warmed up, exhaustion had overtaken her and she had spent her first several hours in blissful slumber. She had then realized that someone needed to let her family know she was okay, which thankfully had already been taken care of. Now it seemed that every time she started to doze off, a nurse would come in and start poking and prodding again. Then she would remember the needle in her arm, something she could hardly stand to look at, and her mind would start racing.

Memories of her struggles escaping Abolstan just served to remind her that she already missed Brent's company even though they had only been apart for eight hours. She supposed that was normal after spending so much time together, but it depressed her to think that she might not see him again. Repeatedly she told herself that the connection she felt to him was probably intensified because of their circumstances, but that didn't stop her from thinking about him.

She had not seen or heard from Brent since they had landed and she had been loaded into an ambulance. Though she knew it had only been the night before, she felt like she had been in the hospital for days rather than hours. The possibility that Brent had already rejoined his team and was headed for the threat in Cairo was too real to dismiss, but she preferred that to the thought of him flying to Washington, where he might be dealing with something even more deadly and elusive than an assassin.

Imagining the chaos that would occur if these terrorists were successful brought tears to her eyes. Her friends used that subway system all the time regardless of what the threat level was on a given day. After going through so much during their teenage years, most of her friends had come to accept that certain things were simply out of their control so it was best not to worry about them.

She had been in high school on 9/11 when the plane had crashed into the Pentagon, and her school had automatically gone into lock-down mode. Barely a year had passed before the area had been terrorized by a sniper who randomly killed people while they gassed up their cars or walked through parking lots. Even a boy walking into a nearby school had been shot. While the search had continued for the sniper, all of the outdoor activities had been cancelled. Again her high school had been locked down each day until she and the other students could barely remember what it was like to eat their lunch outside or walk down the street without fear.

Football games had been held on secure military facilities, often without anyone in the stands. Her soccer league had simply cancelled the rest of the season. Her mind turned to Brent as she realized that he, too, would have gone through some of those experiences. Since he was a couple of years older than she was, she guessed that he would have been in college during the sniper attacks.

When Brent himself suddenly appeared in her doorway, she just stared for a moment, surprised to see him when he had been so heavily on her mind.

"How are you doing?" Brent asked, crossing to the chair next to her bed.

"I'd be better if they would let me out of here," Amy admitted. "What about you?"

"The doctor took one look at your stitches and decided you did such a good job he left them in."

"Yeah, right." Amy laughed. It felt good to laugh again, and she could admit at least to herself that she was relieved to see that Brent was still here and out of harm's way.

"I'm serious." Brent sat down next to her and stretched his long legs out in front of him.

"Just tell me why you're the one who got shot and I'm the one stuck in a hospital bed," Amy said.

"You're prettier than I am," Brent suggested. "I guess they wanted to keep you around."

She glanced toward the door and lowered her voice. "Do you have any experience with taking out IVs?"

"Some," Brent admitted with a grin, but then the smile faded. "Actually, I need to talk to you. We need to know anything you can remember about what the ambassador was working on, what you saw on his desk, anything that might help us with this subway problem."

Before she could answer him, the nurse came back in. "I'm sorry sir, but Miss Whitmore is not supposed to have any visitors."

"That's okay, she isn't staying anyway." Brent stood up and grabbed Amy's chart. He scrawled a name and phone number across the bottom and then signed his name. "Would you please tell the doctor that Miss Whitmore has decided to check herself out? The number of my CO is right here if he has any questions."

"Sir, she can't just leave," the nurse protested as Brent turned to take the surgical tape off of Amy's arm and then removed the IV.

"Just watch me," Amy muttered under her breath, leaning down to slip her shoes on.

Brent bit back a smile, managing a serious face when he turned back to the nurse. He stood and took Amy's hand to help her up. With an air of authority, he said simply, "I'm sorry, but this is a matter of national security."

With that, Brent led Amy past the gaping nurse and out the door.

"Where are we going?"

"We've set up a command center down the road." Brent glanced down at the fatigues she was wearing and shook his head. "It looks like you enlisted without knowing it."

"Yeah, but I think I did basic training the hard way." Amy followed him out into the daylight. Her steps slowed as she looked up into the sky.

Brent glanced over at her. "Are you okay?"

"Yeah," Amy nodded. "It's just that this is the first time in a week that we've been able to walk outside and not worry about someone shooting at us."

"Give it some time. You'll get used to it again." They drove down the street and then he led her inside the building where the squad's temporary command center was located. His voice took on a serious tone when he spoke again. "You know, you probably should go through some counseling after what you've been through."

"The doctor mentioned that too," Amy replied with a shrug. "I'll look into it once I figure out where I'm going to be living."

"I thought you would spend some time at home, at least for a while."

"There are some complications at home I've been trying to avoid."

He caught it then, that sense of someone else. He didn't even try to fight the wave of jealousy that surged through him. Rather than respond, he just continued through the hall and then pushed open the door to the briefing room.

During the twenty minutes he had been gone, six new computers had been set up on two long tables stretching across one wall. Each of the screens had four images on it, apparently feeding from the security cameras at the various metro stations in Washington DC.

Immediately, Amy zeroed in on the video images. "That looks like the metro station at Dupont Circle."

Kel nodded, then shifted uncomfortably. "You probably shouldn't be in here. Why don't we go down the hall and you can tell us what you remember."

Amy let out a little sigh. "If I'm going to be able to help you, I need to see what you already have."

"I'm sorry, but you don't have the proper security clearances," Kel responded.

"We all know that there isn't time for that." Amy folded her arms across her chest and looked Kel in the eye. She sighed and pulled the strings she hated to use. "Look, my father is a senator, and my sister-in-law was in the Witness Protection Program for three years. If there was anything questionable in my past, the government would know about it. I won't know what you're looking for unless I know what you've already got."

Brent stepped to her side. "She's right. We can debrief her later, but we can't afford to hold anything back now."

"I am going to get so busted for this," Kel muttered as he turned to Brent. "Show her whatever you need to."

Five minutes later, Amy was sitting at a desk that has been pushed into the corner nearest the door. In the middle of the desk were all of the operation plans and debriefing notes from the hostage rescue, the background on the terrorists who had been involved, and several analyses of key figures in Abolstan.

Daunted by the task at hand, Amy decided to start at the beginning, scanning through the team's report of the rescue operation. She tried to look at it objectively, but even scanning through the report brought back images of the shot ringing out that she had thought was meant for her. Taking a deep breath, she scanned through each team member's individual report, trying to visualize their side of things.

She didn't notice anything unusual, so she moved on to the reports on the continued violence in the capital city the night that she and Brent had escaped. Halfway through reading them, her mind caught up with what she had read in the first report. She picked it up again and looked at the team members' reports again, this time with a purpose in mind. The two men guarding the hostages had been killed along with two more who had been out in the hall. Another nine had been killed when the SEALs secured the building.

Amy looked around and reached for the closest paper available, which happened to be from the printer hooked up to the computer Quinn was using.

"Can I borrow a pen?"

Quinn grabbed one off of his makeshift desk and held it out to her without even looking up.

"Thanks." Amy sat back down and sketched out the hotel when they had been taken hostage. Two men had come into her room, and one had been outside in the hall. She forced herself to recall what she had seen during those terrifying moments when they were dragged from their rooms, their freedom violated.

Detailing the floor on which all of the hostages had been staying on that fateful day, she drew in little stick figures to represent each of their captors. Two had gone into each of the rooms, she was sure of it, and she distinctly remembered three armed men in the hallway. She looked through the reports one more time to make sure she had done the math correctly. Thirteen had been shot, but she had seen seventeen.

With her sketch in hand, she pushed out of her chair and crossed to where Brent was staring at the security feed from the various subway stations. "When you came in to rescue us, what happened to the other terrorists?"

Brent shifted his focus to her. "What other terrorists?"

"The reports indicate thirteen terrorists were killed. I remember at least seventeen." She put her sketch down on the table and pointed at her little stick figures. "Two came into each room, all at the same time. I remember at least three more were standing guard in the hall. In fact, one of them went to help when they pulled Frank out of his room because the first two couldn't handle him alone."

"That leaves four unaccounted for." Brent stood and motioned to Kel. "During the hostage rescue, were there any terrorists still in the building when we left?"

"No, we cleared the building before the helicopter took off. We didn't want to take a chance of someone being left to shoot us down." Kel gave a careless shrug, ignoring the fact that in essence it had happened anyway. "Why?"

"Because we've got four terrorists unaccounted for," Brent replied, showing him Amy's sketch and explaining her analysis.

"Did all of them take shifts guarding you?"

Amy shook her head. "I don't think so. They changed shifts a lot, but I don't remember the ones in the hall ever guarding us, at least not inside the penthouse."

"Can you remember what they looked like?"

"Sort of." Amy flipped the paper over and did a quick sketch of the one who had been right outside of her room. His face had been emblazoned on her mind, along with the way he had looked at her as though her life was of no importance to him. She held out the drawing to Kel. "If you can get me a pencil, I can probably do a better one, but this should give you a general idea of what he looks like."

Kel's eyebrows rose as he looked at the paper in his hand. A composite artist couldn't have done any better. "Can you do this for the other two who were in the hallway?"

"I can try." Amy fiddled with the pen in her hand. "I didn't see one of them very well, and I'm sure you can imagine that I was a little distracted at the time."

"Tristan! Get me some pencils and paper," Kel shouted across the room. He then turned back to Amy. "Do the best you can."

Amy just nodded as Tristan handed her a dozen pencils and a ream of paper. As she sat down at her desk, Kel called out to her. "Hey Whitmore, welcome to the team."

"Thanks." Amy smiled with a new sense of belonging. She shifted the paper on her desk, picked up a pencil, and got to work.

CHAPTER 12

"Amy, you need to go get some sleep." Brent laid a hand on her shoulder, concerned because she had spent the past four hours sketching the men who had taken her hostage and then devouring as much information as she could from the project files.

"It's going to happen tomorrow, isn't it?" Amy asked wearily.

"We think so."

"Then I want to stay here," Amy said. "Maybe I'll be able to remember something that will help."

"You aren't going to do anyone any good if you don't take care of yourself," Brent insisted. Realizing that he was about to face her stubborn streak, he crossed the room to where Kel was looking over the latest intelligence report. Brent lowered his voice to make sure Amy didn't hear him and said, "I think you may have to order her to take a break."

Kel pushed back from his desk and stood up. "I don't think we're going to be able to get much more done tonight anyway. The subway opens at five o'clock eastern standard time, that's eleven to us." He rolled his neck, trying to work the kinks out of it. "Intel in Washington is going to keep running checks on the emails to that Palm Pilot, but so far we haven't found anyone he was communicating with in the United States. We have another unit that's going to come in here and watch the subway monitors in case someone tries to drop a package during the night."

"Sounds like we have as much covered as we can from here," Brent agreed. "Did anyone think to get Amy someplace to sleep tonight?"

"Quinn," Kel called out.

Quinn turned toward him. "Yeah?"

Kel grinned. "Thanks for volunteering. Call housing and find someplace for our new teammate over there to sleep," he instructed, nodding in Amy's direction. "Also, where did you put those cell phones?"

Quinn dug through a knapsack and fished out two cell phones. "Here you go."

Kel passed them to Brent. "Here's your phone, and we got one for Whitmore so we can keep track of her while she's here." He turned and raised his voice so everyone could hear. "Okay, everyone go get some sleep. We'll start back up at 0600 hours."

"Thanks," Brent whispered.

"It's going to take Quinn a few minutes to track down someplace for her to stay," Kel reminded him. "Why don't you go take her out for some dinner? There's a Jeep out front."

"I might just do that." Brent grinned and took the keys Kel held out to him.

"Give Quinn a call when you're finished with dinner and he'll tell you where she'll be staying."

"Thanks."

* * *

"What do you mean she's not here?" Jim Whitmore growled at the doctor. He was normally a calm, reserved individual. But today had been anything but normal.

"I'm sorry, sir. She just got up and left." The doctor fumbled with the chart he held in his hand. "The nurse said that an officer came in and signed her out."

"Do you know who the officer was?"

"Yes, it was Lieutenant Miller. He gave the name and number of his commanding officer." The doctor scribbled the information down on a piece of paper and handed it to the senator. "Housing should also know where she is staying. I'm sure we can get someone to take you over to the temporary quarters."

"Where's the nearest phone?"

"This way, sir."

* * *

"I'd almost forgotten what real food tasted like after eating those energy bars," Amy said as she spooned the last bite of sherbet into her mouth.

Brent stared at her across the table for a moment before motioning for the waiter to bring him the check. "You must be tired. I should get you over to your room."

"Yeah, I guess I really should try to call my folks again. I still can't believe no one was home when I called."

"I'm sure someone already got word out to them," Brent assured her as he tossed some bills on the table and stood up. He reached for her hand without thinking and led her out of the restaurant.

"How long will you be here before you go back home?"

"About a week." Brent pulled open the door of the Jeep for her and then skirted around the front and got in beside her. "Assuming we're right about tomorrow, it will take about four or five days to finish the reports and debriefings."

Amy watched him as he retrieved his cell phone from his pocket and called Quinn to find out where she was staying tonight. A moment later he put the car in gear and glanced over at her. "Quinn set everything up for you. We just have to swing by and pick up the key."

Amy nodded. She remained silent as they stopped to pick up the key and then drove to the base's temporary housing. She wanted to ask if she would see him again after she left, but she was unable to voice the question. Somehow her wants and needs seemed trivial in the face of a terrorist attack in her backyard.

He pulled up in front of a residential building and got out of the Jeep to show her to the door. "Here we are."

They walked up the short sidewalk together. When they reached the doorstep, Amy turned to thank him for everything, but her mind went blank. He had moved closer without her even realizing it. His eyes were dark, questioning, and little butterflies started dancing in her stomach. Without seeming to move at all, he slid a hand around her waist and drew her closer.

She could almost see his mind racing, his conscience battling between the spark that flashed between them and the ethics he was bound by. She thought she understood the ethics part—his concern that her feelings for him had bloomed from gratitude and dependence. Certain that she knew her own mind and heart, she didn't believe for a minute that she would have developed feelings for just anyone, even after spending days with them in the desert.

Without thinking, she slid her arms around his neck as he lowered his lips to hers. The spark between them exploded, and her entire being focused on this one moment, this one man. A little warning bell sounded in her mind, telling her that what she felt for Brent might overpower her if she wasn't careful.

This wasn't a man who would be home every day at five o'clock for dinner, or whose ambitions she even understood. He was driven to protect, to serve. Duty would always come first, family second. She convinced herself she could never live that kind of life even as she let the sensation of his kiss seep through her.

Suddenly light spilled out onto the doorstep as the door opened behind them. Amy turned to see her father standing in the doorway.

"Dad?" She was torn between wanting it to really be her father in the doorway and hoping that she was just imagining it. Her eyes narrowed as she decided that she wasn't imagining anything. She withdrew from Brent's embrace and turned to throw her arms around her father's neck. "Dad! What are you doing here?"

"Looking for you." Jim Whitmore pulled his daughter close, breathing her in for a moment before he shifted his gaze to Brent. The look turned to a glare. "Are you going to introduce me to your friend?"

"I'm sorry." Amy released her father, noticing the proprietary way he kept an arm around her waist. "Dad, this is Lieutenant Brent Miller. Brent, this is my father, Senator Jim Whitmore."

"Senator." Brent extended his hand and noted the senator's brief hesitation before he reached out to shake.

"It seems I owe you a debt of gratitude for bringing my daughter home safely." His voice was controlled and formal.

"She made the job easy," Brent said simply.

Charlie's voice came from the doorway, and a moment later Amy was scooped up by her older brother. "Thank goodness you're okay."

Amy laughed as he lifted her off her feet before setting her back down. "Charlie, this is Brent Miller. He's the one who rescued me."

Charlie leaned forward to shake Brent's hand, his smile welcoming. "We owe you."

"Not at all." Brent nodded to Amy. "I'll let you spend some time with your family. Would you like me to pick you up in the morning?"

"Please," Amy said simply.

Brent nodded. "I'll see you a few minutes before six."

As soon as Jim had shut the door, he turned to Amy. "What's at six?"

"I'm helping out with a little project tomorrow," Amy answered, not sure how much she should say.

"I was planning on taking you home tomorrow," Jim informed her. "Your mother has been worried sick."

"We can't go home tomorrow," Amy insisted as panic rushed through her. "In fact, I'd feel a lot better if you could talk Mom into going to visit Matt and CJ for a couple of days."

"She's already at Matt's house," Jim said, his eyes narrowing. "Why?"

Amy let out a frustrated sigh. "I can't say. I'm sorry, but it's classified information."

"Amy, I sit on the Senate Intelligence Committee. I have top secret clearance."

"Then you can get the information yourself," Amy replied. "I'm sorry, but I was told specifically not to discuss this with anyone."

Jim stared at her, not so much with disbelief as with admiration. "Let's call your mom, and then we'll talk."

* * *

Tears of relief and joy streamed down Katherine Whitmore's cheeks as she talked to her daughter for the first time since their world had been turned upside down a week before. Amy assured her that she was just fine and that they would come home soon. In fact, she even suggested that they meet at Matt and CJ's house in Florida for a family reunion of sorts.

Matt hovered nearby, and Katherine finally relinquished the phone to him so that he could hear for himself that Amy was safe and sound.

"When is she coming home?" CJ asked as soon as Katherine was off the phone.

"She said it will probably be a few days, but she wants to come visit here first." Katherine wiped the moisture from her cheeks. "I think she wants to have all of us together before she has to start picking up the pieces of her life again."

CJ nodded in agreement.

"I wonder what she'll do now," Katherine said, half to herself. "Maybe she'll finally agree to work for Jim."

CJ shook her head. "I wouldn't count on that. I don't think there's any way she's going to work there as long as Jared is still on his staff."

"Why do you say that?" Katherine asked. Every time she saw Amy and Jared together, Jared was attentive to the point that she wondered if they would decide to get married after all.

"Jared still wants to marry her, so it's awkward for her to be around him." CJ shrugged. "I think she feels like she'll be fighting her way out of a corner all the time if he's around."

"They made such a cute couple," Katherine said as Matt hung up the phone.

"Who did?" Matt asked, sitting next to CJ and putting his arm around her.

"Amy and Jared," CJ answered.

Matt just shook his head. "Jared really isn't Amy's type."

"What makes you say that?" Katherine asked, surprised. Matt had never voiced any negative opinions about Jared before.

Matt looked at CJ as though waiting for her to answer. The only response he got was a shake of her head, and a look that clearly said it was his place to tell his mother what they had both long suspected.

"We've always wondered if Jared was more interested in being married to someone with Amy's social status than in being married to Amy."

"You think he was only interested in her to advance his career?" Katherine shook her head. "I have a hard time believing that. He's such a nice young man."

"Of course he's nice. He's still hoping to tap into Amy's trust fund." Matt pointed out. "And whether or not it's true, that's what Amy thought."

"She told you that?"

CJ sighed. "Not in so many words, but yeah."

"She never said anything about it to us. She just said she needed to get away from the family for a while."

Matt nodded. "I think there's some truth to that too."

"Whatever she does, I certainly hope we can keep her close to home for a while."

"Amen to that."

CHAPTER 13

Brent approached Amy's front door the same way he might have approached a firing squad—with a combination of daring and trepidation. He wished he could say that he regretted kissing Amy the night before, but how could he regret something that felt so right? He knew nothing could develop between them, not with the kind of life he led, but he didn't want to think about that right now. For the first time in his life, his heart no longer belonged to him and he had absolutely no idea how to get it back.

As he said his prayers the night before, he had realized that when she left it would likely tear him in two. He had also recognized it was going to happen no matter how much time they spent together. Brent decided he might as well spend as much time with her as he could until the moment came when her father took her home.

Brent had no delusions of how Senator Whitmore felt about him. The senator felt threatened and wasn't about to befriend the man he had just caught kissing his daughter, even it if was the man who had saved her life.

Despite the fact that Amy was twenty-two and he was twenty-six, when the senator had opened that door Brent had felt like a sixteen-year-old stealing a kiss on a first date. As he knocked on the door now, he once again felt like a teenager, especially when Jim pulled the door open.

"Good morning, sir." Brent met the older man's stare. "Is Amy ready?"

Jim nodded. "We all are."

"Excuse me?" Brent's eyes widened. "I'm sorry, sir, but we are dealing with highly sensitive information. We can't grant just anyone access."

"I realize that." Jim's voice took on an air of authority. "Which is why I already spoke with your commanding officer to make sure my son and I were cleared."

Jim stepped outside, making way for Charlie and Amy to follow. Brent caught sight of Amy and barely kept his jaw from dropping to the ground. A light dusting of makeup accented her eyes, and her lips were tinted a shade darker than normal. Her hair cascaded past her shoulders, contrasting against a tailored white blouse. Her blue floral skirt flowed nearly to her ankles.

Amy looked up and saw him staring. "Are you okay?"

"Yeah, I've just never seen you in normal clothes before."

She smiled. "Dad brought me some of my clothes from home."

Brent turned to open the door of the Jeep for her, wishing for more time alone with her. The senator gave him a stern don't-mess-with-my-daughter look, which he noted and then promptly ignored. After everyone climbed in, Brent moved to the driver's seat.

Rather than speak to Amy, Brent directed a comment to the senator. "You said you spoke with Commander Bennett. Did he bring you up to speed on our situation?"

"Enough for me to understand why Amy didn't want her mother anywhere near Virginia today," Jim responded.

Brent nodded in understanding. He parked in front of their destination and led the way inside. Kel was waiting for them at the briefing room door.

Brent made the introductions and then closed the door behind him.

Kel called out to everyone, "Okay, we're all here, so let's get started."

Jim's eyes widened when everyone left their work stations and moved to the center of the room. Noticing the senator's confusion, Brent turned to him and explained, "We start out every day with a prayer. Today especially, we need all the help we can get."

"Who wants to offer it?" Kel asked.

"I will," Brent said, folding his arms and bowing his head. His prayer was simple and straight from the heart. He asked that each of them would be blessed with the insight needed to protect their country and those who lived in it. When he closed his prayer, he looked up to see tears in Amy's eyes. Before he could say anything to her, Kel took over.

"Whitmore, you already know what to do."

Amy motioned to her dad and brother. "With these two around, you'd better call me Amy."

Kel nodded as she moved past him, and then he turned to Jim. "I'll be honest with you, Senator. Things are going to get tense today. My unit often works intel assignments, but all of us are much more accustomed to being in the field. If any of my men tell you to do something, you do it. We can't afford to have civilians get in the way, not at a time like this."

"We're here to help, not hinder," Jim responded. He nodded at the security monitors. "Charlie and I have spent a lot of time riding the subway over the years. Perhaps we would be most useful observing."

"My thoughts exactly," Kel agreed as he watched Brent pick up a stack of papers from his desk. Kel had made copies of Amy's sketches the night before, and now there was a set beside each computer and the originals were displayed on the wall above them. Beside the sketches on the wall, someone had hung up a photograph of Namir Dagan, the leader of the faction that was currently in control of most of Abolstan.

Brent handed Jim and Charlie each a copy of Amy's sketches. "We aren't sure exactly what we're looking for, but we know that these men may be involved."

"Do we have any idea of how big these guys are?" Charlie asked. "Height, weight, that sort of thing?"

"Amy, can you come here for a minute?" Brent called out.

With a nod, she crossed to where they were standing.

"Give me a guesstimate on the size of these guys."

Amy closed her eyes for a moment and took a deep breath. When she opened them again, she pointed at the man she most feared. "He's about my height—six feet tall—and weighs around one-ninety." She then pointed to the next sketch. "That one was taller and skinnier. Maybe six two, one-eighty. Same with the third one."

"How do you know what they look like?" Jim asked, sincerely shocked to see his daughter providing information in such an off-handed way.

"She's our source," Kel told him bluntly. "As I mentioned to you on the phone, your daughter is currently a valuable member of our team. Most of the intelligence we have came from her and Lieutenant Miller."

"I'll get back to work," Amy said simply and returned to her work station.

"These are the men that kidnapped her?" Jim asked, clearly shaken.

"They're the ones we believe are still alive," Brent answered now. "She thinks there's a fourth out there. That's what she's working on now. She's sketching all of her captors that she can remember. Hopefully with her drawings, we can figure out which ones might still be alive."

Quinn hung up a phone and interrupted the conversation. "Intel confirmed that Dagan is still in Abolstan. He was spotted yesterday in the capital city."

Kel gave him a nod before speaking again to Jim and Charlie. "The subway stations have already closed for the night, and they don't reopen for another five hours. For now, we're just looking for any activity." Kel motioned for them to sit down and then turned to Brent. "Seth still hasn't found anything on that Palm that's going to help us."

"What about customs? Have we gotten the list we needed of all of the entries into the U.S.?"

"Customs isn't cooperating." Kel's voice was clipped. "It's the middle of the night in DC, and it seems the people who can authorize what we need are at home sleeping. We're still looking for someone willing to wake one of them up."

Jim stood once more. "If you're having trouble getting coopera- tion, I may be able to help you with that. What do you need?"

"We need a list of everyone who passed through customs for the past week, particularly East Coast entries," Kel replied. "Amy says she didn't see those three after the hostages were secured. That makes me believe that they started traveling before we got there."

"Point me to a phone and I'll take care of this," Jim said, clearly grateful to be of use.

"One more thing, Senator," Kel said, holding a cordless phone out to him. "Please don't utilize anyone on your staff for information. We'll get you whatever you need."

"Why?"

"We can't risk another breach of security."

"*Another* breach? When was the first one?"

"The press knew your daughter wasn't with the other hostages, and the news broke right after you left for Cairo," Kel explained. "We won't start investigating that problem until we get through this crisis, but we aren't taking any chances."

"In that case, I need the number for customs."

"Quinn!"

"I got it." Quinn held out a paper with a list of phone numbers. "Good luck, Senator. It'll really help if you can get us that list."

"I'll get it."

* * *

Amy stared down at the sketches she had completed and blinked, realizing that most of these men were dead. Her drawings were spread out on the table, staring back at her. She had managed to recall the faces of seven more of the men who had held her hostage, but she had no way of knowing if any of them was the one that was still alive. She sensed someone behind her but didn't look up.

Brent's hand came down on her shoulder, his voice soft. "How are you doing?"

"These are the only ones I can remember."

Brent leaned over, noticing that she hadn't drawn the two that had been in the penthouse when he had come through the window. He tried to recall the faces of the two men who had been standing guard before members of his team had killed them. Retrieving a pen from his pocket, he drew an X in the corner of the page. "He didn't make it out."

"The three on the top guarded us during the first couple of hours." She tapped on the center one. "I remember that one because he's the one that shot Frank."

"Let me show these to the others. Maybe they can help us narrow it down," Brent suggested.

Amy nodded and leaned back in her chair. Though she had only been at it for two hours, she was already exhausted. She watched as Quinn examined the sketches and pointed at two. Seth wasn't able to eliminate any of them, but Tristan identified one that wasn't a problem any longer. Finally, Brent handed the remaining three drawings to Kel. He took his time, ultimately narrowing the possibilities down to two.

Brent moved back to Amy's desk, showing her the two that remained. A moment later the door opened behind him.

"We've got art," Jim announced as he walked into the room with a thick stack of paper in his hand. It had taken a full twenty minutes for customs to agree to give him the information he wanted, and then another hour and a half for them to compile it and send it. "I have it separated by point of entry. I assume you want Amy to look at the DC airports first."

"Yeah," Kel said, turning to Brent. "Brent, make copies of those two sketches. Then you and Tristan can help look through the other points of entry."

Brent nodded and then left the room. A few minutes later he returned and tacked the original drawings on the wall before handing everyone in the room copies.

"Okay, everyone. Let's get to work." Kel divided up the information from customs, handing a stack to everyone except for Seth, who was still working on the Palm Pilot, and Quinn and Charlie, who were keeping watch on the security monitors.

Amy flipped through the papers. Each page contained eight passport photos along with the corresponding names. She sorted the papers into two stacks: those that were clearly not a threat and those that had photos that even slightly resembled any of the men she had identified. She was two-thirds of the way through the stack when she saw the man that she hoped never to see again—Ahmed Alleid.

Amy finished scanning the page and then circled the man in question. "I've got one."

"Are you sure?" Kel took the page from her and compared the circled passport photo to the sketch Amy had done.

"Yeah, I'm sure."

"Seth, notify all of the metro stations that this is one of the terrorists to watch for," Kel instructed. He moved to where the sketches were pinned up and wrote "Ahmed Alleid" at the bottom of the corresponding sketch. "Senator, could you please call customs? See if they know where this guy is staying."

Jim nodded and picked up a phone.

Two pages later, Amy found another one, and then one more. She had located all three of the men she had first identified. Roland Hanover had arrived from London an hour before Orlando Cousette had come in from Paris. "Commander, here are two more."

Jim Whitmore was still on the phone with customs and reached out for the new information to pass along. A few minutes later, he hung up and turned to Kel. "Here are the addresses listed."

"Brent, get the FBI on the phone and send them to pick these guys up," Kel ordered. "Amy, see if you can find our missing man."

Amy nodded as Brent grabbed a phone.

CHAPTER 14

Brent tapped away at his keyboard, hoping his hunch was right. All three of the men Amy had identified had given fake addresses, but Brent was guessing that they were in a hotel nearby. Quinn was sitting next to him, infiltrating the reservation systems of the hotels near subway stations in Virginia while Brent worked on the ones in DC. Tristan had been tasked with Maryland. Charlie continued with the boring task of watching the deserted subway stations on the computer monitors to make sure no one dropped off any packages during the early morning hours in Washington.

"Do you really think they'll be dumb enough to use the same name at the hotel?" Tristan asked as he searched through the hotel guest registers.

"It depends on if they have another set of fake IDs," Brent commented. "They can't possibly know that we're on to them. What are the chances that a hostage could not only identify them, but would also know where to look?"

"True," Tristan said, nodding.

"I think I've got something." Quinn punched up a screen and grinned. "Behold, Mr. Hanover and Mr. Cousette checked in the same day they arrived. According to this, they are checking out today."

"Give me the address. I'll get the FBI over there." Brent dialed the number and held out his hand. He relayed the information to the FBI agent he had been working with and glanced at his watch. It was almost 4 A.M. in Washington, only an hour before the subway would open.

"Ahmed Alleid isn't listed at any of the Maryland hotels," Tristan announced.

"He isn't in Virginia, either," Quinn said.

After getting off of the phone with the FBI, Brent turned back to his computer. He spent another fifteen minutes completing his search only to find that Alleid wasn't at any of the local hotels.

When Brent's phone rang, everyone quieted and listened, trying to piece together the one- and two-word fragments from Brent's side of the conversation. When he finally hung up, he grinned. "They got both of them as well as two vials they think are the biological agent. Our boys are taking it into the lab to be analyzed now."

"If they had two vials, we can assume that each of our missing men is also armed with the stuff," Kel noted. "Do they know how they were going to release it?"

Brent shook his head. "They're still looking into it."

Kel glanced at his watch. "Seth, call out for some lunch for us." He then motioned to the bank of security monitors. "I want everyone to take a computer to monitor. If you're familiar with one of the stations, take one you know."

Amy started to move to the monitors displaying National Airport when Kel stopped her. "Amy, I want you to just stand back and scan all of them. You are more likely to pick these guys out than we are, so I don't want to lock you in to one site."

Amy nodded, glancing at the early arrivals outside the Vienna station. "You know, if these guys are smart, they aren't going to get on the train at one of the busy stations," Amy commented. "I would think they would get on at one of the outlying stations like Vienna or Huntington. No one would really notice them there."

"It's a possibility," Kel agreed. "We've set up some fake construction at a few of the stations that have more than one entrance so that our extra security can try to identify them."

Amy turned her attention back to the monitors. The small crowds outside of the subway grew larger as five o'clock eastern time grew near. When the gates opened, she felt completely overwhelmed. There were so many people, so many places to look.

"Amy, check out this guy," Charlie called from his computer on the end.

She moved to look over his shoulder. "I don't recognize him." As an afterthought she asked, "Why?"

"He obviously didn't know where he was going."

Kel spoke now. "These guys have been in town for a few days. You have to assume that they have traveled the metro several times to determine how to best execute their plan."

Everyone quieted down, studying the screens in front of them. The first hour passed by painfully slowly, but gradually Amy fell into a routine of scanning the monitors in what she hoped was a logical order. Lunch was delivered in the form of sandwiches. Kel relieved everyone for a few minutes at a time so that they could eat without missing anything on the monitors.

Amy managed to eat a few bites, and then she held a water bottle in her hand and sipped from it occasionally.

"I've got an abandoned backpack here," Quinn said.

"Call it in," Kel instructed, moving to monitor Quinn's station while he pulled out his phone.

"Does this guy look familiar?" Brent asked Amy, pointing at a dark-haired man who was carrying a soft-sided briefcase. The man looked from side to side nervously.

Amy put her hand on Brent's shoulder, studying the man he indicated. He did look vaguely familiar, but she couldn't place him. "I don't know."

Kel moved to stand beside Amy and also studied the image.

Amy glanced over at Kel. "I'm sorry. He looks familiar, but I don't remember him from the hotel."

After a moment Kel suddenly let out an exasperated breath and rolled his eyes. "You've seen him on those used car commercials. He's not our guy."

"I knew he looked familiar," Brent muttered. Sensing Amy's tension, he reached up and put his hand on hers and gave it a squeeze.

Kel moved back to look at Quinn's monitor. "What's the status on the abandoned backpack?"

"The transit authority is debating whether to shut down the station or not," Quinn told him.

"Tell them to just do it and let's get it cleared." Kel shook his head in disgust. "It's not like this doesn't happen at least once a week."

"Yeah, but we don't normally go in with hazmat suits on to check them out."

"Just get it done," Kel instructed.

* * *

Jim Whitmore handled stress all the time, but he was starting to think that the tension just might be more than he could handle. The morning rush hour had passed without incident, except for the abandoned backpack that had contained someone's ham-on-rye sandwich and a couple of paperbacks.

Beside him, Charlie had gotten comfortable with his feet stretched out in front of him and his eyes on the screen as he snacked on one of the cookies that someone had brought in. He wasn't sure how many hours had passed since lunchtime, but his stomach rumbled as dinner hour in Italy continued to slip by. Now that they had reached the slow period between morning rush hour and the lunch traffic, Amy had moved back over to her desk to continue looking for that elusive fourth man she knew was out there somewhere.

Jim wasn't sure which he preferred, Amy standing on her feet all day staring at computer screens or her trying to remember the faces of the men who had held her captive. She seemed to be handling things well—too well, in fact. Looking at her, he never would have known she had just gone through a life-threatening experience.

Of course, he couldn't recall seeing her kiss a man in quite the way she had kissed Lieutenant Miller the night before, either. He was sure it was normal for her to become infatuated after what they had been through together, but he would be glad when she got over it. Jim didn't want to see his little girl fall in love with someone who might leave for work one day and then never come home.

The fact that the man clearly had faith in the Lord had brought him up a notch in Jim's opinion, but Brent Miller still wasn't anything like Jared Elliott. Jared was safe, steady, reliable. Brent was just dangerous. Mormon or not, he was the sort that didn't have to go looking for trouble. Trouble was likely to come looking for him.

Jim sensed someone behind him and felt Amy's hands come down on his shoulders to rub away some of the tension that had settled there. "How are you doing, Dad?"

"I'll feel better when all of this is over," Jim admitted. "I'm just glad your brother isn't playing in Washington tonight."

Amy's hands stilled. "Are the Nationals home tonight?"

"I think so." Jim nodded. "Against the Cubs, I believe."

"What if the subway isn't the only target?" Amy turned from her father and spoke to Kel. "Commander, can we find out what time the Nationals play tonight?"

"Yeah, sure." Kel raised his eyebrows but moved to his computer and pulled up the schedule on the internet. "The game starts at seven."

"The subway is going to be packed with people headed to the game as well as the regular rush-hour traffic," Amy pointed out. "Could the game be the target? A lot more people would be affected."

"Quinn?"

Quinn shook his head. "I don't think so. The stuff we're dealing with doesn't have a very big range. It's more effective in tight spaces, not open air."

"Still, we probably should concentrate on the stations that will take most of the traffic to the game," Kel noted.

"Metro Center is always crazy on game days," Charlie commented.

"If this stuff is effective for six hours, we're probably looking at a drop time no earlier than one or two in the afternoon," Kel surmised.

"How long does it take before people start feeling the effects?" Jim asked.

"Supposedly it's pretty quick," Seth piped in. "That means they aren't likely to release it until five or six, when the traffic is the heaviest."

"I just thought of something," Brent said suddenly. He stood, still keeping his eyes on his screen. "Kel, can you take over for me for a minute? I want to make a phone call."

"Sure." Kel traded him places, and Brent headed for his desk. They all listened in as he asked random questions about what their first two suspects had been doing when they were picked up.

After Brent hung up, he turned to the rest of them. "According to the FBI, our two suspects weren't even out of bed when they got there."

Brent grinned. "Not only that, they had requested a late checkout. According to the desk clerk, they weren't checking out until two."

"Then there's a good chance we're looking at the real threat coming this evening," Kel said as he stood and let Brent take his seat once more. "That should give us at least two hours before things start getting crazy."

"Maybe this would be a good time to send out for some dinner," Seth suggested.

"I'm going to get someone to cover these monitors for a while, and then I want all of you to take a break and grab something to eat," Kel told them. He turned to Charlie and Jim. "It's going to be a long night."

Jim glanced back at Amy. "Any ideas of what you want for dinner?"

"Actually," Amy said, "I think I'm going to change and go for a run. I haven't gotten a chance to exercise in over a week."

Three seats down Brent laughed. "Amy, you traveled ninety-seven miles on foot in less than a week. I think that qualifies as exercise."

"Walking around a desert in the middle of the night is not the same as a jog on a secure military base."

Quinn nodded in agreement. "She's got a point."

Brent just shook his head, the grin still in place.

A few minutes later their relief arrived and the first team headed out into the hallway. Brent stepped beside the Whitmores. "Did you want me to give you a ride back to your place?"

"I think I'm just going to head over to the officers' club for something to eat," Jim told him.

"I'll take a ride," Amy said. "I need to grab some workout clothes."

"Me too," Charlie said and slung an arm around his sister. "I think I'll go with Amy."

"Don't overdo it, you two," Jim warned as he walked them out to the parking lot.

"Who, me?" Amy shot back. She would have pulled off an innocent look had he not recognized the mischief in her eyes.

"Yes, you," Jim laughed, letting go of some of the tension. "Charlie, keep her out of trouble."

Charlie grinned. "Sure, Dad."

Jim watched his two youngest children follow Brent across the parking lot to the Jeep. A wave of gratitude washed over him, so great that it replaced the worry and anxiety that had been building over the past week. As he watched them drive away, he prayed that he would be able to find a way to keep Amy out of harm's way indefinitely.

CHAPTER 15

Charlie sat across from his sister, still not quite sure what to think of the situation. Quinn and Brent had met them at the officers' club after he and Amy had finished their run, and now they were enjoying their last fifteen minutes of freedom before they had to report back to reality.

Amy laughed at something Quinn said, making Charlie wonder if it really had been harder on the family while she was missing. He still felt anxious when he thought of what could have happened to Amy when she was in Abolstan. Looking at her, he didn't notice anything different. She was laughing, talking like she always had.

She was totally at ease, even though she was the only woman there. Of course, that hadn't changed much since she was a teenager. She had often tagged along with him throughout his teenage years, at first because he was tasked with watching after her and then because he enjoyed her company.

When she hit about fifteen or sixteen and his friends starting noticing that she wasn't a little girl anymore, Charlie had made a point of keeping her close. He had also made a point of knowing those few boyfriends she had during high school. Nobody was going to take advantage of his little sister.

Across the table Brent leaned over and whispered something in Amy's ear. She laughed at whatever it was and squeezed his hand for a brief moment. Undercurrents rippled between them, and Charlie tried to decide just how he felt about the prospect of his sister getting involved with someone in the military.

Charlie didn't know much about Brent as a person, but he respected what he did know. Dedication and duty sat heavily on Brent's shoulders, but he seemed to be able to shed their weight when it was time to relax. Looking at him and Quinn, Charlie never would have guessed that in less than an hour they would be working diligently to save hundreds, possibly thousands of people from a horrible fate.

As though his internal clock had kicked in, Quinn suddenly pushed back from the table. "We'd better head back."

Charlie stood too. "Might as well."

"You two go ahead," Brent said, still sitting next to Amy. "Amy isn't quite finished with her dinner, and I thought I would grab some drinks and snacks for tonight. We're going to need them."

Charlie teetered for a moment between going with Quinn and staying behind to play chaperone. But he had already taken a step toward the door and there was no way to stay without it being obvious that he just didn't want to leave his sister alone with Brent.

As though Brent read his hesitation, he grinned and said, "Don't worry, Charlie. I promise to behave myself."

With a nod of understanding, Charlie turned and followed Quinn outside.

As soon as they left, Brent looked over at Amy. "Does your brother try to intimidate everyone you go out with?"

She nodded without hesitation. "Between Charlie and Matt, I didn't have a lot of dates during high school. Of course, a lot of guys don't want to go out with a girl who's taller than they are."

"Maybe you just didn't want to go out with guys who were shorter than you," Brent suggested.

Amy laughed. "There was that." She took one last bite and pushed her plate away from her. "I don't think I can eat another bite."

"I'll be right back. I want to put an order in and then I'll drive you back." Brent went to talk to a member of the kitchen staff, requesting food to be delivered in a few more hours. He then crossed to the door where Amy was now waiting for him.

"How much time do we have?" Amy asked. She had yet to replace the watch that had been left behind in Abolstan.

"Ten minutes or so." Brent took her hand and led her outside. "I hope I didn't get you into too much trouble with your dad last night."

She shook her head, a faint blush tinting her cheeks. "I think he was so relieved to see for himself that I was safe, I could have dyed my hair purple and he wouldn't have cared."

"I think he's a little more concerned about me than he would be about purple hair dye." Brent put the key in the ignition but didn't start the Jeep.

Amy looked at him now, uncertainty in her eyes. "He's always been an overprotective father."

"Then I'm glad he isn't here right now." Brent leaned toward her, his lips meeting hers for a brief kiss. When he would have leaned closer, he pulled back instead as he reminded himself that they were in the middle of a parking lot. "I've wanted to do that all day."

"Me too," Amy admitted.

"We'd better get back."

When they arrived back at the conference room, it was packed with people. The men who had come in to relieve them were still manning their posts. The rest of the team had already arrived, all of them huddled next to Amy's desk along with a man in civilian clothes.

Charlie noticed them first and pointed at Amy. "There she is."

Kel moved toward her and handed her a photograph. "Amy, take a look at this picture."

In a gesture of support, Brent placed a hand on her back. He felt her tense as soon as she saw the picture.

"He was there," Amy said. "He's the one who shot Frank."

"What's going on?" Brent asked, taking the photograph from Kel so that Amy could no longer see it.

"Someone from the FBI identified this guy from Amy's sketch," Kel explained. "Apparently they staked out the hotel where they had picked up the other two. He tried to catch a shuttle to the subway station about twenty minutes ago."

"Did he have a vial on him like the other two?" Brent asked.

Kel nodded. "It was identical."

"What about the other man?" Amy pointed at the wall where only two of her sketches now remained. She was hoping and praying that the crisis was really over before it began.

Kel shook his head. "No sign of him. The FBI is informing the transit authority and our surveillance teams of who we're looking for. We don't want them looking for the guys we already have in custody."

"Come on, guys." Tristan called out. "Let's get back to work." He moved back to his computer terminal and relieved the man who had covered for him.

Kel thanked the unit that had taken over for them for the last couple hours as everyone resumed their prior positions. However relaxed everyone might have been over lunch, they were all business now. Between three and four o'clock eastern time, they had two false alarms with abandoned backpacks, but thankfully both were reclaimed before they had to send anyone in to check them out.

As the minutes ticked into the four o'clock hour, tension continued to build. The volume of people traveling the subway increased steadily, and by five o'clock it was difficult to pick anyone out in the crowd. Kel continued to get updates from the security personnel at the various stations, but so far no one had seen the man they were looking for.

Amy looked at the monitor for Metro Center, dread settling in her stomach as she realized that even with all of the extra security, they might not be able to stop the attack. She glanced at the platform where a blue-line train was just pulling out. A couple of people hurried through the sliding doors just as they closed, while a few others moved down the escalator, resigned to wait for the next train.

A man stepped off of the elevator and leaned up against the station wall. Amy's heart stopped, a fragment of memory flashing in her mind. Something in the way he positioned his body took her back to that moment when she was pulled from her room. She closed her eyes, bringing the man back into her mind.

"Can you zero in on this guy?" Amy asked Brent.

Brent didn't hesitate. "Him?"

She nodded, watching as Brent changed the screen so that they were only looking at the one view. Then he zoomed in.

The man's hair was blond, not brown, and he held a cane in one hand. As Brent zoomed closer and then proceeded to add some clarity to the image, Amy gasped. "That's him."

"Are you sure?" Kel asked, moving to her side.

Already Brent had the phone to his ear. "We've got a visual at Metro Center station. Close it down. No one else comes in."

Beside him, Quinn was instructing the police unit at that station where to find the man in question. "Blue-line platform toward Franconia-Springfield."

"Have them stop the blue-line trains in that direction," Kel instructed. "And then have them clear the trains for the other lines and send empty cars to get the rest of those people out of there. With any luck, we can evacuate everyone before he realizes what's going on."

Brent clicked back to the main screen so that they could see more than the one view. "How is he going to release it? He isn't carrying a briefcase or a backpack."

"That cane." Amy pointed to the cane he had walked in with and then leaned next to a bench. "Could it somehow be inside of it?"

Brent nodded. "Look, he's moving toward the platform."

"And leaving the cane behind," Kel added. "It must have some kind of time release in it."

Brent was already instructing his contact at Metro Center. "There's a cane on one of the concrete benches. Tell your men to vacuum-seal it and evacuate the station."

The man glanced at his watch and then up at the monitor that showed how long it would be until the next train. Only seven people remained on the blue-line platform with the man in question—a woman with three boys ranging in age from about six to ten, a couple in their early twenties, and a man who looked like he was on his way home from work. No one seemed to notice that the flow of pedestrian traffic had stopped coming down the escalator behind them. A crowd of people still remained on the other side of the platform, and they could see an empty train approaching to pick them up.

Sensing something was wrong, the man turned just as four men in hazmat suits came storming toward him. Screams echoed as one of them rushed the seven other passengers to the elevator, punching the button to send them upstairs to safety. Another picked up the cane and placed it in a hazmat container, quickly sealing it. Across from them, the train was now full and pulling away.

The man Amy had identified ran up the escalator stairs, and the men in hazmat suits just watched him go.

"Why aren't they chasing him?" Amy asked just as two more men appeared at the top of the escalator, weapons drawn. "Never mind."

Beside her, Kel patted Amy on the back. "Good work, kid."

"Thanks." Amy let out a shaky breath. She stepped back and lowered herself into a chair, afraid that her knees would give way if she stood much longer. She looked up at her sketch and stared evil in the eye.

"Now what?" Charlie asked. "Is that it?"

Kel shook his head. "Not quite. If anyone else is working with the men we've already identified, they won't know that we're on to them." Kel motioned to the bank of computers. "We'll keep monitoring for suspicious activity until the subway closes for the night."

Everyone settled back into their places and the room quieted as they went back to work. Unsure of what an additional terrorist would look like, they couldn't do much more than watch for anyone leaving personal items behind. Minutes ticked by, but the only crime they witnessed was a pickpocket at Dupont Circle.

At seven o'clock eastern standard time, Kel decided it was time to call in another unit to take over. "It's been almost two hours since the attempt at Metro Center. If nothing else has happened by now, I think we're in the clear."

Amy continued to stare at the Metro Center station until their replacements arrived. She couldn't quite believe that it was over and that finally her life and her future were once again hers. She looked over at Brent and wondered if he would want to be part of that future.

CHAPTER 16

"I didn't think your dad would let you out tonight," Brent said when Amy walked through the door of her temporary quarters. She was still wearing the flowing skirt she had put on that morning, but instead of her blouse, she had changed into a plain white T-shirt.

She walked down the steps, smiling when Brent took her hand. "Dad and Charlie were both asleep within ten minutes of getting home."

"You should be sleeping too," Brent commented as he drew her out to the car he had borrowed.

"I'm too wired," Amy admitted. "But I'll understand if you don't want to go out."

"I've gotten kind of used to seeing you in the middle of the night," Brent said softly. "I've missed it."

A faint blush crept into her cheeks, and she looked up at the sky. She guessed that it was about two in the morning, and while her body was exhausted, her mind just wasn't about to shut down. After her dad and brother had fallen asleep, she had called Brent on impulse, just needing someone to talk to. When he had offered to come take her out for a drive, she scribbled a note to her dad and was out the door without a second thought.

"Come on." Brent opened the door for her. "I found the perfect place to hang out."

"I didn't think anything would still be open this time of night," Amy commented, sliding into her seat.

"Trust me," he said before going around the front of the car and getting into the driver's seat.

"Where are we going?" Amy persisted.

"You'll see." Brent drove for a few minutes before turning onto a side road. The road wound through the trees, and finally he pulled off to the side near a little clearing. "Come on."

Amy climbed out of the car as Brent opened the trunk and pulled out a basket. He stepped next to her and took her hand, leading her into the clearing. She didn't see the blanket spread out beneath a tree until she was within a few feet of it.

Brent set down the basket and pulled out a book of matches. He picked up a lantern from the center of the blanket, lit it, and set it back down.

Amy could only stare. "How did you do this? I only called you fifteen minutes ago."

"I was planning on calling you, but I wasn't sure how I was going to get you out past your dad and brother."

"You're not afraid of my family, are you?" Disbelief laced her voice.

"I think it would be more accurate to say that your family is afraid of me," Brent said without thinking. He reached for her hand, and sat down with her on the blanket. "I wasn't sure if you would be hungry, but I brought some food just in case."

Amy watched as he set out the impromptu picnic: crackers, cheese, grapes, and chocolate chip cookies. "You're spoiling me."

"I think after the job you did today you deserve it."

Amy tucked her legs up under her and popped a grape in her mouth. "I wonder if my body will ever figure out what time zone I'm in."

"You really haven't given yourself a chance to adjust yet," Brent commented. "So far you've only spent one night in a real bed in the past week."

"And here I am sitting outside with you instead of taking advantage of the bed that's been offered to me." She laughed. "Maybe I do need to see a shrink sooner than later. I seem to have developed an aversion to easy living."

"I'll think you'll adjust quicker than you think." Brent took two water bottles from the basket and passed one to Amy. "I remember when we went to regionals for swimming my sophomore year. We stayed overnight at a hotel, and we had four people to a room. No one would share a bed, so all of the underclassmen ended up sleeping on the floor. Believe me, I had no trouble sleeping in my own bed when I got home."

Amy leaned back on an elbow. "I would have thought with your height you would have played basketball."

Brent shook his head. "Nope, Mom had been coaching the high school swim teams my whole life."

"I thought most coaches for the boys' teams were men."

"Not at my school. Mom coached both the boys' and girls' teams. Over the years I had learned some important lessons."

"Like what?"

Brent grinned wickedly. "Like that freshmen rarely make the varsity basketball team, and that basketball players don't have girls in swimsuits at their practices. Besides, I didn't want to wait until my junior year to get a letter jacket."

"I have a feeling you were more interested in the girls than in the jacket."

"Probably true." Brent shrugged carelessly. "Not that I could do a whole lot of flirting with Mom standing on deck, but being the coach's son did have some advantages."

"Like having access to the phone numbers for all of the girls on the team?"

Brent laughed. "Have you ever considered a career in intelligence? Not much gets by you."

"It's probably safer than working for the State Department."

"Do you think you'll take another post with State?"

"I don't know." Amy bit into a cracker and considered. "What will happen in Abolstan now?"

"Intel will start gathering information about Namir Dagan and anyone else who is behind the use of biological weapons. Eventually we'll go in and neutralize the threat," Brent explained. Then he redirected the conversation once more. "You know, there are plenty of positions with State that are a lot safer than the one you had in Abolstan."

"I know, but I mostly took the job to get away from home for a while. Now I don't know what I'll do. Even though I was only away for a few weeks, I felt like I was missing out on everything with my family."

"I can tell you're close."

She nodded. "Considering Dad's profession, he did a good job of being around when we needed him most. And Mom made sure that the social side of politics didn't take over our family life."

"That couldn't have been easy to juggle."

"I never realized how many invitations they turned down until I left home. Then all of a sudden they were so busy we could hardly get in touch with them." Amy took a sip of her water. "I have a feeling what happened last week will probably make all of us reconsider what's really important."

"Life and death situations tend to do that to people." Brent frowned. "And your family had more than its share this week."

"I still can't believe my dad and brother were in Cairo."

"I wasn't sure you knew about that."

"I only found out because the DCI sent flowers to thank my brother for saving his life," Amy explained. She considered for a moment. "I guess that means I should send you flowers too."

"I've got a better idea." Brent leaned forward and skimmed his fingers through her hair as the light flickered over her face. Amusement crossed her face when he leaned over and gave her a quick kiss. "Actually," he said, "I owe you for taking care of me after I was shot." With a grin he kissed her again.

Amy was smiling when Brent broke the playful kiss. "Does this make us even?"

"I'm sure I can think of something else I need to thank you for." He leaned forward once more, but Amy put a hand on his chest before he could kiss her again.

"You must have been a handful when you were a teenager."

"Not really. It's hard to get into too much trouble when you always get caught."

Amy just laughed as she popped another grape into her mouth. She looked up at the stars, thinking. Finally, she turned to Brent and asked, "Do we have real threats like the one at the subway often?"

"I'm not sure I can answer that." Brent stretched his legs out in front of him and crossed his ankles.

"Classified?"

"That and I only know about what I deal with."

Amy watched him sitting there in the moonlight. Suddenly he looked so serious. "What can you tell me about what you do? I mean, besides rescuing hostages and preventing terrorist attacks."

Brent shrugged. "That pretty much sums it up. We also spend a lot of time training so that when something does happen we're ready. My unit was specifically created to stay on the East Coast, and there are other SEAL teams that are based out of California. That way no matter where something happens, the military has the right expertise somewhere close by."

"Where will you go from here?"

"We've got a temporary assignment at Quantico for the next few months. Then we'll head back to Virginia Beach. What about you?"

"Day after tomorrow we're going to fly to Miami to visit my brother Matt and his family for a few days. Then we'll go back to Virginia." Amy looked up at the clear sky, wishing this time with Brent would never end. She could feel reality coming too quickly as she asked, "When will you leave?"

"Sometime next week."

Amy hesitated but forced herself to ask, "Will I see you when you get back to Virginia?"

Rather than answer her, Brent shifted closer. Softly he ran his fingers through her hair, watching as her eyes darkened under the moonlit sky. He stared down at her, memorizing every little detail so that he could pull the memory out to warm him on the cold, lonely nights that were sure to come. Her eyes were questioning, her skin pale in the moonlight.

He lowered his lips to hers and brushed them softly, once, then twice. She leaned into the kiss, and he felt like he might drown right there even though water was miles away. He felt her sweetness and her strength as he let her kiss seep through him. He had thought he knew what to expect, but something was different, something he couldn't identify.

She pulled back, uncertainty in her eyes.

"I should get you back." Brent stood and held out a hand. Together they moved through the darkness, both wondering what tomorrow would bring.

CHAPTER 17

Brent didn't settle into a deep sleep until five minutes before someone reached down to shake him awake.

"Come on, Miller. Time to get up." Tristan's voice broke through Brent's foggy, dream-filled mind.

"Go away," Brent mumbled. "We have today off, remember?"

"Not anymore." Tristan picked up Brent's shirt and tossed it at him. "We're wheels up in fifteen minutes."

Brent sat up, forcing himself awake. "What?"

"Kel said he'd brief us on the plane. Grab your gear."

"This isn't happening." Brent swung his legs over the side of the bed, grateful that he had showered the night before. He quickly dressed, packed his things, and then grabbed his cell phone. He glanced at his watch and saw that it was only six in the morning, but he pressed speed dial for Amy's number anyway. He waited anxiously as it rang and rang and rang. Her voice mail came on just as Quinn's footsteps sounded in the hall.

"Come on!" Quinn called from the doorway. "We've only got three minutes!"

"I'm coming," Brent shouted back and hung up the phone. Though it took some effort, he forced Amy from his mind and grabbed his gear.

* * *

She should have known. She had seen how fast he could vanish right in front of her eyes, but still she had let herself believe that Brent was just a normal guy, someone who made her feel like the world was a place made just for them. She still wasn't sure what to make of his almost voice mail message. All day she had waited for him to call back, but her phone never rang.

She had gone through a series of debriefings, as had her father and brother. Reluctantly, she had relinquished the phone Kel had given her to the base commander. She then joined her father and brother on a military transport for the first leg of their journey. Physically and emotionally exhausted, Amy had slept most of the way home. Her dad woke her during their commercial flight so she could eat, but she only picked at her food.

Frustration that she had not heard from Brent had turned to anxiety when she found that his whole unit had left just hours after she had seen him last. Anxiety had settled into worry and apprehension. She knew what his missions could be like and prayed that she would hear soon that he was home safe. Following that thought was the realization that she might not even know when he got home.

All her life she had liked to be in control of her own destiny, to plan out her future. She wasn't sure exactly when Brent had become more important than planning for tomorrow, but as she moved through the airport with her dad and brother, she knew she would much rather have uncertainty in her life if it meant Brent could be a part of it.

Amy tried to shake off her mood as she climbed into the back seat of a taxi. They had taken an earlier flight than they had originally planned, arriving at five in the morning. Rather than call Matt in the middle of the night, Jim had opted to take a cab and surprise the rest of the family with an early arrival.

Amy looked out the window as they drove through Miami. Palm trees swayed in the warm breeze, and she could smell the ocean. Everything looked so peaceful and blessedly normal, yet somewhere in the world something was happening that had taken Brent away from her. She closed her eyes against the onslaught of emotions, a sense of emptiness settling deep within her.

They turned the corner toward her brother's house and Amy sat up a little straighter. "What time is it?"

"A little after six," Jim answered.

"Do you think they'll even be up?" Charlie asked.

"There's only one way to find out," Jim replied. He paid their driver and then helped Charlie get their bags from the car. A moment later he rang the doorbell.

Only a minute passed before the door swung open and CJ's gray eyes lighted with surprise. "You're home!"

CJ moved to hug Amy, and then she hugged Charlie and Jim in turn. "Come in, come in." She pointed to a hallway off to the side. "Just leave your bags there and make yourselves comfortable. Matt won't be home for a couple hours—he had an away game last night. But I'll go tell Katherine that you're here."

"You don't have to wake her," Amy said.

"If I didn't, she'd never forgive me." CJ passed through the kitchen and started up the steps of a closeted stairway. "I'll be right back."

A couple minutes later footsteps sounded on the main staircase. Katherine came rushing in, the ties of her robe flapping behind her. Tears were in her eyes as she moved straight to Amy and pulled her into her arms. Neither of them spoke as a minute passed into two. Finally Katherine pulled back and looked up into her daughter's face. "I am so glad you're home."

"Me too," Amy said. She very nearly believed it.

* * *

"Something's bothering her," Charlie commented as he watched Matt flip hamburgers on the grill in the backyard in preparation of their Memorial Day feast.

"Charlie, she was held hostage, had to walk for days through the desert, and then helped stop a terrorist attack." Amazement filled Matt's voice even as he said the words he knew to be true. "You can't really expect her to get over all of that so quickly."

"I don't, but that isn't what's bothering her," Charlie insisted. "You didn't see her in Italy. She worked with those Navy SEALs like she had been part of their unit for years, not hours."

"Maybe she's having some sort of delayed reaction," Matt suggested as he opened up a package of hotdogs and started adding them to the grill.

"I think what she's having is a broken heart," Charlie told him. "She really fell for the guy that got her out of Abolstan. Ever since he shipped out without telling her, she's been down."

"Maybe we need to find this guy and intimidate him."

"He doesn't intimidate easily." Charlie sat down in one of the deck chairs. "Not to mention that no one knows where he is."

"No wonder she's upset." Matt turned to see the patio door open and watched Amy walk outside. Her hair was pulled back in a ponytail, and she had on only a light dusting of makeup covering up the freckles that were sprinkled across her nose. Not for the first time, Matt thought she could have been a model. Between her height and her natural beauty, he had little doubt she would have succeeded in the career, but she hadn't been interested in such things.

Amy crossed to her brothers. "CJ wants to know how long until dinner."

"Just a couple minutes," Matt told her.

Charlie stood and offered Amy his seat. "Here, sit down. I'll go tell her."

Amy saw the look pass between her brothers, but she sat down anyway. As Charlie went inside, Amy turned to Matt. "I gather he told you about Brent."

"Is that his name?"

"Lieutenant Brent Miller, U.S. Navy," Amy said flatly. "I'm sorry, but I don't know his serial number."

Matt turned and held his hands up. "Hey, I'm not trying to chase the guy away. Heck, I haven't even met him yet."

"It's not likely that you ever will." Amy's eyes misted and she tried to fight it.

"Come here." Matt reached out and pulled her into his arms. "I'm just worried about you."

"I know. I'm sorry." Amy sniffed back most of the tears. "I just don't understand how out of all the guys in the world I have to fall for one who leads an impossible life, one who will probably never have room for someone like me."

Matt laughed. He couldn't help it. "Hey, you're talking to the expert on difficult relationships here," he said. He leaned back so he could look into his sister's face, then reached out and brushed away a stray tear. "If it's meant to be, you'll find a way."

Amy sighed, pointing to the grill in an effort to distract him. "You're going to burn the hot dogs."

"I've got it covered." Matt stepped over and loaded up the serving plate with hamburgers and hot dogs. "I hope you realize that just because you're in love with this guy doesn't mean I don't get the chance to play big brother and make sure he's worthy of you."

As Amy's face paled, he took her hand and led her inside.

* * *

"Since when are you a Florida Marlins fan?" Kel sat down next to Brent in the officer's club and motioned for the waitress.

"Is there something wrong with kicking back and watching a ball game?" Brent asked, avoiding Kel's question.

"I'm just wondering what's going on with you since the Nationals game is on in the other room." Kel looked up at the waitress. "I'll take a Sprite."

Brent remained silent.

"Have you talked to her since we got back?" Kel picked up his soda and took a sip.

"Talked to whom?" Brent kept his face deliberately blank.

"Oh, come on, Brent." Kel hooked an arm over the back of his chair and shifted to look at him. "We all know you're hooked on Amy Whitmore. Why aren't you on the phone right now planning when you can see her again?"

"Because there's no point in seeing her again." Brent's voice was low, but regret hummed through it.

Kel shook his head in confusion. "You're going to have to explain that one to me. You like her, she likes you. Heck, she's even LDS. What's the problem?"

"You tell me." Brent turned on him, anger in his voice now. "How does your wife like it when you disappear for weeks, sometimes months at a time?" He dropped his head into his hands. "I can't do that to her. I just can't."

"Look, I've made enough mistakes in the marriage department for both of us. Don't give up on your own chance for happiness because I did it the hard way."

"How can you say that?" Brent pushed on, looking up again. "How can any woman actually want to be married to someone with a career like ours?"

"I don't know. I married one who didn't," Kel admitted. "She thought I would give up this life, and I thought she loved me enough to let me keep it. It's been generally miserable all the way around for both of us, but that's both of our faults. We didn't talk about it before we got married. Not really."

Again Brent fell silent.

With a shake of his head, Kel pushed back from the table. He took two steps before he turned back. "By the way, church is at ten tomorrow."

Brent nodded and turned his attention back to the television. A few minutes later Matt Whitmore walked to the plate. Brent watched as the pitcher had him on the verge of a strikeout and then threw the wrong pitch. Matt slammed it high over the left field fence. The camera stayed on the field as he rounded the plate behind his two teammates who were already on base.

He had hoped that the camera would flash to Matt's family in the stands and maybe give him a glimpse of Amy. She had said she was going to spend a few days in Florida before heading back to Virginia. That had only been four days ago.

With a shake of his head, he ordered another soda and settled back to wallow in his misery.

CHAPTER 18

Amy followed her escort through the maze of hallways in the Pentagon, finally arriving at Admiral Mantiquez's office. Amy had returned home to Virginia the night before to find that the admiral wanted to meet with her as soon as possible. Now here she was at eight o'clock on a Tuesday morning wondering what in the world this man could possibly want with her.

"Amy Whitmore?" The admiral moved to shake her hand and motioned for her to sit down, then closed the door behind her. He wasn't very tall, probably an inch or so shorter than Amy, and his dark hair was mostly gray. He smiled at her as he moved to sit down behind his enormous desk. "Thank you for agreeing to meet with me on such short notice."

"Your message said it was important," she said simply, smoothing her skirt over her knees.

"I know you went through a series of debriefings in Italy, but I hoped that you could clear a few things up for me," he began.

"I can try."

"First of all, where did you get your information about the planned terrorist attack in DC?"

"I don't know." Amy lifted a shoulder. "My dad mentioned something about that country trying to develop biological weapons, and then I heard the intelligence officer mention that they couldn't transport something safely."

His eyebrows shot up, his voice skeptical. "That's how you knew there was going to be an attack on the DC subway system?"

"I also saw a map of the subway on the ambassador's desk."

He leaned back in his chair, considering. "What exactly are your plans for the future?"

"I'm not sure," Amy said honestly. "The State Department has offered to send me to London, but the job sounds pretty tedious. That's probably terrible to say, but I don't think I want to process the same old paperwork every day."

"How would you feel about processing new paperwork every day?"

"I don't understand."

"I have read Commander Bennett's report about your performance during the subway incident, as well as Lieutenant Miller's report about the rescue." Admiral Mantiquez steepled his fingers together and continued. "For some time I have been trying to fill a support position for this unit, someone to help on intel assignments and run support when they are deployed. Every time we find someone, they quit within a few days. Most civilians underestimate the pressure that comes with the job and find they can't handle it."

"Why don't you just fill the position with someone in the military?" Amy asked, a knot settling in her stomach as she wondered how Brent would feel about her working with him on a regular basis.

"The military is stretched too thin right now. That's why we were slated with a civilian position, to keep our manpower where it's needed most." The admiral leaned forward and looked her in the eye. "I'll be honest with you. The job is only a couple of steps above entry level, but it has potential. You might travel a lot for a few months and then not travel at all for a year. Your days off will vary, although since the whole unit is LDS they attend church on Sundays whenever their duties allow it."

Amy smiled at that. "You sound like you're trying to talk me out of taking the job."

"Not at all." He shook his head. "I just want you to understand what it entails. The job won't be easy, and this unit has a unique temperament, but if you want to be part of something special, you should consider it."

"I don't have to consider it," Amy replied, following impulse rather than logic. "When do I start?"

* * *

Amy showed her ID to the guard and then made her way upstairs to her father's office. She had promised to go to lunch with him after her meeting, and she was already wondering how he was going to take the news. She was nearly to the door to his outer office when she thought of Jared and said a quick, silent prayer that he would already be out to lunch.

The prayer wasn't answered the way she had hoped, and she forced a smile as Jared skirted around his desk and moved toward her. "Thank goodness you're safe." He embraced her, and Amy couldn't help but stiffen. He pulled back, apparently not noticing her resistance, and continued. "Your father said you were coming in today. I thought you would want to take a few days off before starting work, but I'm glad to see you."

Amy shook her head, sorting out his words. "I only came in to meet my dad for lunch. I'm not working here."

Jared's eyes narrowed. "But I thought—"

"You thought wrong." Amy stepped past him and knocked on her dad's door. As soon as she heard his voice call "come in," she pushed the door open and immediately closed it behind her.

Jim was already moving toward the door, and he scooped her up in a hug. "I was hoping that was you."

"Are you ready to go?"

"Yeah, let me just see if Jared wants to join us." Jim reached for the door.

"Dad, if Jared's coming, then I'm not," Amy stated firmly.

"What? Why?" Jim asked, turning back to face her. "I thought you were fond of him."

"Fond of, yes. In love with, no," Amy clarified. "I have no interest in marrying Jared now or ever. The more you invite him along when I'm around, the longer it's going to take for him to understand that I'm really not interested in him that way."

Jim stared at her for a minute and then sighed. "I'm sorry, honey. I didn't mean to keep pushing him on you. I just thought—"

"It doesn't matter," Amy told him. "Let's just go get some lunch."

They walked out of Jim's office, and Jared was standing by the door as though he had already anticipated an invitation. Jim nodded at him and guided Amy to the outer door. "Jared, I'll be back in about an hour."

Jared's eyes widened, but he said nothing as the two left the office.

Twenty minutes later they were sitting in their favorite seafood restaurant overlooking the Potomac River.

"Are you going to tell me how your meeting went?" Jim asked after they ordered.

"Only if you promise not to yell."

"Why would I yell?"

"Promise?" Amy waited until her father reluctantly nodded before continuing. "Apparently the admiral wanted to clarify how I had come up with some of my assumptions."

"And?" Jim asked.

"He offered me a job."

Jim's eyes narrowed. "What kind of a job?"

"It's a support job down at Quantico."

"You're staying here in Virginia?" Jim's smile broke free. "Honey, that's fantastic. Your mom and I will love having you so close by."

"I was hoping you would say that." Amy dabbed a piece of shrimp cocktail into some sauce and took a bite.

Slowly Jim's smile faded. "Wait a minute. Why were you worried I would yell?" His eyes narrowed again. "What aren't you telling me?"

"I'm just not sure you'll like the unit I'm working with."

"Oh, no." Jim shook his head. "Not Miller's unit."

Amy just shrugged and braced against the lecture about to come.

"Amy, those boys are on hazardous duty as often as not. I don't want you involved with them." Jim grabbed her hand across the table. "They are under incredible amounts of pressure all the time."

Her voice took on an edge. "Do you think I can't handle the pressure?"

Jim's voice rose in response. "I don't want you to *have* to handle the pressure."

"You promised not to yell," Amy pointed out calmly. "Besides, I'm only providing support. It's not like I'll be going behind enemy lines with them."

"What happens when one of them doesn't come home?" Jim asked bluntly. "How are you going to handle that?"

"Dad, I'm aware of that possibility. I also know that by some bizarre twist of fate, I helped save people a few days ago." Tears threatened, but she quickly blinked them back. "And as hard as it was to think about what might have happened if we didn't do a good job, I have the satisfaction of knowing that I made a difference in people's lives, people I've never even met."

"There are a lot of ways to make a difference, Amy."

"That's true, and now I know what I'm good at." Amy paused while the waiter arrived to deliver their food. As soon as he moved away, she continued, "This is what I want. I hope you'll be happy for me."

"Do you really think this is a good idea, you working with Brent Miller?"

"I don't know." Amy shrugged, forcing herself to speak her fears. "In fact, that's my only concern about this job, that my presence might in some way make things difficult for him."

"I'm more worried about him making things difficult for you," Jim muttered. "I'm sorry, but I don't trust him with you."

"But you trusted Jared around me. Why is that?"

"He's reliable, steady . . ."

"Arrogant, conceited, boring," Amy finished for him. "You know, I trusted Brent more in the first day I knew him than I have ever trusted Jared. Maybe it's time you let me follow my instincts. Right or wrong, it is my life."

"And whether you like it or not, I'm always going to worry about you," Jim countered.

"That goes without saying." Amy rolled her eyes, the tension between them finally easing. "What do you think Mom will have to say about all of this?"

"I don't think she knows enough about Navy SEALs to be worried. That's probably a good thing." Resigned, Jim asked, "When do you start?"

"A week from Monday. The admiral said it would take that long to push through my security clearance."

"Just promise me you'll always be careful."

Amy grinned. "Dad, I always try."

CHAPTER 19

Brent lengthened his stride as he jogged along a tree-lined path on base and let his mind wander. His unit had returned to Quantico three days ago, but he had yet to settle back into a routine. The rest of his unit had gone for a swim at the base swimming pool for their PT, or physical training, but Brent had opted for a run despite the heat and humidity that was currently consuming northern Virginia. His arm was almost completely healed, but for today he didn't want to confine himself to the pool.

From the time he had run cross country in high school, the freedom of running had always helped him clear his mind. Running allowed him to focus on his problems and, more importantly, the solutions. He had popped in at his folks' house for dinner the night before, hoping to take his mind off of Amy. The diversion had been successful for a few minutes, but once he was back in his car heading back to Quantico, he was thinking about her again.

No one else had ever consumed him so completely. Her face was the first thing he thought of when he woke each morning. He went to sleep each night wondering where she was. He was pretty sure she was still in Virginia visiting her parents, but he couldn't be sure. For all he knew, she had taken a job in another embassy overseas and he would never see her unless she happened to be taken hostage again.

He owed it to her to stay away, but every time he thought of not seeing her again his stomach felt like a ball of lead. Kel's words had been running through his mind for days. Did Kel's marriage struggles really stem from a lack of understanding and communication, or would those problems surface in any marriage dealing with the stress of constant deployment? He couldn't find any answers, even in his prayers at night, although that was probably because his own fears were getting in the way.

He emerged from the woods and went inside to shower and change. After forcing down a sandwich, Brent headed back to his office. He stopped at Kel's office to tell him he was back from lunch, then stepped inside when Kel motioned to him.

"We've got good news," Kel told him. "I just got off the phone with Admiral Mantiquez. He's finally filled our support position."

"He fills the position every couple of months," Brent pointed out. "No one ever lasts long enough to get up to speed, much less be useful."

"He's convinced that this civilian is up for the task."

"I hope so. It would be nice to have the help for a change."

"Isn't that the truth," Kel agreed. "The admiral told us to take the weekend off. He said we deserve it after the pace we've set for the past few weeks."

"We'll see how long that lasts."

"I'm sending everyone home early today," Kel said. "Go ahead and close down your office. Just make sure you have your phone with you in case the admiral changes his mind."

Brent nodded and moved into his office. He started to turn off his computer, but instead he logged on and did a quick search. After scribbling down an address, he shut everything down and headed for his car. For the first time all week he felt like he was looking forward instead of back.

* * *

"Are you sure you don't want to come with us?" Katherine asked from Amy's bedroom doorway. "The Whites would love to see you."

"Thanks, Mom, but I really just want to stay home and relax for a while," Amy responded. "It's too tiring having to repeat the same story over and over again."

"Okay, but call me if you need anything." Katherine moved back into the hallway, and a moment later her heels echoed on the wood in the entryway below.

As soon as she heard her parents drive away, Amy headed downstairs to the living room and turned on the television. Charlie had left for the beach that morning with a few friends, and for the first time in what felt like forever Amy could just be alone. She hadn't realized how much her family had hovered over her since her return until she finally had a chance to spend an evening without them.

Grabbing the remote, she flipped through the channels looking for her brother's game. When she finally realized that it wasn't scheduled to start for another hour, she decided she could root for the Nationals for a while. She considered heating up a frozen pizza and quickly decided against it. Her last experience in her mom's kitchen had involved a fire extinguisher and buying her mom a new set of curtains. She had only been sixteen at the time, but she didn't trust her luck lately and decided against taking any chances.

With a sigh, she picked up the phone and ordered a pizza and then turned her attention back to the game. Twenty minutes later the doorbell rang and Amy grabbed a few bills from her wallet to pay the pizza delivery guy. Her jaw dropped open when she pulled the door wide and saw Brent standing just over the threshold.

For a moment, Amy just stared at him. For nearly two weeks she had worried and wondered about Brent. Now he stood in front of her looking like a regular guy. He was dressed in khaki shorts and a white polo shirt, his tanned arms looking even darker against the light color. All of the worry of the past two weeks melted away, leaving only a remnant of doubt and insecurity. When the pizza delivery boy walked up right behind him, she struggled to regain her composure. She exchanged cash for the pizza and turned back to Brent. "I'm sorry. Come on in."

Brent only hesitated a moment before he stepped into the open foyer. An oversized picture of the temple dominated the wall, the round table beneath it adorned with a basket of silk flowers. He followed her into the enormous living room, where she set the pizza down on the coffee table.

"I hope you don't mind me just dropping by," Brent said when she turned back to face him. "I managed to find your address, but I didn't have your phone number."

"Of course I don't mind." Amy motioned for him to sit down. "I'm just surprised to see you." Her insecurity crept in when she added, "I wasn't sure I would see you when you got back." Before he could respond, she stepped toward the kitchen. "Can I get you something to drink?"

"Just water, thanks."

When she came back in and handed him his drink, he pointed at the pizza box. "Are you going to share some of that?"

"Maybe." Amy's eyes brightened. "I suppose that's the least I can do since you drove all this way."

He looked around as Amy opened the box. "Where's your family?"

"Charlie headed for Ocean City this morning, and Mom and Dad are at a friend's for dinner." She tore off a paper towel from the roll she had set on the coffee table and pulled a piece of pizza from the box. "I hope you like mushrooms."

"As long as there aren't any anchovies." Brent reached for a slice, using the top of the box for a plate. "Can I assume that you didn't have any plans for tonight since we're sitting here eating pizza?"

Amy nodded. "This is the first time since I've been home that my family has left me alone. They've been driving me crazy."

"I can leave you alone too if you want." His voice was almost sincere.

"That's not what I meant." Amy rolled her eyes. "They're hovering, you know? It's like they're afraid that if they can't see me I'm not going to be here when they get back."

"I'm sure that's normal." Brent took another bite. "Sometimes the families of hostage victims are actually more traumatized than the victims themselves. They get so worked up over what might happen that they have trouble accepting the actual outcome of the situation."

"I suppose," Amy agreed reluctantly. "I guess I'm just tired of being the center of their attention. I'm ready for them to get back to their own lives and let me live mine."

"What's next for you?" His voice was casual, but his eyes sharpened as he waited for her answer.

"State Department offered me London, but I turned them down," Amy replied. She knew she should tell him about her new job, but her insecurity held her back. Would he be happy that he would see her often, or would he hate being around her every day?

Well aware that he would find out eventually, she kept her response neutral. "It looks like I'll be sticking around here for a while after all."

Brent just nodded and glanced up at the television when someone struck out.

Amy pulled her feet beneath her as she settled back on the couch. She had hoped Brent would be happy that she was staying in Virginia, but his expression was unreadable. He pointed to the TV and made a comment about the game.

With a little sigh, Amy let herself be content to sit beside him and talk baseball. When Matt's game started, she changed channels, flipping back to the Nationals game on the commercials until the Nats went down by five runs and Brent decided it was too painful to watch.

When the Marlins game went to a commercial during the seventh-inning stretch, Brent finally asked, "Is it weird watching your brother on television?"

Amy shrugged. "Not really. Maybe a little at first, but it isn't really much different from picking up a newspaper and seeing Dad's picture."

"That just seems so strange to me." Brent stretched an arm out along the back of the couch, his fingers playing with the ends of her hair. "I think the only time I've ever seen anyone in my family in the newspaper was when one of us made all-area athlete. None of us have ever been on TV."

"I don't know what it's like to not have cameras around." Amy smiled. "The funny thing is that the paparazzi seem to love my family, and we never doing anything to really talk about. It's not like any of us have ever gotten arrested, or done something really stupid to embarrass Dad."

"No, you just survive a hostage situation and then help save the country from a terrorist attack." Brent nodded, not quite able to keep a straight face. "And let me see if I have this right. Your brother Matt married someone in the Witness Protection Program right after she exposed a huge smuggling ring, then he made the major leagues. Your sister-in-law medaled in the Olympics, and Charlie just graduated at the top of his class and is heading to law school."

Amy shrugged. "And then there's me."

"Yeah, let's talk about you." Brent shifted closer. "You were the player of the year in basketball your senior year of high school, you went to BYU on a full scholarship and graduated in the top ten percent of your class." He shook his head, his eyebrows drawing together. "Definitely an underachiever."

Amy couldn't help laughing. "Sounds like you've done your homework. Is this what you do when no one is trying to blow up the country?"

"It was slow yesterday." Brent wound a lock of her hair around his finger.

"I see." Amy's eyebrows lifted. "I guess I sound pretty good on paper."

"You're better in person." Just as he started to pull her closer, the rumbling of the garage door sounded. With a sigh, he shifted away from her. "I gather that's your parents."

Amy nodded, turning toward the kitchen when she heard the door open from the garage. The moment Katherine stepped into the living room, just a step ahead of her husband, Brent stood up. Amy followed suit, focusing on the surprised look on her mother's face rather than the annoyance on her father's.

"Mom, you haven't met Brent Miller," Amy said as Brent shifted from behind the coffee table. "Brent, this is my mother, Katherine."

Katherine moved forward and took Brent's outstretched hand. "Thank you so much for what you did for my family." She covered their joined hands with her free one, her expression welcoming. "We can't tell you enough how grateful we are to have Amy home."

"I was just doing my job, ma'am." As Katherine released his hand, Brent nodded to Jim. "Hello, Senator."

"Lieutenant." Jim moved forward and shook Brent's hand, but only because his manners were so ingrained. "I didn't expect to see you tonight."

Amy didn't give Brent a chance to respond, instead drawing everyone's attention to the television. "Hey, Dad. Matt's coming up to bat."

Katherine hurried over to sit down so she could watch. Reluctantly, Jim turned his attention to the television as well.

"Brent, come sit back down," Amy suggested. She felt his hesitation and reached for his hand and pulled him down beside her.

As soon as they were sitting, Brent pulled his hand away, careful to keep his distance. They all watched together as Matt managed a single, then a teammate struck out to end the inning. When the game ended, Brent stood up. "I should get going."

Amy stood also. "I'll walk you out."

When they stepped out onto the front porch, Brent pulled out his cell phone. "Any chance I can get your phone number?"

A smile slowly crossed her face as she reached for his phone. She put her number into memory for him, and then handed it back as she looked up at him. "Brent, I'm glad you came by."

"Me too." Brent glanced over at the living room window and stepped back. "I'll try to call you tomorrow." With that he turned and disappeared into the night.

CHAPTER 20

Brent pulled up in front of the Whitmore home, as intimidated by its size now as he had been last night. Quite simply, the house was huge. Logically he knew that Amy came from money. He had just never considered exactly how much money. Huge oak trees stood like soldiers next to the street in front of the house, and a circular driveway arced in front of the main entrance.

He had waited until nine o'clock this morning to call her, grateful she had given him her cell phone number so that he wouldn't have to worry about waking up the rest of the house on a Saturday morning. He hadn't gotten home until midnight, but for the first time in weeks he actually slept well. By seven o'clock he was up and watching the clock, counting down the minutes until he could call and make plans with Amy.

He had hoped to at least talk her into going out to dinner, but when she had suggested going horseback riding to Great Falls, he had thrown a change of clothes in a bag and was now looking forward to spending the day with her.

Their time together the night before had not been what he imagined. He had expected her to demand answers from him about why he had left so suddenly in Italy, or why he hadn't called her when he got back. He hadn't realized how much he had dreaded those questions until he was on his way home from her house and recognized that she had never asked them. Could she really understand that his job was like that sometimes—here one minute and gone the next?

That they had been able to just hang out and watch a ball game, or two ball games, actually, had been so normal. He couldn't remember the last time he had just hung out with friends like that except with the guys in his unit. Amy expressed her opinion about baseball just as forcefully as any of his buddies, but Brent found he enjoyed bantering with her a lot more than if he had been debating with Quinn or Tristan.

Brent stepped from his car and jogged up the steps to ring the doorbell. The smile on his face faded when Jim Whitmore answered the door rather than his daughter.

"Good morning, Senator," Brent said as he watched Jim's tension level shoot up. "Is Amy ready?"

"Ready for what?"

"We're going for a ride this morning."

Jim leaned against the doorjamb rather than inviting him inside. "Do you really think this is a good idea? Obviously my daughter has developed some sort of infatuation with you, something I understand is quite common in a rescuer-hostage situation. I had hoped you would be smart enough to keep some distance between you, at least long enough for Amy to sort out her feelings."

Brent braced against the truth of the senator's words, afraid to reveal that he had gone through this same argument in his head a dozen times. Each time he came back to the same truth: he couldn't stop thinking about her. He kept his voice low and even when he responded. "No one is more sure about their own feelings than Amy is."

"How can you say that? How can you possibly think you know my daughter?" Jim asked bluntly. "You were only with her for a few days."

"I realize there are a lot of things I don't know about Amy. That's why I'm here, so that I can learn what she's like when life is normal."

"Your life isn't ever going to be normal," Jim pointed out. "I can't say I want that for my daughter."

"With all due respect sir, that isn't for you to decide." Brent stood up a little straighter. "If you know your daughter at all, I think you realize that Amy doesn't want ordinary. I don't think she ever has."

"She doesn't know what she wants right now."

Stung by the cold reception, Brent turned to walk away, but something pulled him back. He looked back at Jim and took a deep breath. "Did you know that Amy stitched me up after I was shot? Did she tell you that she went out by herself to cover up my blood trail to make sure no one would find us?"

Jim's eyes widened, but he remained rigid. "I know that Amy is intelligent and that she did what she needed to in order to survive."

"It was more than survival with her," Brent said, realizing the truth of his words as he spoke them. "She thrived when we were out in that desert. You saw for yourself how she performed during the subway attack. She will never be ordinary, whether I'm a part of her life or not."

Before Jim could respond, his wife appeared at his side. "Good morning, Brent." She nudged her husband aside and reached out a hand. "Please come in. Amy will be down in a minute."

She gave her husband an admonishing look and pulled Brent inside before he could decide he didn't want to spend the day with Amy after all. As soon as Jim closed the door, Katherine continued, "Amy mentioned that you were going to ride down to the falls today."

"That's right, ma'am."

Katherine smiled, beauty and elegance exuding from her. "We haven't ridden up there in quite some time."

"You're welcome to join us," Brent suggested and had the satisfaction of seeing the surprise on the senator's face. "As I was just mentioning to your husband, I'm looking forward to finding out what Amy is like when she isn't in crisis mode."

Amy descended the stairs a moment later, grateful that her mother was keeping her father in check.

Jim turned to her and said, "Brent just invited us to ride along with you to the falls. Do you mind?"

Amy glanced over at Brent and suspected that he was waging a battle her father didn't know how to fight. "That's a great idea. It's supposed to be gorgeous out today."

"Why don't you two go saddle up the horses while we go change," Katherine suggested. "I'll pack a lunch for us."

"Sounds good." Amy turned to Brent and motioned to the kitchen. "Come on. It's this way."

Brent followed her out the back door and up a narrow path through the trees. "I hope you don't mind that I invited your parents along."

Amy just grinned. "Trying to get on Dad's good side, huh?"

Humor lit Brent's eyes. "After the way we first met, it feels like an uphill battle."

They stepped into a clearing where the stable was situated next to a large pasture. In the corral next to the stable, a bay gelding stood in the shade of the building. Amy turned back to Brent. "I know you can ride, but do you know how to saddle a horse?"

"Yeah, just tell me which saddle you want on what horse," Brent said as he followed her through the stable and into the tack room.

Amy pointed at a western saddle. "You can put that one on the palomino. She's in the second stall."

Rather than reach for the saddle, Brent just stared at her. "You know, I don't know if I'll get a chance to be alone with you again today."

Amy smiled slowly, turning toward him. Just as Brent moved closer, Jim's voice echoed through the stable.

"Hey, Amy. Can you hand me a lead rope?"

Brent let his head drop, fighting back a combination of frustration and laughter. He reached up and grabbed a lead rope that was hanging on the wall. Turning, he stepped out of the tack room and held it out to Jim. "Here you are, sir."

"Thanks." Jim was dressed in jeans and a plain T-shirt, but he still carried an air of authority.

Brent turned back and picked up the saddle Amy had indicated along with another lead rope. By the time Katherine arrived, they had finished saddling up four of the horses. Katherine divvied up portions of their lunch to be put into saddlebags and then led her horse outside to mount.

They started off at an easy pace, Brent and Amy both appreciating the ease of riding with a saddle and bridle rather than just makeshift harnesses. The day was warm, broken up by an occasional breeze. The trail narrowed in places, forcing them to ride single file. Finally they arrived at a clearing across from the falls. Water cascaded down the rock face, the sound a distant rumble.

Jim spread out a blanket for them to sit on, and Katherine started setting out food. When they all settled down, the conversation flowed easier than Brent had expected. Jim was even cordial, making him wonder if Katherine had warned him to behave or if he was finally warming up to him.

When the conversation turned to his profession, Brent concluded that the politician was just setting him up.

"Is your father in the military, Brent?" Jim asked casually.

Brent reminded himself to stay at ease and took a sip of water before answering. "No, he worked for a government contractor in DC before he retired last year."

"What made you decide to join the Navy then?" Jim persisted.

"My mom, actually."

"Your mom was in the military?" Amy asked now.

"No, the CIA." Brent leaned back, a little more willing to share information now that Amy was asking the question. "She quit working before I was born, but I got a glimpse of the kind of work she did when I was a teenager. It made me decide I wanted to be part of protecting the freedoms we enjoy in this country."

"You are in a very honorable profession," Katherine stated before her husband could continue his interrogation. "I'm sure your parents are very proud of you."

"Most of the time." Brent shrugged. "Although I think I'm still in the doghouse with Mom since I mowed down her garden last month."

Amy laughed, trying to imagine him doing something as simple as mowing his parents' lawn. "I hope she didn't have much planted."

"The chives took the worst of it." Brent bit into one of the finger sandwiches Katherine had packed and nearly managed to hide the spark of mischief in his eyes. "The good news is that my nephew gets to do lawn duty from now on. It will make a good summer job for him."

"How old is he?" Katherine asked.

"Twelve." Brent grinned. "He's been trying to start his own lawn mowing business so he can start saving up for his mission and college."

Amy studied Brent for a moment before asking. "Does he know that you mowed down your mom's garden on purpose?"

"It was his idea," Brent admitted, the words coming out of his mouth before he realized Amy had seen through him.

Amy threw him a line before he sank any deeper. "So you were just being a supportive uncle."

"Something like that." Brent turned from Amy and spoke to her mother. "Sister Whitmore, these sandwiches are wonderful."

"Thank you, Brent." Katherine gave him the gift of a genuine smile and then stood up. She turned to her husband. "I think I'm going to take a little walk. Jim, why don't you come with me?"

Jim hesitated for a second before standing and taking his wife's hand. "I'd love to."

"We'll be back in a few minutes," Katherine said casually as they started toward a wide path through the trees.

Brent waited until they were out of sight before he leaned toward Amy, lowering his voice. "I can't believe your dad left us alone."

Amy grinned. "Maybe he's decided to like you after all."

"Oh, I doubt that." Brent shook his head as he reached for her hand. "He just knows that if he says you can't go out with me, you'll do it anyway just to spite him."

Amy laughed, lacing her fingers with his. "What makes you say that?"

"Let's just say I'm a trained observer. I don't think you like to be told what to do, and your father knows it." He skimmed his thumb over hers. "The last thing he wants right now is for you to decide to keep me around."

Amy's eyes met his, confusion and hope shining from them. For a fleeting moment she wished she had the nerve to ask him if he wanted her to keep him around.

Oblivious to Amy's insecurities, Brent changed the subject. "What time do you have church tomorrow?"

"I'm not even sure," Amy admitted. "I've been debating which ward to go to. If I go to my parents' ward I'm going to be smothered by people asking me if I'm okay, but I'm not sure the singles ward would be much better."

"There's a singles branch that meets down in Fredericksburg. We don't meet until three in the afternoon, but if you want, I'd be happy to come pick you up." Brent lowered his voice. "I don't think many people down there know you."

Amy nodded. "Let's hope." A beeping noise startled her, and she watched as Brent pulled his cell phone from his pocket. "Is everything okay?"

"It's probably nothing," Brent said as he accessed the flash message. His eyes widened as he read through the information sent to him by

Admiral Mantiquez's office. He quickly stood and extended a hand to Amy. "We need to find your parents."

"What's wrong?"

"Two of the other hostages from Abolstan were just killed."

"What?" Amy's jaw dropped at the startling news. "How?

"I'll tell you in a minute. First we need to find your parents."

CHAPTER 21

Brent didn't mince words when he found the senator and Katherine standing on top of a ridge looking out over Great Falls. "Senator Whitmore, what kind of security system do you have at your house?"

"What?" Jim looked at him, confused. "Why?"

"It's important, sir."

Impatiently, Amy answered for him. "It's an enhanced system in the house, installed by the government when CJ was in Witness Protection. There's also a secondary system on the perimeter of the property."

"Infrared beams?"

Amy nodded. "We keep the system on in the house any time we leave, but we only use the perimeter alarms at night."

Jim folded his arms across his chest. "Would someone please tell me what's going on?"

"Two of the other hostages were just killed. We have to eliminate the possibility that the remaining five hostages could also be targets."

"What would someone gain by killing me or the others?" Amy asked, dumbfounded.

"I don't know." Brent shrugged. "But we have to make sure you're protected until we can check it out."

Jim pulled out his cell phone. "I'll call and have Secret Service send over a couple of agents. They can check out the house before we get back."

"I would rather you waited on that for a little while."

"Why?" Jim asked, surprised.

"The easiest way to get past your security system would be to send in someone disguised as Secret Service. Someone intercepts a phone call and shows up a couple minutes later. By the time the real agents show up, it's too late." Brent looked over at Amy. He tried to think of her as just another assignment but failed completely. He couldn't let anything happen to her. A plan forming in his mind, he turned back to Jim. "I have an idea, but I need your complete cooperation."

The muscle in Jim's jaw twitched with irritation. "I will do whatever is necessary to protect my family."

Brent kept his eyes on Jim's. "That's what I needed to know."

* * *

"I still don't understand why you think I'm in danger," Amy said as Brent led her to a picnic table in the park next to Great Falls. After Brent made several phone calls, they had ridden to the picnic area near the road. A few yards away, Jim and Katherine were tying up the horses.

Brent continued to scan the area, his gaze finally landing on the nearby parking lot. "The first victim was shot leaving the hospital. A few minutes later the second victim received a phone call telling him about the incident, and he called the police for protection. When the police arrived, he was already dead."

"You think someone showed up pretending to be the police and killed him?"

"There's a reason Trojan horses work, and it wouldn't be the first time someone used this approach."

"But why come after any of us in the first place?"

"Retribution, probably." Brent shrugged, glancing at her for a moment before turning his eyes back to the road. "It hasn't been confirmed, but we think that one of the men killed during the rescue attempt was Namir Dagan's brother. In fact, it was one of your sketches that caught someone's attention at the CIA. They believe one of the confirmed dead was Lieb Dagan."

"This just seems so farfetched." Amy shook her head in disbelief as two cars approached.

Brent stood, shielding Amy from the road. Jim and Katherine came to stand beside Amy. Brent turned and said to Jim, "Keep them here. I'll be right back."

Brent moved forward and shook hands with the six men who emerged from the cars. A few minutes later, he returned with four of the men and introduced them as Secret Service.

"These men will stay with you here while we flush out any problems at your house."

Jim looked at him, confused. "I don't understand. I thought you said you didn't want me to call Secret Service yet."

"I contacted them through secure channels. When they tell you, I want you to make a call to Secret Service as though you just found out about the two hostages. If anyone is out there waiting to impersonate them, we'll know it within a few minutes."

Jim nodded, understanding dawning. "Just let me know when."

Brent glanced at Amy before speaking to her protectors. "Keep them safe."

The men nodded and set about deploying their manpower to do just that.

* * *

Leaves rustled in the summer breeze. A bird chirped in the distance. The sound of children laughing rang out down the street along with the noise of a passing car. A man walking a German shepherd passed by on the sidewalk in front of the Whitmore home, glancing for a moment at the quiet surroundings.

Brent peered through the shrub he was hiding behind, listening for any sound that didn't belong. He saw a shadow move in front of the living room window, a shadow he knew to be Tristan giving the appearance that there was someone home. The whole team had arrived within an hour of receiving Brent's call.

From his perch in the top of an oak tree, Kel watched the traffic on the street, occasionally glancing over at the front of the house. He watched two cars drive by. He checked his watch and shook his head. Nearly five minutes had passed since the senator had made the phone call to the Secret Service. If something didn't happen within the next ten minutes, they likely had made the trip to the Whitmores' home for nothing.

A plain black sedan approached on the street, slowing as it neared the Whitmores' driveway. "I've got something," Kel said into the mike on his earpiece. He looked through his binoculars and counted two inside the car. "Two confirmed in the car."

Seth's voice came over the line a moment later. "We've got confirmation that Secret Service did not send anyone else out."

Silence hung in the air once more as the car slowly pulled into the driveway. The curtain moved inside as Tristan played his part. A moment later, two men stepped out of the car, one with jet-black hair and the other blond. Both were dressed in the dark suits common to Secret Service agents. They even had the subtle bulges beneath their jackets and the earpieces for communication. Slowly they scanned the area before the dark-haired man moved to the front door. The other man stayed by the car, his eyes sweeping the yard.

The man by the door rang the bell. He waited patiently while Tristan peeked out from behind the curtains once more, and then his footsteps sounded in the entryway. As the door creaked open, the man moved for his inside pocket as though reaching for identification. The movement stopped immediately when he looked up to see Tristan holding a pistol to his forehead.

In the same instant, Seth moved forward with his weapon also trained on the man by the door as Brent and Quinn emerged from opposite sides of the yard, weapons aimed at the blond man standing by the car.

The man by the door found his voice first. "What's the meaning of this? Senator Whitmore sent for us."

"I don't think so," Tristan drawled as Seth reached into the man's pocket and pulled out a semiautomatic pistol.

Seth shook his head as though scolding a naughty child. "That doesn't look like identification to me."

Seth and Tristan secured the first suspect as Quinn apprehended the second, shoving him against the car while instructing him to assume the position to be searched. Brent kept his weapon trained on the blond as he moved forward to look into the back seat of the car. He saw the figure crouched down in the back seat, gun in hand, just in time to jump out of the way. Brent dove for the ground as he shouted, "Gun!"

Quinn dropped down to the ground next to Brent just as a gunshot shattered the rear window. The man Quinn had been searching immediately broke free and took off across the side yard toward the trees. He turned to shoot at Brent and Quinn but he never got the chance. From his post twenty feet away, Kel pulled the trigger of his rifle and dropped him in one shot.

An instant later the man in the back seat scrambled out of the car, squeezing off a round of gunfire to keep the SEAL unit at bay as he started toward the backyard.

"Check Blondie," Brent yelled at Quinn, referring to the man Kel had shot. Knowing that Quinn would comply, Brent scrambled to his feet and started after the man sprinting around the side of the house.

Brent was within fifteen yards of catching him when the man turned and aimed his gun once more in Brent's direction. Anticipating the shot about to be fired, Brent stopped abruptly and dove behind a mature oak tree in the backyard. His back pressed against the thick trunk of the tree, Brent crouched down and waited as shots were fired in his direction.

A rapid burst of gunfire sounded. It was over in an instant, the silence of the backyard once again broken only by quick footsteps. Satisfied that the terrorist was once again retreating, Brent peered across the yard in time to see the man duck into the woods. Perfectly aware of the threat this man was to Amy, Brent angled across the yard at a dead sprint, glancing back in time to see Seth trailing behind him.

Their training took over as both men moved quietly and steadily through the trees, listening for the man they were tracking. Brent stayed in the lead, and several minutes passed before he finally caught sight of his target. Now winded, the man still held his weapon in his right hand as he reached a small clearing.

Brent picked up a stick and tossed it a few feet away. The moment the man turned toward the sound, Brent pounced forward and kicked the weapon free of his hand. As the man bent down to retrieve the weapon, Brent dove forward and used his body to knock him to the ground.

The man bucked to get Brent off of him, but Brent just sat up and shoved a knee into the middle of his back, pulling one of the man's arms behind him. He heard Seth approaching to back him up and fought against a grin when Seth squatted down beside them, and deliberately cocked his revolver.

Seth waited for the man to turn his head, waited for the acknowledgement in the man's eyes that his struggles were in vain. Then he said, ever so casually, "Now, I think it's time you cooperate."

Brent patted the man down, confiscating a pistol, a knife, and a fake set of Secret Service identification papers. A few minutes later when the police arrived to take the prisoners into custody, Kel stood looking down at the forged documents.

"It isn't a very good forgery. Looks like they didn't want to take the time or spend the money for the high grade stuff."

"Or they knew that their IDs weren't going to be looked at closely anyway," Quinn commented. "After all, their victims were expecting them."

"What's the status on the other hostages?" Brent asked Kel, glancing briefly at the real Secret Service agents who were currently sweeping the area.

"Three of them are still in the hospital, and the security has been increased there. The Brits took our advice and pulled the same stunt at the other hostage's place in London. They only sent two assassins for her."

"Now what?" Brent asked.

Kel shrugged. "Secret Service will provide protection for the Whitmore family for the foreseeable future, and customs will red-flag anyone coming into the country who has been in Abolstan in the past couple of years."

"Hopefully this attempt was the one and only," Quinn said, though he didn't sound very convincing.

"Thanks for trying, but we all know better than that." Brent shook his head. "Dagan is ruthless. No matter what battles he is fighting in his own country, if he wants revenge, he isn't going to stop until he gets it."

"I don't think it's just revenge he's after," Seth interjected. "He knows one of the hostages helped stop that subway attack."

"Even if he did make that connection, that's water under the bridge," Quinn pointed out. "Why go after the hostages now? The damage has already been done."

"Unless the subway attacks were just the beginning." Brent looked at Seth, concerned that he might be right. "He thinks the hostages have details about another attack."

Kel dropped a hand on Brent's shoulder in a gesture of support. "It doesn't matter what his reasons are. We'll get Dagan eventually. It's only a matter of time."

* * *

"I can't believe this is happening." Katherine sat down on the living room couch, gripping her husband's hand.

"Everything is going to be okay." Jim patted her hand with his free one and looked over at Brent. "I appreciate what you did today."

Brent simply nodded.

Amy leaned against the arm of a chair and looked from her dad to Brent. She sensed the lingering tension from both men and was afraid of what it meant. "You think something like this will happen again."

"I wish I could tell you that this failed attempt will be the end of it, but Dagan isn't known for giving up," Brent told her, his voice serious. "The Secret Service is already assigning agents for your protection."

"Hopefully just their presence will keep Dagan's men from trying again," Jim suggested, trying to hide the doubt in his voice.

"I hope so," Katherine added.

"Me too," Brent agreed, though he was relieved to see the doubt in the senator's eyes. Brent took a step toward the door. "I had better get going. I have some reports I need to take care of before church tomorrow."

Amy stood. "Thank you again for everything."

"My pleasure." Brent gave her a quick smile. He turned back to the senator. "Senator, you should probably change the codes on your security system."

"Oh, I will."

CHAPTER 22

"I just don't understand why you don't want to go to church with us." Jim adjusted his tie, annoyed that his daughter was skipping to go off with Brent Miller again, especially after the scare they'd had just the day before and the lingering threat of a repeat performance. "Everyone really wants to see you."

"Dad, you keep telling me that it's going to take some time for me to get over what happened in Abolstan, but then you get mad when everything isn't normal." Amy let out a frustrated sigh. "I feel like I can't win."

"After yesterday, I think it's going to take a while before any of us feel normal again."

Amy closed her eyes and took a deep breath. She still couldn't believe that someone would try to kill her because of a grudge any more than she could believe two of the other hostages were dead. Hearing about the men who had been sent after her still seemed surreal, and she already dreaded having two Secret Service men following her around everywhere. More, she worried that they would serve as a constant reminder of how her day could have ended yesterday had Brent not been with her. "I don't want to think about it, okay?"

"I just don't understand why you couldn't go to the singles ward here."

"Then I would have to deal with Jared. I hardly call that an improvement," Amy said as the doorbell rang.

"What's wrong with Jared Elliott?" Jim asked, his voice rising. "The man's been in love with you for years."

"No, he's been in love with my trust fund for years," Amy returned evenly. She picked up her purse, pulled open the door, and stepped outside, shutting the door behind her. She nodded at the two men guarding her door and turned to Brent, "Ready?"

Brent looked at her, confused, but nodded. "Are you okay?"

"Yeah." Amy headed for his car, impatience shimmering from her as the two special agents got into their car and prepared to follow them. "Just trying to deal with those problems I tried running away from."

They were almost on the beltway before Brent broke the silence. "I should have called and asked you earlier, but my mom invited us to dinner after church tonight. That is, if you're up for it."

Amy nodded, trying to shake off her mood. "I'd like that," she said, but then thought of her dad once more. "I have to ask, though, are your parents going to be as tough on me as my dad is on you?"

Brent laughed. "Are you kidding? My mom was so excited when I mentioned you to her that she even decided to forgive me about her garden."

"Happy to help." Amy grinned, her previous argument with her father temporarily forgotten.

When they arrived at the church in Fredericksburg, the parking lot was nearly empty. Brent helped her out of the car, keeping her hand in his as they walked inside. The opening hymn was just starting when they took their seats, but Amy was surprised that only about forty people were in the chapel. Her protectors followed them inside and took seats in the back.

She shook her head at the thought that she needed protection inside the chapel, but still she glanced around the room before training her attention on the pulpit.

Two members of the congregation spoke, followed by a member of the stake high council. The talks were predictably on temple marriage, and Amy wondered if she just always happened to pick the ward that had chosen that topic, or if it was used more frequently in the singles wards.

As soon as sacrament meeting ended, Brent slipped an arm around Amy's shoulder. "We just stay here for gospel doctrine class."

She was just starting to relax, thinking that this might be a stress-free evening after all, when the teacher singled her out and asked her to introduce herself. Reluctantly, she stood up. "I'm Amy Whitmore. I'm just visiting from northern Virginia."

She felt the ripple of whispers go through the congregation as she sat back down. Awareness dawned in the teacher's eyes as he stumbled over his words. "Well, um, welcome."

The teacher then asked the two men in the back to introduce themselves, and Amy could feel a blush rising to her cheeks as one stood, nodded at Amy, and said simply, "We're with her."

Beside her, Brent ran his fingers lightly over her back. He leaned closer, and she expected him to make some funny comment. Instead, he said simply, "I'm glad you're here."

After the closing prayer was said, Brent stood and led her into the hall, anticipating his friends and acquaintances wanting to meet Amy. "Do you want to go to Relief Society, or would you rather just head straight to dinner?"

"Dinner sounds nice," Amy agreed quickly.

As soon as they were in the car, the two agents quietly trailing them, Brent commented, "I'm sure things will calm down after a couple of weeks."

"I guess I didn't expect people down here to know who I was," Amy admitted. "Especially since the problem at my house yesterday was kept out of the news."

"That's true, but not many people are reported to have fallen from a helicopter one day and then reported fine two days later."

"What?" Amy's eyes widened, and she turned to face him. "That was on the news?"

"Yeah." Brent glanced over at her. "I'm sorry, I thought you knew. Someone leaked information out while we were still trying to get out of Abolstan."

"Mom said something about how she couldn't watch the news anymore, but I just thought it was because of the hostage situation in general." Amy rolled her eyes with disbelief. "No wonder that destroyer was looking for us when your team pulled us out. Who in the world could have been dumb enough to leak that information?"

"I don't know, but that's one of our top priorities next week," Brent admitted. "In fact, Kel put me in charge of the investigation since I'm the only one they know couldn't have slipped up. Unfortunately, this is just the latest in a string of security breaches over the past couple of years."

"I hope you find whoever it was."

* * *

Brent hadn't been exaggerating when he'd told Amy that his mom was excited about her coming to dinner. She had set the table with the good china, polished the silverware, and had even made Zeke, her beloved black lab, stay in the backyard. Even now Zeke was lying on the deck, looking mournfully through the glass and waiting for someone to let him back in.

The two agents who were following Amy around had opted to wait outside rather than intrude, so for the moment Amy felt almost normal.

"Sister Miller, you have a beautiful home," Amy said as she and Brent sat down on the stools next to the breakfast bar that separated the modest kitchen from the family room.

"Thank you. We actually moved in here about a year before Brent was born. I imagine he's one of the few around here that spent his entire childhood in one house." She glanced up as the front door opened. "Oh, good. That must be your father. He had a meeting after church."

"Am I late?" Tom Miller asked as he entered the kitchen and kissed his wife's cheek.

"Right on time." Dana Miller smiled up at her husband. "Tom, this is Amy Whitmore."

"Good to meet you." Tom stepped closer and reached over the counter to shake her hand. His dark eyes were quietly appraising, his smile warm.

"It's nice to meet you." Amy said as she shook hands with the tall, lanky man who looked a great deal like Brent.

Dana glanced at her watch. "Dinner is just about ready. Brent, why don't you get the drinks."

He nodded, crossing the kitchen and pulling glasses out of the cabinet. He glanced over at Amy and asked, "Do you just want water?"

"Yes, thank you." Amy stood and crossed to him. "I can help you put the drinks on the table."

Brent handed her two glasses and then proceeded to fill two more before leading her into the dining room.

A few minutes later they all sat down to eat. After the blessing was said, Brent's mom dished out the chicken parmesan. Brent eyed it suspiciously, cutting off a small bite to sample.

Pleasantly surprised, he cut off a larger bite, considering. His father didn't make Italian food, and his mother didn't make food period. As he prepared to enjoy the meal before him, he spoke to his mother. "This is really good, Mom. Who made it?"

Amy's eyebrows rose at the subtle insult.

Noticing her expression, Brent explained, "Mom doesn't cook."

"He's right." She nodded and motioned to her husband. "Tom does most of the cooking. I'm much better at dialing for take-out, but today our neighbor down the street cooked for us. She heard Brent was bringing a friend to dinner and decided it had been too long since we've had her chicken parmesan."

"Pass along my compliments." Amy smiled. "It's delicious."

"Do you cook, Amy?"

She shook her head. "Not at all. I'm afraid my homemaking skills are definitely lacking."

"But you can sew," Brent pointed out.

"Only out of absolute necessity."

Conversation was easy, and Brent found himself oddly unsettled at how comfortably Amy chatted with his parents on a wide variety of subjects. After dinner, she helped clean up the kitchen before she let Brent take her home.

When Brent pulled up into the Whitmores' driveway, he reached out and toyed with her hair. "Thanks for making time for me this weekend."

"I can't believe the weekend is already over." Amy shifted to face him. "I assume you're back at work tomorrow?"

Brent nodded. "Hopefully I'll be able to track down that leak before anything else comes up."

"Let me know if there's anything I can do to help on this end. After what we dealt with when CJ was in the Witness Protection Program, I can guarantee that no one in my family said anything."

"That's good to know." Brent nodded, then glanced over at her front door, where a light was burning brightly. "If I didn't know better, I'd think your dad was waiting by the door for you."

"I do know better, and I'm sure he is." Amy laughed. "I'm sorry he's been so difficult. I think he's gotten worse since I moved out of the house. Now that I'm staying here, at least for now, he seems to think he needs to protect me." She glanced back at the Secret Service agents getting out of their car and moving to stand by the front door. "I'm starting to think that protecting me has risen to a new level."

"In that case . . ." Brent edged closer. "I'd better not wait to kiss you good night."

Amy met him halfway, leaning into the kiss that held warmth and promise. Brent shifted, changed the angle of the kiss, and was suddenly thankful that he was sitting down. He could run five miles and barely break a sweat, but suddenly, he wasn't sure his legs would be able to function. Forever hovered on the edge of his mind, evoking a fear greater than he would have felt had he been facing a dozen armed men.

When he stepped out of the car a few minutes later, he was grateful his knees didn't give way beneath him. Taking Amy's hand, he led her to the door. He managed a smile when Jim opened the door to welcome his daughter home. Brent greeted the senator, acknowledging the not-so-subtle look in his eye, the look that clearly said "Stay away." As he started home, he wondered how long the senator would let him date his daughter before he waged a full-scale war.

CHAPTER 23

Brent stared at the computer screen, convinced that he was going to start seeing phone numbers in his sleep. For three days he had been tracing phone calls for everyone who had access to the information that he and Amy had been left behind. He had started with the easy part first and cleared his team so that they could help in the research.

Tristan and Seth had interviewed all of the hostages who had survived the weekend. They found that the British woman had been the confirmation for the reporter who originally released the information. According to her, she had been instructed before being released from the hospital not to discuss the fact that Amy and Brent had not returned with them. When the reporter had indicated that Amy and Brent had already been rescued, she had assumed that the gag order no longer applied. That was when she had mentioned how worried she had been that they hadn't survived the fall.

Now he was concentrating on every call to the reporter during the day. So far only three numbers were unidentified. His phone rang and he snatched it up, hoping that Kel or Quinn was having more luck than he was. "Lieutenant Miller."

"Lieutenant, this is Doug Valdez from the FBI. I had a message to call you."

Brent flipped through his notes, refreshing his memory that Doug was the government liaison with the hostages' families. "Yes, Agent Valdez. I am investigating the leak to the press about Amy Whitmore's rescue. I was hoping you could help shed some light on who had access to that information in your agency."

"Just me, and I didn't speak to anyone about it except for the senator," Doug informed him. "The only reason I was asked to act as liaison was because of my prior relationship with the Whitmore family. I was the agent-in-charge for CJ Whitmore when she was in the Witness Protection Program."

"That makes more sense," Brent said, more to himself that to Doug. "I was wondering why someone in the FBI was involved in a military operation." Brent hesitated a moment and then continued. "Was the senator always on his home phone when you spoke to him?"

"For the first several calls, yes. The last time I talked to him he was at his office. That was when he told me he and Charlie were going to Cairo."

"Could someone in his office have overheard the conversation?"

"I doubt it. The senator is extremely conscientious when it comes to security," Doug told him. "Nothing irritates him more than the press getting hold of privileged information. Unfortunately, this isn't a new problem."

"Was he on an open line the last time you spoke to him?"

A long pause. "I tried calling his private line first, but it was busy, so I called the office number."

"Who answered the phone when you called?"

"It was a man," Doug told him. "And I don't think it was Jared."

"Jared?"

"Jared Elliott," Doug offered. "I can't imagine he would have leaked any information out, especially after all Amy has done for him."

Brent hoped his voice sounded professional when he asked, "Exactly what is his relationship with Miss Whitmore?"

"They were engaged," Doug replied.

"I see. Well, thank you for the information," Brent managed to say before ending the call. He swallowed hard, a ball of lead sinking in his stomach. He closed his eyes, focusing on the fact that he had said "*were* engaged," past tense.

Pushing back from his desk, he walked down the hall and stepped into Kel's office. He was on the phone, but he waved him in. When he ended the call, he turned to Brent. "Did you find anything?"

"Maybe." Brent leaned forward and put both hands on the chair across from Kel. "Has anyone done bios on the senator's staff?"

Kel shook his head. "I doubt it. Everyone on his staff has at least a secret security clearance because the senator is on the Senate Intelligence Committee. Why, what have you got?"

"As far as we can tell, the only hostage who was available to the press was the Brit. She admits to talking to the press, but she insists that the reporter approached her and already had a good deal of information." Brent straightened. "The aircraft carrier standing by was under a communications blackout, official use only, so we know it wasn't anyone from there. The admiral didn't inform anyone on his staff of the situation, and our team is clean. That leaves the senator's staff."

"But the senator didn't tell his staff that his daughter wasn't with the other hostages."

"At least not intentionally," Brent corrected. "Agent Valdez from the FBI said that the one time he talked to the senator in his office was right before he left for Cairo. It's possible that someone was listening in on the conversation."

"Then I guess we'd better start on those bios," Kel said with a nod.

Brent nodded. "Agent Valdez said a man answered the phone when he called, but that doesn't necessarily mean that he was the leak."

"See if you can match up any of the staff members' phone numbers to one of those to the reporter, and I'll have Tristan pull the background checks."

"You might want to have Seth take a peek at bank records too," Brent suggested. "An exclusive like that was probably worth something."

Kel glanced at his watch. "I'm meeting my wife for lunch at noon. Let's meet at eleven and see what everyone's got."

Brent nodded in agreement and headed back to his office. He looked up the home and cell phone numbers for each member of the senator's staff, disappointed when none matched the three unidentified numbers to the reporter. He proceeded to check the phone numbers for the senator's office, again coming up empty.

Not sure how else to narrow down the suspects, Brent looked up Senator Whitmore's private number, took a deep breath, and dialed the phone. The senator answered the phone with a simple "hello," throwing Brent off for a minute. He had expected a more formal greeting.

"Senator Whitmore?" Brent started. "This is Lieutenant Miller."

"How did you get this number?"

"I utilized my resources," Brent responded. "I'm sorry to use your private line, but I need some information and I thought it best not to use an open line."

The senator's voice softened fractionally. "What kind of information?"

"The day you left for Cairo, can you tell me if everyone on your staff was in that day?"

"As far as I know, but if you'll hold on I can check." Papers rustled in the background for a moment, and then Jim's voice came over the line once more. "Melissa, my assistant, was out that day, and Jared, my press secretary, was out of the office most of the day sending out a press release about my trip. Our fax machine was broken, so he was working in an office down the hall. Why do you ask?"

"I'm just covering all the bases," Brent replied, making notes by the two staff members' names he'd mentioned. "Thank you for your help, Senator."

Brent ended the call before the senator could turn the questioning around on him, and then he studied the list of the senator's staff members. He glanced at his watch, gathered his files, and headed to Kel's office.

"Haven't you figured it out yet?" Quinn asked him when he walked in. "I am so sick of this investigation."

"I think we've at least narrowed it down," Brent said, passing on what the senator had told him.

"You can rule out Julia Hernandez, too. She's out on maternity leave until next week," Quinn told him.

"Assuming that Jared Elliott wasn't in the office, that only leaves David Ackman and Colton Reilly." Kel leaned back in his seat. "Seth, what have you got on them?"

"No one had any large deposits into their bank accounts during the past two weeks," Seth started. "If a payment was made, it must have been in cash."

"What time did Valdez talk to the senator?" Kel asked Brent.

Brent scanned through his file. "The senator talked to Valdez a little before ten o'clock."

Kel turned to Seth. "What kind of financial activity do you have for the reporter that day?"

Seth rustled through some papers. Then a slow smile spread over his face. "At 12:16 P.M., the reporter charged lunch to her company's credit card at a restaurant that's only a few miles away from the Capitol Building."

Brent grinned. "The senator left his office around eleven to go pack for his trip to Cairo."

"Tristan, check out the security logs at the Capitol for that day. See if any of the staff members left around eleven. Quinn, make a visit to the restaurant and see if anyone can identify Ackman or Reilly." Kel turned to Seth. "You crosscheck the senator's staff's credit card records to see if we can narrow this down any more."

"I'll check out the unlisted phone numbers at the Capitol," Brent volunteered. "Maybe one will match those unidentified numbers."

"Just make sure you keep them out of trouble," Kel suggested, motioning to Tristan and Quinn. "I'm going to lunch."

* * *

Brent shook his head in frustration as he and Tristan studied the security logs of the Capitol. Security officers buzzed in and out of the building's security office as both men came to the same realization: both of their prime suspects had left the building within minutes of each other during the time in question. Even the receptionist and Jared Elliott had left during the critical window of time.

"It could have been anyone," Tristan finally said as he pushed back from the table.

"Basically," Brent agreed as a security officer approached.

"We identified two of those phone numbers you were looking for," the officer told them. "One is for a conference room, and the other is from Congresswoman Donlan's office."

"Thanks," Tristan said as he stood. "Maybe we'll have more luck with these."

"I'll check out the conference room," Brent told Tristan. "You see if the congresswoman remembers talking to the press that day."

Tristan nodded as they stepped out into the hall and he headed in the opposite direction of Brent. When Brent found the conference room upstairs, it was being used. He noticed two men in dark suits flanking a door a short distance away. Curiously, he walked down the hall, passing only four doors before he was standing in front of Senator Whitmore's office. He was debating whether or not to go inside when his cell phone rang.

He nodded a greeting to the two men guarding the door and walked a few yards farther down the hall before picking up. "Miller."

"The congresswoman said she sent out several press releases that day, and she remembers being interviewed by that reporter," Tristan told Brent. "Her story matches the phone records. It looks like that call happened around ten."

"What time was the call from the conference room?"

"Quarter after ten."

"It's only a few doors down from Senator Whitmore's office."

Another call beeped through. "Hold on, I've got another call." Brent flipped to the other line to find Quinn calling.

"I found the waitress who served the reporter at the restaurant that day," Quinn said. "She said the reporter was sitting with a good-looking man in his twenties with light hair."

"Is she sure it was that day?"

"Yep. She only works one day a week. She even remembers the reporter passing a thick envelope to him," Quinn informed him. "In fact, he was dumb enough to open it and she said it was full of cash."

"Get her info so the FBI can get an official statement," Brent instructed. "Then you can come meet me and Tristan over here."

Brent clicked back over to Tristan and updated him on the new information. "I want you to call the FBI and get them over here to conduct a search of the senator's office. Hopefully we'll find a trace of that money."

Brent had barely hung up when the phone rang again. This time Seth was on the other end. "What have you got?"

"I ran credit card activity on both of our prime suspects."

"And?"

"And I think I've found our culprit."

Brent listened as Seth detailed the credit card information for several members of the senator's staff. A grin crossed his face as all of the clues finally started pointing in one direction. "Call Tristan and fill him in."

"What are you going to do?" Seth asked.

"I'm going to wait around for the feds to arrive."

CHAPTER 24

After showing his ID to the men in the hall, Brent waited for nearly forty-five minutes outside Senator Whitmore's office before he finally got the call that the FBI had arrived with the search warrant. Impatiently, he pushed open the outer door of the senator's office and took a good look around. A woman he guessed to be about his mom's age sat at the reception desk, a phone to her ear. Across from her was another desk, the man who occupied it also on the phone. Brent glanced at the nameplate and turned to the third desk, the one right beside what he assumed to be the door to the senator's office.

Pretty boy was Brent's first impression as he summed up the twenty-something-year-old man who was currently tapping away on a computer. *Jerk* was his next thought.

The receptionist hung up the phone and turned to Brent. "Can I help you?"

"No, thanks." Brent shook his head, keeping his position just inside the door. "I'm supposed to meet someone here, but it looks like I'm a few minutes early."

The woman glanced at her appointment book. "Did you have an appointment with Senator Whitmore?"

"No, not with the senator." Brent shook his head. Anticipating that he was making the receptionist nervous, he considered his options. He could either announce that he was here to bring Pretty Boy in for questioning, or he could skirt around the truth. "I was planning on picking his daughter up for an early dinner."

Brent had the satisfaction of seeing Jared Elliott's hands freeze on the computer and his head turn toward him. Despite the fact that

Brent had already answered the receptionist, Jared asked, "Is there something I can help you with?"

"No, thanks," Brent said casually.

"You said you have a date with Amy Whitmore?" Jared started.

"That's right."

"I find that difficult to believe." Jared stood and stepped out from behind his desk. "I'm Amy's fiancé."

Brent's first thought was that no one else was going to marry Amy if he could help it. Even as that thought startled him, Brent rocked back on his heels, keeping his voice and his posture relaxed. "That's funny, she didn't mention it on any of our dates last weekend."

Jared's jaw dropped, but whatever response he had planned died the moment Jim Whitmore opened the door. When Amy followed him out of his office, Brent prepared to make his earlier excuse a reality. He saw the surprise in her eyes but moved forward as though she had been expecting him.

"Hi, honey." Brent ignored the warning look in Jim's eyes and kissed her cheek. "I hope I'm not late, but I got hung up at work. You did still want to go get some dinner, didn't you?"

Amy played along. "That sounds great."

"Amy, I thought you were coming with me to the Mitchells' dinner party tonight," Jared said, looking sincerely shocked.

"No, you assumed I was coming. You never actually mentioned it to me." Amy turned to Brent and gave a little shrug. "Jared has a bit of trouble understanding the word 'no.'"

"He has a lot of trouble understanding the word 'integrity,'" Brent added.

"What's going on here?" Jim finally asked.

"As I mentioned to you on the phone, I have been investigating the leak about your daughter's rescue." Brent motioned to Jared. "We found it."

"That's absurd," Jared insisted, leaning casually against his desk.

Jim shook his head in denial. "What makes you think Jared is involved?"

"The reporter who broke the story received a call from the phone in the conference room down the hall," Brent replied. "Two hours later, the reporter charged lunch at a restaurant just a short distance from here."

"Anyone could have used that phone," Jared pointed out.

"Yes, but the only people who could have gained access to the information about Amy and who also matched the waitress's description are you and Mr. Reilly over there."

Colton Reilly's eyes widened, but before he could defend himself, Brent did it for him. "Since Mr. Reilly was using his credit card in Georgetown at the same time the reporter was having lunch, that just leaves you."

"Perhaps you should consider taking a class in law," Jared suggested with a haughty tone. "All of this is purely circumstantial."

"That's true until the waitress identifies you." Brent had the satisfaction of seeing Jared's face pale. "And then of course there's your own credit card activity."

"What about it?" Jim asked before Jared could defend himself any further.

"He was using his cards frequently until the day you left for Egypt. His last charge was at the gas station down the block, which happens to be conveniently located on the way to the restaurant where the reporter ate lunch. The timing fits perfectly." Brent nodded toward Jared. "Since that day, he hasn't made a single charge. Makes me think he came into some cash."

Jared stepped forward, squaring off against Brent. "I don't have to listen to any more of this. I'm not saying another word to you without my lawyer."

"That sounds reasonable," Brent agreed. But when Jared tried to move to the door, he reached out and grabbed his arm. "But you aren't going anywhere until the FBI gets the chance to talk to you."

"Don't try to stop me," Jared said through gritted teeth. He slapped at Brent's hand, but Brent's grip didn't falter.

Brent checked the urge to slam him up against the wall, barely. Instead his voice was deadly calm when he said simply, "Mr. Elliott, I'm a Navy SEAL. Threats don't work on me."

The door opened and Brent watched two FBI agents step inside. "I believe these gentlemen are here to see you," he said to Jared. With some regret, he let one of the agents take custody of Jared as the other presented a warrant to Jim.

"Start with Mr. Elliott's desk," Brent instructed. "We're looking for a plain envelope. It might even have some cash still in it."

The agent nodded in response and started opening Jared's desk drawers and riffling through them. He searched the desk in vain, but when he searched the pockets of Jared's jacket, he pulled out an envelope containing almost a thousand dollars in cash.

Amy's eyes widened in shock as her father stepped forward.

"How could you do such a thing?" Jim accused, closing the distance between him and Jared. "You could have gotten her killed!"

Jared just stared at him, refusing to answer.

Suddenly compassionate to the shock and betrayal Jim was suffering, Brent nodded to the FBI agents and watched them escort Jared from the office. He then laid a hand on the older man's arm. "Senator, perhaps I can convince you to join me and Amy for dinner."

For a long minute, Jim stared at the door the FBI agents had just disappeared through. Slowly, he turned to face Brent and shook his head. "No, thank you. You two go ahead. I have a few things I need to take care of."

Amy slid an arm around her father's waist. "Dad, are you okay?"

"Yeah, thanks," Jim answered, though not convincingly. He started toward his office before turning back to face Brent. "By the way, I think it's about time you started calling me Jim."

"Thanks, Jim." Brent nodded, a silent understanding reached. "Did you want me to bring Amy back here after we eat, or shall I escort her home?"

"I have some late meetings, so I would appreciate it if you could get her home safely."

Amy reached up and kissed her dad good-bye and then followed Brent out into the hall. "I can't believe Jared was the leak."

"I can't believe you were engaged to the guy."

"I was young and stupid," Amy replied easily. She took three steps before she turned back to face him. "How did you know I was engaged to him?"

"I never reveal my sources."

"That I can believe."

* * *

Brent sat across from Amy at the McDonald's adjoining the Smithsonian's National Air and Space Museum. After the FBI took Jared into custody, Quinn and Tristan had headed back to Quantico, leaving Brent to spend time with Amy. Brent considered himself beyond lucky that he had insisted on driving his own car instead of carpooling to DC with Quinn. Brent glanced around the restaurant to see that Amy's security detail had taken their positions nearby. "When I offered to take you out to eat, I didn't mean McDonald's."

"But I wanted McDonald's." Amy dumped her french fries out of the bag and proceeded to squirt ketchup on them. "Besides, how often do you get a chance to just hang out at the Smithsonian?"

"I don't think I've been here since I was in high school," Brent admitted. "It's funny how those of us who grow up around DC don't actually take the time to come and see all the things that attract the tourists."

Amy lowered her voice and leaned closer. "Probably because we're so sick of dealing with the tourists."

"True," Brent laughed. "Now what? Do you want to go out and do something after dinner?"

Amy nodded at her security detail. "I don't think my friends over there will want me to play tourist tonight." She looked out through the wall of glass separating them from the oppressive heat and humidity outside and considered their options. "How about catching an early movie?"

"We can do that." Brent smiled. He collected their trash and dumped it into a trash can, then held out his hand to Amy. Together they made their way back through the crowded Air and Space Museum.

The heat enveloped them when they walked outside and turned toward the parking garage where Brent had left his car. Brent stopped long enough to talk to Amy's security detail, telling them where he was parked so that one of them could go get their car and meet them at the parking garage.

Despite the heat, the sidewalks were crowded with tourists and the occasional local. In the distance a baby cried, and on the grass a couple of kids were throwing a Frisbee.

As soon as they made it to Brent's car, Brent turned to Amy. "Did you want to find a movie theater here in DC, or would you rather go to one near where you live?"

"Let's go into Great Falls," Amy suggested. "I rode in with Dad this morning, so I don't have to worry about picking up my car."

Brent nodded and pulled out onto the street. They fell into easy conversation, and once again he was surprised at how comfortable he was around her. He thought of his earlier instinct that he wasn't going to let anyone else marry her, and a new sense of determination to spend time with her settled through him. His stomach clenched at the realization that he couldn't imagine a life without her, and he wondered if it was possible to fall in love in such a short period of time. Just as he felt the tension settling over him, Amy said something to make him laugh and he pushed those thoughts aside. He promised himself he would analyze his feelings later. Much later.

Instead, he debated with her about the Nationals' chances of making the playoffs, and speculated on the new players the Washington Redskins football team had picked up in the off season. When they arrived at the movie theater a few miles away from Amy's house, Brent was relieved to find that they even liked the same movies.

The theater was empty when they chose their seats for the evening showing of the latest comedy.

Amy settled down in her seat and turned toward Brent. "Now that your latest project is done, what happens next?" she asked, offering Brent some of her popcorn. "Will your unit stay in Quantico, or will you move back down to Virginia Beach?"

"The training course we're conducting at Quantico will last for another three months. After that we'll probably head back to Virginia Beach." Brent shrugged. "With this job, you can never be too sure."

"Can I ask you a question?" Amy asked tentatively.

Brent nodded.

"Why were you assigned to uncover the leak? I would have thought an investigation like that would have been turned over to the FBI or Naval Intelligence."

"That's usually true. I think it was partly your father's doing, actually. Congress is so fed up with leaks that they wanted to make sure the investigating officer couldn't have possibly been involved. Besides, intelligence is a big part of our job. Every once in a while, the powers that be like to throw a case like this at us and see how we perform."

Amy shook her head. "I still can't believe it was Jared. I don't think I've seen Dad this shaken up in a long time."

"Your whole family really should look into some kind of counseling. Your dad and brother have had their share of stress over the past few weeks," Brent said as another couple walked in and sat down a few rows in front of them. He glanced back at the special agents in the back of the theater and added, "Not to mention having a security team tagging along behind all of you now."

"Mom already arranged for counseling," Amy told him. "I think she's worried about how Dad is since the whole thing happened. Of course, she's just as worried that I seem too normal."

"Everyone reacts to things in their own way," Brent replied. "We have to go through a psych evaluation every six months for that reason. No one wants to find out the hard way that someone is having trouble dealing with the pressure."

The lights dimmed as a few more people entered the theater. Brent reached his arm around the back of Amy's seat and drew her closer. She leaned her head against his shoulder, feeling so completely normal that she could almost forget about the terrorists, the subway threat, and even Jared.

They laughed together at the movie, both grateful to be able to laugh again. The movie was almost over when Brent sat up and reached for his cell phone. She looked over to see him read the lighted display. He leaned over and whispered, "I've got to go make a call."

Amy nodded, then watched him leave the theater. She turned her attention back to the movie for about a minute before she decided to follow him out. When she reached the lobby, Brent was already heading toward her.

"I'm sorry, but I've got to go," Brent told her.

"Where?"

"I can't say." He nodded at the theater door and the two men who had just emerged from the theater. "If you want to stay and watch the rest of the movie, I'm sure the Secret Service can take you home."

Amy shook her head. "That's okay. Do you have time to drop me off at home on your way?"

Nodding, Brent took her arm and started outside. "I'm really sorry about this."

Amy got into the car and turned to look at him as he started the engine. "Brent, I understand. We both know that your job isn't exactly nine-to-five."

Brent gave a brief nod, already concentrating on where he would be going. A few minutes later he pulled up in front of her house. He turned his attention to Amy for a moment. "I'll talk to you later."

"Be safe." Amy reached over to give him a quick kiss good-bye.

"Always."

With that, Brent pulled away and disappeared down the street.

CHAPTER 25

Brent scanned the dark water, listening to the water ebb and flow around him. Even the moon was dark, and hazy clouds blocked the stars from his view. He turned his attention back to the only visible light for miles, the lamplight coming from the windows of the white yacht that was now only a half mile away.

He sensed Quinn beside him, not so much because he heard him but because he knew that was where he was supposed to be. Beyond Quinn were the other members of the squad. Steadily and stealthily they moved toward their objective.

The owner of the yacht, Fahid Ramir, was suspected of a number of crimes in the United States, among them providing weapons and training to known terrorists. Ramir himself was an American-born citizen, but his family still lived in the Middle East, and the latest intelligence showed that while he was American by birth, Ramir was anything but loyal to his countrymen. Intelligence also indicated that Ramir was on board his private yacht for a pleasure cruise with his family and that only two bodyguards had accompanied him.

Brent reached the yacht first, grabbing hold of the thick chains of the anchor while Quinn reached for the ladder at the back of the vessel. Simultaneously, they boarded the vessel with Seth and Kel right behind. Tristan had drawn the short straw and was waiting in the SEAL boat, ready to move in at their signal.

Dark as the night in their wetsuits, they drew their weapons and prepared to move forward. When Kel gave the command, they spread out and prepared to take over the vessel and hold those on board for questioning.

Silently, Brent moved downstairs with Seth right behind him. The first cabin they checked was empty, but when they moved to the second, they got more than they had bargained for. Four armed men were positioned around the room, one of them holding a boy of about nine or ten in front of him, a handgun aimed at the terrified boy's head. A couple was sitting on a couch in the center of the room, and the woman was sobbing.

The man holding the boy looked up as Brent and Seth entered. Brent saw the intent in his eyes and didn't hesitate. He fired, his shot merging with another. He could only watch in horror as his target collapsed along with the now lifeless child. His training clicked in when one of the other men turned his weapon toward Brent. The woman's cries merged with the gunfire as Brent and Seth neutralized the remaining threats.

He already knew, but Brent forced himself to move forward and check the boy for a pulse. The woman already had him in her arms, her dress stained with his blood. Her eyes looked up into Brent's, her hopes and prayers to be left unanswered as Brent shook his head and uttered a useless apology.

Behind him, Seth laid a hand on his shoulder, a gesture of comfort as well as a reminder. Despite the tragedy, they still had a job to do. With a subtle nod, Brent straightened and proceeded to help his team secure the rest of the boat. When they had finally completed their task and were on their way back to their ship, Brent closed his eyes and fought the images that just wouldn't go away.

* * *

"Are you okay?" Seth asked when Brent opened the door to their quarters on board ship.

"Yeah," Brent replied, referring more to the fact that the ship psychologist had cleared him for duty rather than whether he was able to deal with what had happened. He laid down on his bunk and closed his eyes but immediately opened them again. Because Seth had been there and understood, he let himself speak. "I can't get that kid's face out of my mind."

"I know." Seth shook his head. "But there wasn't anything you could have done to save him. If we hadn't gotten there when we did, the boy's parents would probably be dead right now, too."

"How could intel be so wrong?" Brent asked, frustrated. "No one had a clue that Ramir was holding that family there, or that he had a small army on that boat with him."

"It happens," Seth said simply. "It sure would have been nice to have had Amy Whitmore on intel for this one."

At the mention of her name, Brent propped himself up on his elbow and looked across the room at Seth. "What do you mean?"

"She sees things more like we do, not just what everyone expects her to see."

Brent shook his head and leaned back onto his pillow. "I doubt she could have made much of a difference this time."

"Maybe not, but we might have at least gone in a little more prepared for what to expect," Seth suggested. "Are you going to see her when we get back?"

Brent had been asking himself that same question for the past thirty-six hours since he had watched that little boy die. She had been completely understanding when he had been called in to work three days ago. He imagined she expected him to call when he got back, but he thought he knew her well enough to know that she wasn't going to sit around waiting by the phone until then either. Feeling Seth's eyes still on him, he shrugged. "I don't know."

"If you're not planning to hang onto that girl, you may need to get back in there and have your head reexamined," Seth told him. "She's one of a kind."

He could feel the truth of Seth's words as panic welled up inside him. Wanting the conversation to end, he forced himself to close his eyes, hoping that he could finally find some peace. Thoughts rattled around in his mind—first memories of the mission, then his analysis that nothing he could have done would have changed that boy's fate. Still, he felt a fresh wave of panic when the moment that the shots echoed flashed into his mind. When he let himself think of Amy, he felt another wave of panic rolling through him.

He couldn't love her, he assured himself, even though he knew it was a lost cause. He had never met anyone like her, and Seth was more right that he could possibly realize. She really was one of a kind. She was the only woman he had ever loved. And in time, she might come to love him, too.

For a brief moment, he let himself consider what life would be like if they married. He would be gone more often than not, never being able to tell her where he was or when he was coming home. If by some miracle they managed to have kids, she would basically have to raise them on her own. Once again the vision of the woman holding her lifeless son flashed into his mind. She had been helpless to stop his fate, just as Brent would be helpless to protect Amy and whatever children they might be blessed with.

Tears sprang to his eyes as he realized that if he truly loved her, he had to let her go. She deserved a rich, full life, one with a husband to share it with. She was entitled to have a husband who could fit into her lifestyle, one that included backyard barbeques and horseback riding on the weekends. He could never give her that, only a brief illusion of it every few months or so.

He waited until he was sure his eyes were dry before he opened them and looked over at Seth, who was sitting at the desk. "How soon do you think we'll get sent back to Virginia Beach?"

"I wouldn't worry about it yet," Seth told him, assuming that Brent wanted to stay at Quantico a while longer. "I think it's going to be at least another month or two."

Brent just nodded, wondering how in the world he was going to be able to stay away from Amy when she was only an hour away.

* * *

Amy really hated to shop. She reminded herself of this about six times on her way to the mall on Saturday morning, and another dozen times as she carried clothes in and out of various dressing rooms. Since she was six feet tall, most clothes just didn't fit right. She browsed through racks of clothes, her security detail following closely.

The majority of her wardrobe was still in Abolstan, and it was highly unlikely she would ever see any of it again. Yesterday her parents had pointed out the obvious—that she needed an entire new wardrobe before she could start work in just two more days. She had been managing for the past month with the few clothes she had left at her parents' house, but she had to admit she was getting tired of doing laundry every three days. In her wallet was her father's credit card, something she hated to use, but for once he had insisted and she had let him.

Frustrated that yet another store didn't have anything that fit her, Amy crossed over to the men's section and pulled two pairs of Levis off of a set of shelves. She checked the size on the label and then moved to a rack of T-shirts. Within ten minutes, she was able to round out her casual wardrobe to include jeans, workout clothes, and a couple of shirts. After paying for her selections, she then left the store in search of work clothes.

She wondered briefly what Brent would think if he realized that a good portion of her clothes came from the men's department. She didn't think he was the type to care, unlike Jared, who had been appalled that Amy would stoop to buying men's clothes instead of just having her clothes tailor-made.

Her father was still upset about everything that had transpired with Jared over the past few weeks. To give him some time to find a replacement for Jared, Amy had helped out in his office for a few days. If nothing else, it gave her something to take her mind off of the fact that she felt smothered by the presence of the Secret Service and the fear that someone might really want her dead.

Twice already she had been forced to stay home when potential associates of Namir Dagan had been discovered in the U.S. Each time, Amy felt like the house was closing in on her a little more. As much as she hated shopping, at least today she had successfully made it out of the house.

Though they had only attended one family counseling session so far, it did seem to help them deal with the stress a little better. If nothing else, her dad was recognizing that he had been as traumatized by the hostage experience as he thought Amy should be.

In her private session with the psychologist, Amy had found comfort in knowing that it was okay to have adjusted well. Admittedly she still had some apprehension at times, and occasionally a bad dream would startle her awake. But overall the psychologist agreed that she had moved past the experience and was ready to move forward. Now she just had to figure out how to find some kind of normalcy with two men following her around everywhere.

She walked past several stores, slowing when a dress in a store window caught her eye. Hopeful that she might be able to at least find one outfit she could wear for work, she walked into the shop, smiling when she realized that the store clerk was nearly as tall as she was.

"May I help you with something?"

"I sure hope so," Amy said with a smile. "I'm looking for work clothes, and I'm having a little trouble finding things that are long enough."

With a sincere smile, the girl nodded in understanding. "Let's start over here."

Amy followed behind her, pleased that the store carried clothes in tall sizes. She tried on one thing after another, enjoying herself for the first time all day. Four skirts, six blouses, and three dresses later, Amy noticed an elegant cocktail dress. Her mind turned to Brent, and she thought it would be nice to have something dressy to wear in the event they went out to the officers' club or an upscale restaurant.

She tried on the dress, first in a midnight blue and then in a cream. She chose the cream, and wondered if Brent would approve. Her hair was down today, but she imagined she would wear it up in some sort of elegant hairstyle with this dress. She moved to buy shoes to go with the dress, for once choosing heels instead of flats like she normally did.

She hadn't heard anything from Brent since he dropped her off at her house three days earlier, but she hadn't really expected to. For all she knew, he might be back by Monday when she started work or he could be gone for the rest of the month. She hoped that once her clearances were in order, she would always know exactly where he was and when he was coming home.

CHAPTER 26

Her clearances took longer than expected and it was Wednesday before Admiral Mantiquez called and told her when and where to report. To her surprise, he instructed her to report to the Pentagon instead of Quantico on Thursday morning.

She started her day with a brief meeting with the admiral. Frustration seeped through her when she realized she would spend her first month in training. The admiral couldn't even tell her where her new unit was at the moment, except that they weren't stateside.

By the time she arrived home after her first day of work, her head was spinning with rules, regulations, and acronyms she wondered if she would ever understand. She walked into the kitchen just as the phone rang. She plucked it up, grinning when she heard her oldest brother's voice on the other end.

"Matt! What are you doing home this time of day?" Amy asked, knowing that her brother's baseball schedule usually kept him out of the house every evening.

"Actually, I'm at the stadium, but I have a while before the game will start," Matt explained. "Tell me what's going on in your life. News is you haven't heard from your lieutenant."

"Does Dad call and give you hourly updates on my life or what?"

"Well, yeah." Matt laughed. "You'll have to let me know when he gets back so I can meet him."

"You just want to check him out," Amy accused, but there was humor in her voice.

"Same thing," Matt said carelessly. "Do you have any idea where he is?"

"No clue." She poured herself a glass of milk, considering for a moment before she decided to confide in her brother. "I don't know how you and CJ handled it, not knowing when you would see each other again. It's only been a week, and I'm going crazy."

"Yeah, but when CJ was in Witness Protection we knew we weren't going to see each other for months or longer. It wasn't like we were waiting around for a phone call," Matt said. "For you, there's no way of telling if he'll be gone for a day, a week, a month . . ."

"Or forever," Amy finished for him with a sigh. "I keep asking myself if I can live like this. I've only known him for a few weeks, and this has already happened twice."

"It'll be different now that you're working with his unit," Matt reminded her. "By the way, how does he feel about working with you?"

"I don't know. I haven't told him yet."

Surprise laced Matt's voice. "Why not?"

"I don't know." Amy dropped into a chair. "At first I was so excited to see him and I just wanted a chance to be normal for a while. I guess I was afraid that talking about his work would remind him of why we met and make him think that I'm only interested in him because he saved my life."

"Is that why you're attracted?" Matt asked with the bluntness only an older brother could get away with.

Amy rolled her eyes. "I don't remember giving you and CJ the third degree when you brought her home."

"You were too busy playing basketball and pretending to stay out of trouble."

"I didn't get into trouble," Amy said innocently.

"Much." Matt saw through her and directed the conversation back to his question. "You didn't answer me. If you had met your lieutenant under different circumstances, would you have gone out with him?"

"Probably," Amy replied. "I'm not sure I would have been as understanding about why he just disappears and can't call or anything for days at a time, but I would have gone out with him if he had asked."

"Then I think it's time you tell him about your new job. It's better that he hears it from you than from someone else."

"What if he doesn't want me there?" Amy asked, voicing her fears for the first time.

"From what I've heard about him, I'm sure he will."

* * *

"We're about done here if you want to go ahead and take off," Kel told Brent as they stored equipment from their earlier obstacle course training.

"What?" Brent finished storing his rappelling harness before turning to Kel.

"I just thought you might have plans tonight."

Brent shrugged. "Like you said, we're almost done here."

Before Kel could respond, Tristan walked up behind them. "Hey, Brent. Are you and Amy going to the dance tomorrow night up in Oakton?"

"I wasn't planning on it," Brent said, evading the question.

They had returned to Quantico over a week before, and he knew that everyone thought he was spending his free evenings with Amy. Even though he thought of his teammates as brothers, for once he didn't think they would understand his decision. Except for Kel, none of them had ever been in love. They would never understand what it was like to care so much for someone that their happiness was more important than anything, even their own. Even Kel's situation probably wouldn't help him understand Brent's decision. Kel's sense of duty conflicted with the life his wife wanted, and both of them still struggled with the lack of communication they had experienced before they married.

Brent had tried calling Amy twice over the past week to break things off, but each time he had received her voicemail and decided against leaving a message. When he noticed a photograph of her in the society page of *The Washington Post* earlier that week, he decided maybe a phone call wasn't necessary after all. The photograph had been taken at some White House dinner over the weekend, and she had been sandwiched between her father and some political aide. Brent's jaw clenched at the memory of the way the aide's hand had rested so comfortably around Amy's waist.

Tristan closed the storage locker and snapped Brent back to the present. "You two really should come. Maybe Amy can introduce us to some of her friends."

"We'll see." With that he turned away and got back to work.

* * *

Amy stepped into the cultural hall at the Oakton Stake Center and instantly wished she hadn't come. Independence Day was only two days away, and the cultural hall was decked out in red, white, and blue, reminding her too much of Brent and his dedication to serving his country. She tried not to think of the dangers of his job or where he might be right now. Instead, she let her eyes adjust to the dimmed lights and glanced around at the many familiar faces.

The girlfriend that had bullied her into coming to the dance was waiting for her just inside the door. She immediately dragged Amy across the room to meet a friend of her boyfriend. The poor guy looked as surprised as Amy was to be party to their friends' obvious matchmaking scheme. Reluctantly he asked her to dance, and Amy promised herself that she would find some excuse to spare both of them from any of their friends' expectations.

She had barely made her escape when one of Jared's friends cornered her and wanted to talk about exactly what Jared had done to get arrested. Even though Amy insisted that she wasn't at liberty to talk about it, the friend persisted and Amy finally made the excuse that she needed to go to the restroom.

What she had hoped would be a brief reprieve turned out to be anything but. She opened the door to the restroom to find a few of the women from her singles ward inside. Instantly she was bombarded with questions. What was it like when she was held hostage? Did she really fall out of a helicopter? How did she manage to get home? And then there was her favorite, "Is Charlie dating anyone right now?"

Using a combination of diplomacy and avoidance, Amy finally managed to break free from the inquest in the restroom only to find Tristan walking through the door into the foyer. Her eyes widened when Quinn and Seth followed them inside without Brent. Her first horrifying thought was that something had happened to him on his last mission. When Tristan approached with a smile on his face, other doubts started creeping in.

"Hi, Amy. I didn't think you were going to be here." Tristan reached out and shook her hand. "Brent acted like you weren't going to come."

"Really?" Amy asked casually even as her heart broke neatly in two. She knew in that moment that Brent didn't want to see her anymore. She had convinced herself she could live with the doubts, the insecurity, the waiting for the call she hoped would never come. Now she had to live with the fact that she had fallen in love with a man who didn't love her in return.

Oblivious to the battle waging inside her, Seth stepped beside Tristan and asked, "Where is Brent? Is he inside?"

She wasn't sure how to answer without letting them see how deeply hurt she was by what their presence meant. Had she not seen them, she would have just assumed that Brent was still on assignment. Drawing on all of her strength, she kept her voice light when she answered, "Actually, I'm not sure. A girlfriend had asked me to come with her before I had a chance to make other plans."

Tristan grinned at her. "In that case, save me a dance."

"Sure." Amy agreed even though all she wanted to do was go home and cry.

She kept up the pretense for nearly an hour before anyone realized a thing. When Seth noticed Amy trying to dodge the attentions of the elders quorum president, he moved in and rescued her by asking her to dance to the slow song that was just beginning.

"I'm surprised Brent didn't show up here tonight," Seth commented casually. "If he knew how many guys you've had to fight off, I think he would probably stick to your side like glue."

Amy didn't say anything, but Seth felt her tense. He looked down at her, and for a long moment he said nothing. Finally, he spoke softly. "Did he even call when we got back?"

She shook her head and sniffed back the tears that she refused to let come. She took a deep breath, hoping her voice was steady when she finally spoke. "Would you mind walking me out to my car? I really don't want to be here, but I doubt I can make it past my friends without some help."

"No problem." Seth nodded and took her hand to lead her across the cultural hall and then through the foyer where her protection detail was waiting. The two men followed Amy and Seth out into the parking lot and headed for their car as Seth escorted Amy to hers. "I assume you don't want the rest of the guys to know about our talk?"

Amy shook her head, focusing on digging her car keys out of her purse. When finally she found them and unlocked the door, she turned to look at Seth. "Thanks for walking me out."

"You're welcome." Seth took a step back toward the church and then hesitated. He turned back, his voice carrying just a hint of a southern accent. "I can't give you details, but the last mission wasn't an easy one for Brent."

"But he's okay?"

"Yeah, he's okay."

Amy nodded, and without a word she got in her car and drove into the darkness.

* * *

Brent walked into the office on Tuesday morning, his mood surly. He had let his mom rope him into dinner the night before, and her endless questions about Amy had been more than he could take. He had finally made excuses to get out of attending the fireworks display at one of the local churches. Instead, he had gone home to sulk. He was tired of everyone assuming that he and Amy were a couple even though he had only known her for barely more than a month. To hear his mother talk, one would think she expected to hear wedding bells any minute.

He saw Quinn first and nodded a greeting rather than taking the effort to speak.

"Hey, Brent." Quinn stepped into his path rather than letting him just walk by him. "We missed you at the dance Saturday."

Brent shrugged and started to move past him.

"You know, you really should have come," Quinn continued. "We did what we could to help Amy fight the guys off, but some of them were pretty persistent."

Brent looked at Quinn now, considering. His already lousy mood darkened, but he managed to say, "I'm sure she appreciated that."

Before Quinn could continue the conversation, Brent continued down the hall to his office. He was nearly to his desk when he noticed Seth standing just inside the door.

"Did you need something?" Brent asked briskly.

Without a word, Seth closed the door and then turned back to face Brent. "What's going on, Brent? What happened with Amy?"

"Since when does everyone think they have the right to intrude on my personal life?" Brent shot back irritably. He pushed the button to turn on his computer in the fleeting hope that Seth would just go away. He should have known better.

Seth just stared at him, watching him with those deep, dark eyes. He took his time about answering, but when he spoke, Brent felt the truth of his words spear through him. "I'm your friend, and I'm worried about you. I know you have feelings for this girl, but I can't figure out why you're trying to blow it."

Brent ran a hand over his face and let out a sigh. "I don't want to talk about this, okay?"

"No, it's not okay," Seth shot back. He was usually a man of few words, but when the situation called for it, he could spar with the best. "You fall in love with an incredible girl and then you break her heart. What is wrong with you?"

"I can't let her live like this!" Brent's voice rose. "I owe it to her to let her get on with her life—a normal life."

"Maybe she doesn't want a normal life," Seth suggested mildly.

"What do you expect me to do? Marry her?" Brent asked, and then he rushed on when he saw the answer in Seth's eyes. "Would you really want someone sleeping beside you when a nightmare wakes you up, a nightmare you can't even talk about?"

"If you love each other, you both owe it to yourselves to talk this out," Seth insisted. "How can you say you love her, but then not give her any choices about her own future?"

Brent just shook his head. "Please." His voice softened. "Can we please end this discussion?"

"Suit yourself." Seth rested his hand on the doorknob. "But if I were you I would at least talk to her."

Brent watched him leave, grateful that he closed the door behind him. He leaned back in his chair and just let himself stare into space. *Seth doesn't understand,* he told himself. He was doing Amy a favor by leaving her alone and letting her get on with her life. He shut his eyes against the images Quinn had painted of Amy dancing with a bunch of other men. *She's better off without me,* he assured himself. *She couldn't possibly be happy married to a Navy SEAL.* Eventually he would get over her. After all, supposedly time heals all wounds. He very nearly believed it.

CHAPTER 27

Her training was nearly done. Amy walked beside her escort through the halls of the original headquarters building of the Central Intelligence Agency. They passed by the wall where portraits of past directors hung neatly and then turned the corner and moved through the glass-encased hallway to the new headquarters building.

Today she would finally get to work on a case that related to her new job. Even though she had done well in her training, doubts were creeping in as the day drew closer that she would start working with Brent's unit. She knew now that he didn't want to see her. Of that she had little doubt. She just had to figure out a way to live with his decision.

Her heart ached, something she had never known was physically possible. She forced herself to go through each day wondering if she could possibly do this job knowing that she would have to see Brent every day. After the time they had spent together, she knew he cared for her, at least to some extent. She just hadn't wanted to consider that he really might not be the marrying type.

With four of the five men in his unit single, she wondered now if all of them kept their relationships from getting too serious because they knew their careers would always come first. For all she knew, Brent had backed off from her because he didn't want things to get too serious. She wondered if he knew that she had already completely fallen for him.

Over a month had passed and she hadn't heard anything from him—not even a courteous phone call to let her know he was okay. She thought that maybe she could have convinced herself that he was just on assignment somewhere if she hadn't seen his friends at the dance.

After talking with Seth, she had made some casual inquiries as to how many positions existed like the one she was slated to fill. She had found that there were three others that were currently vacant, but the one with Brent's unit held the highest priority.

Understanding that she would be filling an important role within that unit, she had decided to take the job and then request a transfer as soon as someone else became available who was qualified to replace her. All of the other open positions were located in California rather than Virginia, but she was willing to make that move if it meant she wouldn't have to face Brent every day.

She tried to push him out of her mind as she was shown to a conference room. A woman was already sitting at the table with a file open in front of her. When she noticed Amy, she stood up and moved to shake her hand. "You must be Amy. I'm Glenna."

"Nice to meet you."

"Let me show you what we've got here." Glenna motioned for her to sit down and slid a file to her. "Basically, we're taking the raw intelligence on a recent case and preparing an intel report as though we are getting ready to send a SEAL unit into a combat situation."

"So this is like a test, to see if I can put the pieces together?" Amy asked.

Glenna nodded. "In a manner of speaking. Management likes to conduct these reviews every so often to help evaluate our intelligence-gathering and interpretation processes. I was chosen to help you because I just transferred from another office and I don't have any firsthand knowledge either. The combat situation is an actual scenario that the unit you will be working with went through recently."

Amy pulled a notepad out of her briefcase as Glenna gave her some basic instructions. A few minutes later she sat down and started reading through the first file. She noticed a date, realizing that this must have been the mission that had called Brent away so suddenly when they were at the movies together.

Other than breaking for lunch, the two women worked silently beside each other throughout the morning and into the afternoon. Only an hour after lunch Glenna closed her file and pushed back from the table. "I'm done except for typing up my report. Are you close to being finished?"

Amy nodded. "I'm getting there."

"Go ahead and use that computer when you're ready," Glenna said, pointing to a PC in the corner of the room. "I'll be back to check on you when I finish."

Amy nodded and turned back to finish reading the bio on Fahid Ramir and his family. She scribbled a few more notes and then moved across the room to type up her report. She tried to imagine what Brent and his team would need to know if they were going into a potentially hostile situation. The answer was simple: everything.

Once she got started, everything just flowed from her mind to her fingertips and finally into the computer. When Glenna came in, Amy didn't break stride, afraid that she might lose her train of thought as she approached her conclusions. Ten minutes passed before she finally finished and turned to see Glenna sitting at the table waiting for her.

"Done?"

"I think so," Amy said, and she hit the print button. "Now what?"

"Now we get to meet with someone familiar with this situation and defend our findings." Glenna told her.

With a nod, Amy collected her report from the printer. She skimmed over it while Glenna went to find the person they were supposed to meet with next. Amy stood when Glenna returned with a man in his forties. She introduced him simply as Kyle.

Kyle motioned for Glenna to sit down next to Amy, and he chose a seat across the table from them. "Glenna, why don't you go first."

Glenna nodded, beginning by going over the basics, when the yacht had set sail, who was rumored to be on board, the eyewitness account that Ramir had been seen on board before the yacht set out. She then went on to make her assumptions, many of them based on the interview with an eyewitness.

As Glenna continued, Amy started to question whether she had read too much into the reports. Her list of assumptions, or rather possibilities, was extensively longer than Glenna's, and their analyses of how many people were on board varied greatly.

When finally Glenna finished, Kyle turned to Amy. "How does your report compare to Glenna's?"

Amy glanced over at Glenna, recognizing that Glenna had significantly more experience and was more likely to have made an accurate analysis. For a brief moment, Amy was tempted to say that their reports were similar, but she just didn't have it in her to lie. "Actually, we have a lot of differences."

Kyle nodded and leaned forward. "I know it's difficult, but try to pretend that you haven't already heard Glenna's analysis and tell me what you think."

"Our basic facts agree," Amy started. "But I'm concerned about what time the yacht set out. Leaving in the middle of the night suggests that something was going on they didn't want anyone to see."

"Like what?"

"I don't know exactly," Amy admitted, and she flipped to the second page of her report. "The receipt from the local market makes me think that we are dealing with at least twice as many people as what the eyewitness reported. And they ordered hot dogs and macaroni and cheese."

"Hot dogs?" Kyle asked, an eyebrow lifting.

Amy nodded. "According to the bio on Ramir, all of his children are already grown, and none of them have children of their own. It makes me ask why he would order hot dogs, especially since its doubtful his family would eat pork because of their religion. Besides, that isn't something that one would usually find on the menu on board a luxury yacht."

"If you had to speculate, what does this tell you?"

"It tells me that someone else was on board besides Ramir's family, most likely including at least one child between the ages of two and ten. The hour they departed suggests that some of the people on board may not have been there of their own free will."

Kyle nodded and pushed back from the table. "Thank you, ladies. I think I have heard enough."

"Did you want us to consolidate our reports?" Glenna asked, also standing.

Kyle shook his head. "That won't be necessary. I'll just take a copy of your individual reports."

Amy shuffled her notes together and slipped them into a file along with the finished copy of her report. "Is that it for today?" she asked Kyle.

"Yes. Glenna can show you out, and then I believe you will report to your new job tomorrow." Kyle walked to the doorway and then turned back. "By the way, the child was nine."

Amy smiled, pleased that her analysis hadn't been completely off after all. As she studied Kyle's face and realized he had used past tense when he referred to the child, her smile faded. "Was?"

Kyle gave a brief nod and continued out of the room.

Amy felt a wave of grief wash over her as she thought of the child whose life had been cut short. Her next thought was of Brent. He had been there. He knew that an innocent life had been taken, and he had had more than just a brief mention of the tragedy. He had lived it.

Beside her, Glenna turned to face Amy. "Is he saying that a child was killed because no one noticed hot dogs on the grocery list?"

"I think so."

Nervously, Glenna turned and gathered up the files they'd been using. When she turned back, a sheen of tears were in her eyes. "I read right over that grocery list and didn't notice anything at all. I mean, I thought it was weird for rich people to eat hot dogs, but . . ." Her voice trailed off.

"I think in cases like these, it's best to give too much information than too little," Amy said gently. "The people relying on this information don't assume anything. That means we can't either."

"If I didn't know better, I would swear you were the one who'd been working here for five years instead of me." Glenna shook her head. "Where did you learn so much?"

"In Abolstan."

CHAPTER 28

"Looks like you were right." Kel dropped a file marked "Top Secret" on Brent's desk in front of him. "Intel did mess up this time."

"What?" Brent looked up, his eyes sharp. "How did we get them to admit that?"

"CIA had two people do intel reports based on the original information available before we moved in." Kel sat down in the chair across from Brent. "One of the reports was almost identical to the one we got. That's the other one."

Brent flipped open the file and scanned the report. His eyes widened when he saw the mention of the grocery list, including the quantity of food as well as the fact that hot dogs were on the receipt. "Hot dogs." Brent shook his head. "How did everyone miss that?"

"They had an eyewitness that saw Ramir's family board the yacht. The source was reliable, so everyone just skipped over the information they thought wasn't important," Kel replied. "The good thing is that this case will be used to illustrate how important these mistakes are and how to avoid them."

"They need more people like the one who wrote this report," Brent said, flipping back to the first page. He noticed Amy Whitmore's name on the author line just as Kel spoke.

"The CIA doesn't get her." Kel waited for Brent to look up at him before continuing. "We do."

Brent's eyes widened. "What?"

"She starts tomorrow." Kel stood up. "Get with Seth and figure out where we want her to set up. One of you can share an office with her, or you can double up so she can have her own."

"You can't be serious," Brent managed, still trying to catch up. "Amy Whitmore is filling our support position?"

"That's what I said. Admiral Mantiquez had to do some fast talking on our behalf to keep one of the California units from snatching her from us."

"This isn't happening," Brent muttered to himself.

"Oh, it's happening all right." Kel turned toward the door. "I want an office set up for her before our training session this afternoon."

Brent could only stare as he watched Kel walk out the door. He shook his head, his mind still trying to comprehend the situation. *I can't do this,* he thought to himself. He was used to working through hopeless situations, overcoming impossible odds. But suddenly he wasn't sure he could face this kind of impossible odds.

How could he get over her if he had to see her every day? He had already chastised himself for his behavior in the desert. More than once he had fought the temptation to kiss her when they were in Abolstan. If he could barely maintain a professional distance in a hostile country, how in the world could he steer clear of her under normal circumstances?

He tried to consider the current dilemma of where to set up her office. Tristan and Quinn were already sharing one of the four offices allotted to his team while they were temporarily stationed here at Quantico. As the commanding officer, Kel needed to keep a private office. That left the options that Kel had already spelled out. The thought of sharing an office with Amy was just too uncomfortable, and though he trusted Seth completely, he didn't like the idea of Amy spending her day in an office with him either. Reluctantly, Brent got up and crossed the hall to Seth's office.

Seth had the phone to his ear, but he motioned for Brent to come in. "Just make sure it gets here before ten thirty," Seth was saying. "I'll be here, thanks."

Seth hung up the phone and stood up. "So do you want to move or do you want me to?"

"It doesn't matter." Brent felt himself give up the fight. He was emotionally drained and he didn't want to make any more decisions today, especially about Amy Whitmore.

"In that case, let's get your stuff moved over here," Seth suggested. "I've got a desk and computer coming this morning, and the phone guys will be here this afternoon to take care of the phones while we're out."

"Fine." Brent turned back to his office and prepared to pack up his desk to make room for the woman he thought he had already shut out of his life.

* * *

Amy showed her new ID at the main gate, followed the guard's directions to the building where she would be working, and parked her car in the employee lot. Now that she was working on a secure military base, the Secret Service agents assigned to her had scaled back their hours with her. On work days they would merely follow her to the front gate and then return to escort her home at the end of the day, when their surveillance would continue as usual.

Threatening clouds loomed on the horizon, a few sprinkles hitting the windshield as she grabbed her briefcase and did a quick search for her umbrella. Realizing that she must have left it at home again, she pushed open the car door and headed across the parking lot. She was still twenty yards away from the building when the heavens opened up and the rain started sheeting down around her.

She hastened toward the door, thankful she wasn't wearing heels. Still she managed to get drenched as she made her dash inside. She pushed her wet hair out of her face and glanced down at the water pooling at her feet. Self-consciously, she stood on the doormat and let the water drip off of her for a minute while she considered what to do next.

When three more people rushed in behind her, all of them in a similar state, including the one holding an umbrella, Amy decided that some things just couldn't be helped. Turning to the woman standing beside her, she asked, "Can you tell me where the ladies' room is?"

"Down that hallway on the left," she said, wringing out her hair. "Just don't use all of the paper towels."

"Deal," Amy laughed and moved in the direction the woman had indicated. She found the restroom and used a combination of the hand dryer on the wall and some paper towels to help her go from drenched to merely wet. She tried not to think about the time she had spent that morning putting on her makeup and fixing her hair. Instead, she wiped off the mascara that had pooled under her eyes and went to find her new office.

She found Kel in his office, his door hanging open. She knocked on the doorjamb, and he immediately stood. "Welcome aboard."

"Thanks." Amy shook his outstretched hand, noticing his subtle assessment of her now-soaked clothing.

"Come on." Kel stepped out into the hallway and motioned to the door next to his. "We made room for you in here."

She stepped inside, her shoes squishing as she walked, and looked at the simple furnishings. A computer sat on top of a plain wooden desk, and an empty set of shelves was across the room next to a file cabinet. Two mismatched chairs were in the room, one behind the desk and the other situated across from it. Amy set her briefcase down on the desk and turned to face Kel. "Where do you want me to start?"

"First, I'm going to scrounge up some fatigues for you. You're going to be miserable if you have to sit in those wet clothes all day," Kel said. "Then I'll get a copy of our office procedures and training schedule so you can get familiar with what we have planned for the next few weeks."

Amy just nodded as he disappeared back out into the hall. Rather than sit down and soak her chair, she moved to open the file cabinet. The first drawer held only two files; one contained the training schedule Kel had mentioned, and the other a list of contact numbers.

She turned when Kel rapped on her door and stepped inside holding out some dry clothes. "Here you go. These should fit you."

"Should I ask where you got them?" Amy asked tentatively.

Kel grinned. "Let's just hope Quinn doesn't get caught in the rain, too."

"Thanks," Amy laughed. She motioned to the filing cabinet. "I found a copy of the training schedule. I'll read over it after I change."

"Good," Kel replied. "We're going to be out of the office this morning, but I should be back around lunchtime. If you run out of things to do, go ahead and run over to the exchange and the officers' club and familiarize yourself with the base."

"Don't worry about me," Amy assured him. She made her way back to the ladies' room. By the time she returned, Kel was long gone and there wasn't any life in any of the offices near hers.

She settled down behind her desk to start her first day and decided that maybe she could handle this after all.

* * *

Brent rushed down the hall and glanced at his watch. He had less than fifteen minutes to report to the helipad, and suddenly it was his job to find a copy of the flight authorization he had faxed in personally the day before. He rounded the corner, stepped into his office, and stopped short.

Sitting behind the new desk in his old office was Amy Whitmore dressed in army fatigues, her damp hair hanging loosely over her shoulders. She looked up, at once completely professional. "Hello, Brent. Did you need something?"

"Uh, sorry." Brent started to back out of the office and uttered a simple explanation. "I was just looking for a copy of our flight authorization."

"I already faxed it in." Amy stood and picked up a paper from her desk. "But here's a copy for you just in case they lose it again."

"How did you . . ."

"Someone called looking for it." Amy glanced at her watch and put the paper in his hand. "You had better get going."

Brent took the authorization from her and calculated how long it would take him to drive back to the helipad. Awkwardly, he nodded at her. "Thanks."

He raced down the hall, out of the building, and into the Jeep he had commandeered to make the trip across base. The helicopter was ready on the pad when he pulled up. Kel was waiting, motioning for him to join the rest of the team on board.

"Amy already faxed it over," Kel told him, jogging alongside him.

"Yeah, I know." Brent climbed in and took his seat. As they took off, he closed his eyes and tried not to think about just how good Amy looked in uniform.

CHAPTER 29

The first three weeks went by smoothly—unexpectedly so, in Brent's opinion. Of course, they had spent two and a half of those weeks in the field for a training exercise. Still, he hardly saw Amy at the office, and when he did see her she was professional and casually polite. If he didn't know better, he would have never guessed that they had spent days together alone in the desert or that they had spent hours talking before he left for his last assignment, not to mention sharing some unforgettable kisses.

He had just finished showering after a five-mile run when Kel walked in.

"Grab your gear. We're heading out in an hour," Kel told him. "Everyone's meeting at the helipad."

Brent nodded, wondering where they were headed this time. Forty-five minutes later he walked over to the helicopter, where Quinn and Seth were already storing their gear. Brent started to get on when he heard another vehicle pull up. He turned to see Kel and Tristan getting out of a car followed by Amy. Once again she was wearing military fatigues instead of one of the business suits or dresses that she usually wore to the office.

Brent turned to Seth. "What's she doing here?"

"Coming with us."

Kel moved in quickly. "Everyone on. It's time to go."

Brent started to voice his objection, but Kel silenced him with a single look. There wasn't time, and like it or not, Amy was coming with them to wherever they were headed. Whether it happened by coincidence or design Brent wasn't sure, but somehow he ended up sitting next to Amy.

He saw her close her eyes as they started to lift off, heard her control her breathing the way he had taught her when she needed to relax in tense situations. Instinctively, he reached over and laid his hand over hers, his stomach somersaulting when she turned her hand over and linked her fingers with his.

He could only imagine what she was thinking, whether she was remembering her first trip up in a helicopter, the one in which she ultimately landed the hard way, or if it was the way the helicopter jerked and evaded when they had finally gotten picked up over the ocean. The breathing techniques seemed to be working, and gradually he could feel her beginning to relax.

"Are you going to tell us where we're heading?" Quinn called out to Kel as they headed southeast.

"I don't know yet."

* * *

"Kel, you can't let her come with us," Brent insisted, fighting to keep the panic out of his voice. "She's a civilian."

They were already on board the aircraft carrier USS *Harry S Truman* and were expected to set sail in less than an hour. Quinn and Tristan were storing their gear, Seth was showing Amy around, and Brent was now praying he could talk some sense into his commanding officer. Kel checked something off of the list he held before looking up at Brent.

"Relax, kid. We're not taking her into a combat zone," Kel insisted. "She's not going to leave the ship."

"Right. She'll stay on an aircraft carrier that could be deployed at any time," Brent clarified, sarcasm dripping from his voice. "That's so much better."

Kel stood a little straighter, taking on an air of authority he rarely found necessary. "Like it or not, she's the best intel officer we've ever had in this unit. One of the objectives for this training mission is to see if a civilian can function effectively as an intel officer on board ship. Like it or not, your girlfriend is coming with us."

"She's not my girlfriend."

"That's your problem," Kel stated simply. "One way or another you'd better get your head on straight. If you don't think you can do your job with Amy around, tell me now."

The muscle in Brent's jaw twitched. "I'll do my job."

Kel simply nodded. "Tell everyone to meet in the briefing room in an hour. Amy too."

With a nod, Brent turned and went in search of his team.

* * *

Amy sat quietly near the back of the boardroom. She was one of only a few women in the room crowded with Navy personnel. She was also the only civilian, though the uniform she wore helped disguise that fact. Beside her, Seth pointed out the key personnel she would be working with. He had already introduced her to the commander of the air group and promised to show her how to find her way to the main areas on the ship she would need access to.

Brent slipped into the room just as the briefing was beginning. Amy didn't see him but rather sensed him taking the seat behind her that Quinn had saved for him. They had been working together now for weeks, and still her heart beat a little faster every time he was around. He generally avoided her, so they weren't together often, but every once in a while she saw something in his eyes that made her wonder if he still had feelings for her.

Of course, she was probably just imagining it. She knew she should try to move on, let herself go out with other guys in the hopes that she would get over him. The more she told herself to do just that, the more she realized that she was too far gone. Despite her best intentions, she didn't know how to fall out of love with this man.

She tried to focus on the words being said, the mission they had been called here to do. Her eyes widened as she realized that this training mission would put them in the Mediterranean Sea, just a few hundred miles off the coast of Abolstan. This time the SEALs weren't here to rescue hostages but rather would spend their time updating their qualifications for their flight status and conducting a number of other training exercises in the area. The ship's positioning was simply a matter of precaution in case hostilities in the area once again required U.S. intervention.

Behind her Quinn asked a question. Amy glanced back at him, instead finding herself looking into Brent's eyes. She felt her cheeks flush and quickly turned back to the front of the room. She closed her eyes for a moment, annoyed with herself. Somehow she had to find a way to get over him, or she really was going to have to put in for a transfer.

When the briefing wrapped up, Kel moved from the front of the room to where the rest of his team was sitting. "I want everyone to meet in our boardroom so we can go over our schedule and make sure we have everything we need."

They moved down the narrow hall to their temporary office. When Amy stepped inside, she looked around, surprised by the duality of the room. Computer terminals were set up on opposite ends of the room, three on each side. In the corner near the door, a television sat on a high platform. A couch stretched across the back wall, and a round table was set off to the side. Amy imagined it could be used as either a work table or as a place to eat if the need arose. A couple of other chairs were situated facing the television.

As soon as they were all inside their boardroom, Kel gave them their specific assignments. "Quinn and Brent, work up the mission plans for next week. Seth, make sure Amy knows how to access the cable traffic and the latest intel reports. Tristan, check the training schedule and make sure everyone gets enough flight time to stay current on their qualifications."

Amy and Seth moved to one side of the room, while Quinn, Brent, and Tristan each claimed a computer on the other side of the room.

"Can I ask a stupid question?" Amy asked Seth as she sat down at the computer on the end. She glanced over at Seth and continued. "Why did we only get an hour to get ready to leave? Obviously the Navy planned this exercise days ago."

"Actually, they probably planned it weeks ago," Seth commented. "They like to do that sometimes just to make sure we really can deploy without warning when we need to."

"Does this happen a lot?"

"It's hard to say," Seth told her. "Sometimes they really do wait until the last minute before they decide they want our squad to come along. Whatever the reason, we don't usually get a lot of warning that we're shipping out."

"I'm just glad I took him seriously when Kel told me to keep a bag packed and in my car."

"Definitely good advice." Seth laughed. "Especially when you don't live within five minutes of the base."

Amy nodded and turned to log on to the computer. Seth walked her through the process of accessing the secure cable traffic and the intelligence reports she would need. After they reviewed the cable traffic pertinent to them, Seth stood up.

"Come on. Let's get started on that tour I promised you," he said, motioning toward the door.

"What are the chances that I won't get lost at least once during this cruise?"

"None." Seth laughed and pulled open the door. "Don't worry. We'll draw up a map for everything you need to know."

Amy glanced back at Brent, the thought crossing through her mind that Seth couldn't show her everything she needed to know. As hard as she tried to convince herself that the reasons didn't matter, she needed to know why Brent had stopped caring for her. With an inward sigh, she stepped into the hallway prepared to deal with the challenges that she could conquer.

CHAPTER 30

Her first week on board the *Truman* Amy got lost more times that she cared to count. But gradually she learned her way around, and the number of wrong turns she made each day was now down into single digits. The crew was helpful and apparently accustomed to new personnel getting lost regularly.

The rest of the squad spent most of their time in the air or engaged in other training exercises. Amy worked with the personnel on board to make sure everyone completed their qualifications on the various aircraft on board. She seldom saw any of them except when they popped in for prayer each morning and to check their schedules.

Brent rarely said more than two words to her, and Amy often waffled between wanting him to come in so she could see him and hoping he stayed occupied elsewhere so she could pretend she wasn't thinking about him. Though she hated to admit it, she had little doubt that Brent didn't want her on board. During the first few days she came to realize that he wasn't the only one.

The first time she met the executive officer, Commander Dunnan, he gave her a curt nod and then spoke with Seth briefly before turning his attention elsewhere. Amy thought perhaps he was just busy and wasn't the type for small talk until she overheard him talking to Kel. She had taken one of her many wrong turns their fourth day out and had been just about to turn the corner toward the mess hall when she heard Dunnan's voice.

"I don't care who her father is, she shouldn't be allowed to just roam the ship."

Kel's voice was placating. "Come on, Al. She has top secret clearance just like the rest of us, and she's not going to get in anyone's way."

"How can you be so sure?" Dunnan shot back. "Civilians have no business being involved in day-to-day military operations. We have too much at stake out here to let some woman come on board so she can play soldier."

"It's not like that and you know it," Kel snapped. "Outside of the members of my squad, she's the best intel officer I've ever had. Like it or not, you're going to have to deal with it."

"I still think you're making a mistake having her here."

Amy had ducked into a stairwell to avoid being seen when footsteps had sounded toward her. Since then she had decided to steer clear of the commander as much as possible, but Kel apparently had other ideas. Every time someone had reports or any other business for Dunnan, Kel sent Amy to take care of it. She deliberately kept her interactions with him as short and concise as possible, but it didn't take much for people nearby to realize that the man didn't like her.

The excitement and novelty of being on a ship had worn off quickly as Amy spent much of her time alone in the squad's boardroom. Between the cold shoulder she continued to receive from the executive officer, or XO as he was more commonly called, and Brent's apparent apathy toward her, she was starting to wonder why she was even here. She had too much free time on her hands, and even her daily workouts and her frequent emails to her family didn't completely diminish the feeling that she just didn't belong.

She walked toward the mess hall to get some lunch, looking forward to some human companionship for a few minutes. She had made a few acquaintances during her first week, but when she walked in she was surprised at how few people were sitting down eating. Instead, a crowd huddled around the television playing in the corner of the room.

Amy felt the tension hanging in the air as she moved closer. On the screen, she saw images of a bus in London, bodies hanging lifelessly out the windows. On a nearby sidewalk a woman was sprawled beside a baby stroller.

Amy felt her eyes tear as she considered that such a young life may have been cut short. She blinked hard, trying to piece together the tidbits of information.

The sailor beside her shook his head. "Who would do something like this?"

Amy swallowed hard and forced the words out of her mouth. "What happened?"

"Someone released a biological agent on a bus in London. Everyone within a hundred yards was killed."

Amy immediately tensed, remembering vividly the attempt in the United States. She looked at the man beside her. "Have they said who is responsible?"

He shook his head. "It only happened an hour ago."

Without a word, Amy rushed out of the mess hall and headed for her team's boardroom. When she opened the door, Kel and Seth were standing in the middle of the room staring at the television.

"I just heard," Amy began, anger combining with sorrow as she glanced up at the horrific images once more. "Dagan's responsible, isn't he?"

"Nothing has been confirmed," Kel started, pausing as he looked over at her. "But it sure looks that way."

Amy turned away from the terrifying scene on the television and logged onto her computer. She glanced at the day's schedule long enough to see that Brent and Quinn were currently in an F-14 somewhere over the Med, and that Tristan was most likely still sleeping after returning from a flight early that morning.

She had just sat down to read the new cable traffic when Kel spoke. "Amy, you and Brent have the most firsthand knowledge of Abolstan of anyone on board. It looks like this is about to become command central as soon as intel confirms that Dagan is behind this attack."

"That could take hours, even days."

"Don't worry," Kel said. "An ensign is on his way down now with a detailed map of Abolstan and the surrounding area along with all of the recent aerial photos. Somehow we've got to figure out where they're making this stuff so we can destroy it."

No sooner had he spoken than the door opened. The ensign was about Amy's age, and he looked around anxiously until he recognized Kel as the commanding officer in the room. "Here you are, sir."

"Thanks." Kel motioned for him to set the map and the thick envelope he carried on the work table.

After setting down his packages, the man turned to Kel once more. "Is there anything else, sir?"

Kel nodded. "I'd appreciate it if you could run down to the mess hall and grab some lunch for us. I have a feeling it's going to be a while before we make it there ourselves."

"Yes, sir."

By the time the ensign left the room, Seth had already dumped out the aerial photos and started sorting through them while Kel rolled open the map and tacked it to the oversized bulletin board on the wall.

"How do we go about this?" Amy sat across the table from Seth and picked up a box of colored pushpins.

"We use those pins to code the map, marking it with the locations of the military installations. Blue pins for ones with naval bases, white for ones with air capability, and so on," Seth explained. He showed her how to identify the photographs, comparing them to the locations on the map.

Slowly, meticulously, they coded the map to identify where various military assets were located. When they had reviewed all of the latest photos, Kel stood with his hands on his hips staring at the map. "They could be making this stuff anywhere."

Amy moved to stand beside him, her mind whirling. "Before I was taken hostage, an intel officer at the embassy said it was dangerous to transport the evidence to the United States. I have to assume he meant the biological agent."

"Yeah," Kel responded. "He wouldn't have wanted to take the risk of it getting released on board an aircraft."

"But the terrorists all transported it safely," Amy pointed out. "I don't understand how they could transport it, but we couldn't."

"There must be something that makes it unstable that the intel officer was concerned about," Seth suggested.

"That could be anything: the altitude, air pressure, heat . . ." Kel trailed off as they all looked at each another.

Seth's eyes darkened. "If the biological agent is unstable in hot or cold temperatures, he wouldn't have been able to transport it in his baggage because the baggage compartments aren't climate controlled."

Kel nodded in agreement. "Call our friends at the CIA and find out everything they know about this stuff."

"I'm on it."

While Seth headed for a phone, Amy and Kel turned their attention back to the map.

"If it's sensitive to hot or cold, it probably isn't being produced anywhere in the desert. The temperatures are too extreme," Amy suggested, remembering vividly how cold the nights had been when she and Brent had traveled through that part of the country.

"That would eliminate most of their military installations." Kel tapped on the map where three pushpins were located, two on the coast and one about twenty miles inland. "Only these three are located in the milder climate."

Seth hung up the phone and grinned. "Our boys at CIA are sending us the report on the biological agent. Apparently it doesn't like high temperatures." He rocked back on his heels. "It also seems some of the components that go into it can't develop in the presence of salt water."

"Then this must be the place." Kel removed the green pin that had identified it as a military base and replaced it with a red one to distinguish it from the others. "That was almost too easy. Amy, find the photos of this one."

Amy nodded, shuffling through the photos as Kel called out which map grid she was looking for. After searching for a minute, she finally found the right one and pushed the others aside. "Got it."

"Let's take a look." Kel sat down at the table as Seth and Amy looked over his shoulder. The photo showed two clusters of antiaircraft guns, several unidentified buildings, and a number of tanks positioned around the perimeter of the facility.

Seth tapped the center of the photo. "Since there isn't a runway, they must be getting their air support from one of the nearby bases."

Kel nodded. "Take a look and find out which one is the closest with air combat capability."

As Seth checked the map and started shuffling through the photos once more, Amy glanced up at the television and the most recent newscast. She took a deep breath and forced herself to ask, "How many more attacks do you think they have planned?"

Kel looked at her, hesitating a moment before confirming her fears. "I would expect two or three more if they're using a plan like the one they had in DC."

"I just don't understand how these people think. What motivates them to kill innocent people?"

"It's their way of sending the world a message." Kel glanced up at the television for a moment before continuing. "The United Kingdom and the U.S. were the most outspoken countries about stopping Abolstan from developing biological weapons. They started out by taking some of our people hostage, and now they're waging war on us."

"Then we have to assume they'll eventually try for another target in the U.S."

Kel nodded. "I expect that as soon as we can identify Abolstan as being behind this, we'll strike before they get the chance."

Seth stacked all but two of the photos and set them aside, then laid the remaining two in the center of the table. "These two are close enough to provide immediate support. One is a small airbase, and the other is the naval base on the coast that is probably their most heavily armed base in the country."

The door opened and the ensign walked in along with a seaman carrying their lunch.

Seth picked up the aerial photos and set them beside one of the computers to make room for the food. The two men had barely set the trays down when Kel started barking out orders. He sent the seaman down to wake up Tristan, and the ensign was recruited to track down the executive officer while they continued to gather their facts.

As soon as they left the room, Kel turned back to Amy and Seth. "Seth, I want you to get on the phone with the CIA or whoever can tell us what to expect if we blow up the plant where they're making this stuff. Basically, we need to know where the kill zone is so we can see what kind of civilian casualties we can expect.

"Amy, I know it won't be easy, but see what you can find out about the situation in London. Start by calling the intel officer at our embassy there. Make sure they know that they should expect more attacks, and let's see if we can help identify who's responsible." Kel picked up a sandwich and moved to a computer. "I'm going to start working on a mission plan in case we're right about this." He motioned to the food on the table. "Grab something to eat while you have the chance. It's going to be a long day."

CHAPTER 31

Brent's first reaction when he heard the news was gratitude that Amy hadn't taken that assignment in London after all. His second thought was that it was time they put a stop to Namir Dagan and the terror he was unleashing on innocent civilians.

The minute he and Quinn had returned from their training flight, someone had been waiting with the latest updates on the situation along with orders for them to report immediately to their commanding officer. They had quickly changed out of their flight gear and headed straight for their boardroom.

Brent pushed the door open and was surprised to see Commander Dunnan, the XO, sitting at the table shoulder to shoulder with Amy. Neither of them even looked up, and Brent moved closer to see the papers spread out in front of them.

Amy tapped one of the papers in front of her. "I'm telling you, this has to be the route they're taking to transport this stuff out of there."

"You want me to take out a road even though we don't know if they're responsible?" Commander Dunnan asked in a condescending tone.

"Actually, taking out the bridge here would be better," Amy answered with a shrug, ignoring Dunnan's skepticism and his tone. "They can just reroute if the road is damaged, but if they can't get past the river, the only way to get the stuff out would be by helicopter."

Before Brent managed to find his voice, Quinn asked the question, "What are we working on?"

Dunnan glanced over at him and tapped the stack of photos in front of him. "These are the latest satellite photos of Abolstan. Assuming the theory is correct and Dagan is responsible, we are working up a strike plan." He nodded at the map. "We think we know where they're manufacturing their biological weapons, but the president isn't likely to authorize a strike until we can identify the culprit."

"Which is why we need to take out this bridge," Amy insisted. "We don't even have to claim responsibility. With the accuracy of our weapons, I'm sure some mid-range weapon could take care of it in one shot."

Dunnan let out a sigh. "We still need authorization."

Brent listened half-heartedly to the debate while Kel brought him and Quinn up to date on the situation. He turned to see Amy push back from the table, and from the look on her face he wondered if she was debating calling for authorization herself. When she picked up the phone, he was relieved when she didn't start the conversation with, "Hello, Mr. President."

Sitting beside her, Seth hung up the phone and pushed out of his seat. "We just got the estimate on the kill zone if we blow up the plant." He held out the satellite photo and tapped a finger on the map. "They estimate that the vapors from the explosion would affect everyone within a twenty-mile radius."

"The closest village is just outside that range," Kel said with a shrug. "It's risky, but the villagers should be okay."

Brent sensed Amy standing beside him. He looked down at her, startled by how pale she was. "Are you okay?"

She shook her head, and a tear spilled over. "The CIA just confirmed two more attacks. One was in Edinburgh, the other in Belfast."

"What?" Brent stepped back so he could see her more clearly as everyone stopped talking.

"When?" Kel interrupted.

"One was only fifteen minutes ago, the other a few minutes before that." Amy drew in a shaky breath and continued. "One of my contacts at the CIA was keeping track of the live satellite images from the base we've identified. Three cars just left the installation and are heading for the border."

Dunnan grabbed the nearest phone, motioning to Amy at the same time. "Find out how long it will take for those cars to reach the bridge." He then updated the captain with Amy's new information, detailing the plan to eliminate the bridge.

Amy made her call, and she had her answer in less than thirty seconds. "Their ETA at the bridge is twelve minutes."

"I don't know if our patrol is close enough to take out the bridge before then." Dunnan shook his head as he once again relayed the information to the captain. He hung up a moment later and turned to Kel. "I'm going to head back up to CIC." He glanced at Amy and added, "That's the Combat Information Center. I want you to keep me informed of any new developments." With a nod to Amy he turned and left the room.

* * *

Amy dialed the phone for the twentieth time in an attempt to connect with someone in London's Center for Disease Control. Apparently everyone was so busy dealing with their three tragedies that no one was actually in the office to take her calls. She hung up after yet another unsuccessful attempt.

She anxiously glanced up at the clock. Only seven more minutes before the three cars would reach the bridge. She knew it was unlikely that they could prove Abolstan responsible for the attacks in the next seven minutes, and she prayed silently that the Navy would succeed in destroying the bridge to eliminate any imminent threats until they could prove who had caused this nightmare.

Her eyes swept the room, and she knew that the rest of the team was working just as hard. Each of them was concentrating on different aspects of the strike that would destroy the weapons plant, none of them paying attention to the news that hummed in the background. Amy let out a little sigh as she let herself look up at the television screen.

In her mind, the most logical way to confirm that Dagan was responsible was to identify the biological agent that was used in the attack. Since they already had a sample of the deadly substance in the United States, all they should have to do was compare the sample with the weapon used today.

She had already contacted the CDC, and they had faxed over their report of the drug to her as well as to their counterpart in London. The substance they had confiscated in Washington was a new derivative of some drug with a name she couldn't begin to pronounce. Most of the information they had about it had come from a source in Abolstan that had caused the intelligence officer there to arrange for the meeting with the DCI.

The report listed the various technical data that could be used to match their sample to samples being taken at the scene of the first attack. As she watched the television, a reporter came on the screen dressed in a hazmat suit. His voice was muffled as he pointed to the scene behind him, the site of the first attack. The camera showed several people working in the area, all wearing the required hazmat suits.

With a flash of inspiration, Amy snatched up her phone once more. The call to her father's secretary only lasted a minute, and two phone calls later she was speaking to the producer for the news broadcast she was currently watching. The beginnings of a smile lighted her face as the reporter signed off and the scene shifted to Edinburgh.

When her phone rang two minutes later, she sighed with relief as she spoke to the reporter who had just been on camera. When she explained she needed to talk to one of the British scientists, he was eager to help. A minute later one of the scientists currently taking samples on site came on the line. Amy relayed how critical it was for them to identify their samples and compare them to the samples obtained from the attempted subway attack in DC. She hinted at the possibility of more attacks if they couldn't gather the information quickly.

Amy agreed to send her report from the CDC to their makeshift command center, pleased that the scientist promised to gather the initial analyses and make the comparisons immediately. With a little sigh, she leaned back and prayed that this would all be over soon.

CHAPTER 32

Kel hung up the phone and turned to face the rest of his team. "Our patrol was two minutes late. The cars had already crossed the bridge."

"Did they still take out the bridge?" Tristan asked.

Kel shook his head. "They didn't want to alert anyone that we've identified their location." He pointed to the map. "Intel is trying to keep track of the three cars, but we only have about an hour before the first one gets to a heavily populated area. Once that happens, we're going to be hard-pressed to keep tabs on them."

Brent leaned back against the table. "Then we're going to have to plan a simultaneous attack on three moving targets as well as the military base."

Kel held up his notes. "Here are the projected routes of the vehicles. Let's figure out when the best time to strike is so that we can keep this stuff away from the populated areas."

* * *

The phone rang and Amy snatched it up, pleased to find that the British scientist was on the line. She grinned when she received the news and rattled off her email address so that he could transmit the official findings.

"We've got our confirmation. The Brits have matched the substance used in the London attack with the samples we confiscated in DC."

Kel nodded his approval. "Call up to the XO and let him know. Let's get the strike plan ready now. We don't want to miss this time."

Ten minutes later they were all staring at the maps trying to see something that wasn't there: the perfect timing. At any given time, at least one of the three cars would be near some kind of populated area, and they had no idea how much of the biological agent was being transported in each vehicle.

"Where would the least civilian casualties occur?" Kel voiced the question that none of them wanted to hear, much less answer.

"Right here." Tristan tapped the route of the car on the northern-most route. "There's a medium-sized town right beside the road, but the other two cars aren't near any kind of populated area at that time."

Quinn shook his head with disgust. "I wish there was a way to get the villagers to leave so that they'd be out of the kill zone."

"Actually, I have an idea," Brent said, breathing new life into the team. "When Amy and I were in Abolstan, we came across a village that had been abandoned just a few hours earlier because of a nearby battle. If we make it look like there's fighting nearby, they should head the other direction."

"How do you plan to do that?" Amy asked.

"A couple of well-placed missiles should do the trick," Brent suggested. "In fact, we should probably do the same thing in Abolstan to get the villagers to move away from the kill zone when we go in to strike there."

"That's a good idea," Kel said, nodding in agreement. "Amy, call the XO and tell him we're ready. Everyone get suited up and meet in the briefing room in five minutes. The rest of the pilots should already be in there standing by."

"What do you mean, 'the rest of the pilots'?" Amy asked, apprehension shooting through her as understanding dawned. She had never considered that this squad would be going into combat with the other pilots on board.

"We've got the most firsthand data, and we know more about the targets than any of these flyboys on board," Kel explained. "That means we're going along."

* * *

Amy had never seen anything like it. Briefing the pilots had only taken about three minutes, but those three minutes had been charged with an excitement level Amy couldn't compare to anything she had ever witnessed. These men were in essence going to war, and they were eager to do it. Not eager to kill, but eager to protect.

She sensed that the images they had all seen on television that day probably fueled their need to get out and do something, and for them that something was to exact revenge in a way that could protect their country and so many others from experiencing anything like this again. Assignments were given out—who would take out which target, who would intercept any enemy fighters, and so on. Then suddenly they were dismissed.

As the men filed out of the room, Amy caught a glimpse of Brent. She shifted uncomfortably when he returned her stare. Then he disappeared in the crowd filing out the door. Brent and Quinn had been tasked with firing the shots near the village by the military base to hopefully save innocent lives. She looked at the now-empty room, realizing that all she could do was pray that they would be successful and that they would all come home.

* * *

The sky was crystal clear, blue above and blue below all the way down to the Mediterranean. Brent had scored the pilot's seat in the F-14 since he had been next on the training schedule, and Quinn was operating as his navigator in the seat behind him.

"I always get stuck in the back seat," Quinn complained grumpily as he looked over the complex instrumentation he would use to help Brent achieve their objective. "How come you always get to fly on the real missions?"

"Because it's always my turn," Brent said simply, suppressing a grin. He could always count on Quinn to keep him loose. "Time to intercept?"

"Two minutes," Quinn replied. "The bombers are in place and are thirty seconds behind us."

"That's cutting it pretty close," Brent observed.

"We don't want the base to have too much warning. We can't be sure those antiaircraft guns aren't already waiting for us."

"How long will we be in range of the guns?"

"Fifteen seconds." Quinn checked in with the other team members, and then suddenly the target was right before them.

"Incoming!" Quinn shouted as the antiaircraft guns started firing. "Roll right!"

Brent rolled to the right as bullets flew within inches of the belly of the plane. He made another turn to avoid the steady stream of ammunition. His heart pounded and his fear surfaced briefly before he pushed it aside. Seconds ticked by slowly as he used a combination of instinct, skill, and luck to evade the bullets sparking in the sky around him. Finally he made it out of range and picked his target, a large tree a half mile from the village. From the corner of his eye he saw one of the Navy pilots take out one nest of antiaircraft guns. "Missile away."

"Let's get outta here," Quinn said as the bombers came into view.

Brent didn't respond as he navigated out of the kill zone to rejoin the squadron that was flying cover. He was moving too fast to see if the villagers heeded their warning, and he hoped that the estimated size of the kill zone was accurate.

Twenty seconds later, the bombs dropped and the military base ceased to exist.

* * *

Amy stood wide-eyed as she tried to decipher the pilots' voices as they reported in. She stood in CIC watching the intricate details that went into running a military operation. Each officer seemed to know exactly what to do, who to report to, and how to disseminate their information.

The first round of cheers startled her, but she shared in the joy when she heard that the military base had been completely destroyed.

The next few minutes seemed to take forever. Amy found it difficult to understand the overlaying messages as the pilots were given the precise locations of their targets. As she watched, officers communicated with members of the intelligence community to help guide the fighter pilots while also tracking a squadron of enemy planes being sent to intercept them.

The first two suspicious vehicles were neutralized just as they reached the Turkish border. Seconds later, the plane targeting the third car missed its objective as it came under fire from enemy planes. Amy understood little about what was happening except that several Navy planes were in the middle of a dogfight as the third car passed over the Turkish border. She turned her attention back to the radar screen where Commander Dunnan was now hovering. Communications overlapped as enemy planes were shot down, a tense voice rattled off a series of technical data, and the tracking continued on the third and final car. Tension was rising rapidly, and Amy struggled to understand the situation.

Suddenly, Dunnan turned to Amy. "Have all of your boys finished their weapons qualifications?"

Amy nodded. "What's wrong?"

"Enemy fighters have intercepted our planes that were after the third car. I'm diverting your team to finish up the job," the XO told her. "Who had the best accuracy rating from your team?"

Amy's heart lurched into her throat as she answered. "Lieutenant Miller."

Dunnan turned from her and rattled off the instructions Amy feared. Brent was being sent to intercept the last remaining threat, and in so doing, would have to pass through a war zone.

* * *

"I don't see the target," Brent said as he passed over the road heading toward the Turkish border. On his starboard wing, Seth was piloting another F-14 with Tristan in the back seat.

Behind him, Quinn rattled off the newly received directions and then checked the road himself. "I don't see it either."

Seth's voice came over the radio. "All I see is a truck up ahead."

"That doesn't match the information we received." Once again Brent studied the terrain below. Miles of open space stretched from the road to a ridge of mountains rising in the east. To the west the Mediterranean Sea glistened below them. Brent couldn't fathom how the car could have possibly disappeared from sight. "This doesn't make any sense." He spotted the semi-truck and considered. "The car has to be inside that truck."

"It's possible," Quinn admitted from the back seat.

"I hate to be the bearer of bad news, but we've already crossed into Turkey, and we aren't authorized to take out a truck." Seth's voice of reason came over the radio.

"Then get authorization," Brent suggested as he checked their location. "And you'd better make it quick. We only have ten minutes before the next town."

* * *

"How could we have lost it?" Dunnan's voice was tense as he studied the map in front of him.

Unsure of her current role in the situation, Amy stepped closer and looked at the map as well. Just sixteen minutes before, the planes had confirmed their target before diverting to engage enemy fighters. Three minutes ago, Brent had found no trace of the car. She considered Brent's analysis that the car was likely inside the tractor trailer and set about looking for any other possibilities.

Beginning from where they lost contact, Amy studied the terrain. The road followed the coastline of the Mediterranean, so there weren't any places to hide on that side of the road. On the other side was open desert leading to a mountainous region. Again, in the short span of road where they could have lost their target, there weren't any roads branching off of the main route. In fact, the only place they could have lost sight of the car was a single tunnel where the mountains abutted the road.

"When did that truck show up?" Amy asked finally.

Dunnan didn't respond, but the officer who was communicating with intelligence turned to answer. "It's been in front of our target the whole time."

"I assume it was going slower than the car we were targeting."

"Yeah," the officer responded. "One of our concerns was whether or not to let the car pass it before striking."

Amy turned to the XO. "Commander, the car was probably loaded into the truck inside this tunnel." She tapped on the map. "Either that, or the car is hiding in the tunnel."

"We have to confirm where the car is before we strike."

"We don't have time," Amy reminded him.

Dunnan turned to face her. "What do you suggest?"

"This stretch of road is isolated," Amy started, tapping her finger to the map. "If we take out the road right here in front of the truck, we'll stop the truck's forward motion, and then we can take out the road right before the tunnel to keep it from reversing course." Amy pointed at her suggested targets. "If the car is hiding inside the tunnel then it can't go anywhere either."

Reluctantly, Dunnan nodded. "Both sections of road are close enough to the mountain that a vehicle shouldn't be able to get by," he admitted. "That would give us time to send a couple of helicopters in to check out the tunnel."

Amy nodded. "Our troops would have to be outfitted with hazmat suits, just in case, but I doubt the driver is going to release the biological agent . . . unless he plans to kill himself too."

"Which is definitely a good possibility." The XO turned and relayed the suggestion to the captain. A moment later, the locations of the new targets were sent to Brent and Seth. At the same time, two fighter helicopters were deployed to help neutralize the final threat.

Two minutes later, Brent's voice came over the speaker confirming that the road had been destroyed in the two locations.

Amy waited anxiously as the minutes drew out while Brent was among the fighter pilots flying cover for the two helicopters entering the area. Suddenly, Brent's voice came over the radio. "Target acquired!"

"Where did it come from?" Dunnan asked one of his officers.

"It just emerged from the tunnel, sir."

A split second later, Brent's voice sounded again. "Missile away!"

A brief moment passed before one of the officers informed the XO, "The target was destroyed."

"Alert the Turkish border patrol of the situation. Make sure they know about the truck stranded out there," Commander Dunnan instructed. He turned to Amy, who was still trying to comprehend that the threat was really over. "You and your boys did a good job today."

"Thank you, sir." A surge of satisfaction flowed through her as she fought back a smile. "I guess I'd better get out of your way."

She took two steps before the XO called out to her.

"Hey, Whitmore." He waited until she turned and then said simply, "Welcome aboard."

CHAPTER 33

Brent didn't realize he was looking for her until he found her. Amy stood on deck looking out at the dark ocean, her hair pulled back in a ponytail. She had changed out of her fatigues and was in her own clothes again: jeans and a T-shirt. Above her the flight deck was quiet, at least for now.

She rubbed her arms against the chill of the wind coming off of the water but made no move to go inside. He considered leaving her alone, but his body moved forward anyway. He was only a few feet away from her when she sensed his presence and turned to face him.

Surprise registered in her eyes, but her voice was completely professional when she spoke. "Did Kel need me for something?"

"No." Brent shook his head. "I doubt he'll need anything until morning."

She nodded and turned to look back over the ocean. They stood there in silence until finally Amy turned back toward him. "I guess I should go in and get some sleep."

"You don't have to go," Brent heard himself say. "If you want to be alone, I can leave."

"I thought it was you who wanted me to be alone." Amy's voice was low, the words nearly lost in the wind.

Brent's eyes met hers. He saw the loneliness that mirrored his own. He felt the sizzle of attraction that he had been trying so hard to ignore these past several weeks. He knew he should turn away. If he didn't do it now, he wasn't sure if he would ever really be able to. As though his body wasn't listening to his reasoning, he stepped forward.

Her eyes met his, challenging, even daring him to stay. She'd never asked why he didn't call, not once. Now, he could see the questions there in the depth of blue, right along with the challenge for him to finally be honest with her. Giving in to his feelings, he heard a sigh escape, barely registering that it had come from him. Then suddenly the words were tumbling from his mouth.

"Do you have any idea how hard it's been for me to stay away?" He moved closer. "I wake up every morning thinking about you. You're the last thing I think about when I go to bed at night."

Amy's breath caught in her throat as his arm wrapped around her waist and drew her closer. She felt the truth of his words as his lips touched hers.

He drank in her sweetness, colors exploding in his mind as she responded to his kiss. She overwhelmed his senses—the softness of her hair, the feel of her hand on the back of his neck, the scent of her combining with the ocean air. He forgot about the frustration of the past few weeks, the difficulty of watching her each day, entrenching herself in his unit as a valuable, respected member.

Images flooded his mind: the first time he had seen her play basketball with some of the Marines on base, the way she chatted with the secretaries in the next office like they were lifelong friends, the first time she had offered morning prayer. The attraction he had first felt for her had deepened to include a respect and appreciation that continued to grow each day.

He heard her sigh, and panic overwhelmed him. He drew back, staring down at her. He had perfection in his arms, but what would happen tomorrow if he didn't come back? Or the next day? Fatalities in the teams were lower than the general public probably realized, due in part to the intense training, but the possibility still existed that one day he would leave on a mission or a training exercise and wouldn't come home. She deserved better than that.

Her big, blue eyes stared up at him, clouding with confusion as Brent released her.

"I can't do this," Brent heard himself say, even though his heart was shriveling at the thought of life without her. "You deserve someone better, someone who can come home to you every night. I can't be that kind of man."

Something flashed in her eyes but was quickly banked. She folded her arms across her chest, her voice even. "I don't believe I ever asked you to be anything but what you are."

"I'm sorry. This is my fault." Brent took a step back. "I never should have let myself be alone with you."

"You are such an idiot," Amy stated mildly despite the hurt she showed in her eyes. "You think you have the right to decide what I want my life to be like."

She stepped closer to the rail and then turned back before she continued. "Do you really think that by staying away from me it would be easier if something happened to you?" She shook her head and then continued, talking more to herself now than to him. "Actually, it would be worse. If we were married at least I'd have you in the next life. I guess you don't care for me enough to give me that."

Brent's eyes widened at her casual mention of marriage, and he saw the moment when she realized she had spoken her thoughts aloud. With a sigh, she forced herself to look him in the eyes. Her voice was soft now. "You might want me to find someone else, settle down, have kids. That would make it easy for you because then I would be out of your life, somewhere that you wouldn't have to see me. But that's never going to happen. I can't marry someone else when I'm in love with you."

"Amy," Brent said, even as she fought the tears that sprang to her eyes.

She just shook her head, stepping away from him and toward the door. "I'll talk to Kel. He can help me transfer to one of the units in California. It may take a couple of weeks, but you should be able to steer clear of me for that long."

A new sense of panic flooded through him, but all he could do was watch her go.

Brent stared at the hatch Amy had disappeared through for several long minutes before turning his gaze out to the open sea. Was it possible that instead of giving Amy the chance for a normal life, he was robbing them both of any chance of happiness? A memory flashed in his mind, the argument he'd had with Jim Whitmore when Brent had insisted Amy didn't want a normal life.

Moving to the rail, Brent bowed his head in prayer. Questions tumbled out of him, fast and furious. Was he really the man Amy was supposed to marry? Could they really find a way to balance family and his career? Tears welled up in his eyes as he asked the question that had been haunting him for weeks. Why did that little boy have to die?

Brent ended his prayer, struggling against his tears. He just stood there, staring out at the ocean. Slowly, a warmth spread through him as he realized that the little boy who had died so tragically was no longer suffering. He was in the Lord's care, away from the fear and pain that had taken him from this world.

The realization that the Lord would watch over him and Amy during their lives overwhelmed him for a moment. Didn't his unit start each day with a prayer for that reason? They all knew that whatever happened, their Heavenly Father had the power to protect them from danger, just as He had the power to take them from this world. His heart jumped into his throat as he considered that—just maybe— the Lord had put Amy in his path for a reason.

His eyes lifted from the dark ocean to the stars above as he considered his future in a new light.

* * *

Amy walked into her temporary office to find it empty. She dropped into the chair in front of her desk and decided it was probably best she didn't find Kel tonight. He'd already had a long enough day fighting terrorism and deserved a little time off. Her time with Brent kept running through her head over and over.

She was a fool to think that he had changed his mind about her. She had honestly believed when he kissed her that everything was finally going to fall into place. How could he say that he thought about her all the time and then spend so much time avoiding her? What was he so afraid of?

For weeks she had tried to pinpoint exactly when Brent had lost interest in her, or more accurately, when he had decided he didn't want to be interested anymore. She thought that she had been more than understanding when the call had come while they had been at the movie together, but obviously that had been the beginning of the end. He had dropped her off at her house and then just disappeared from her life. Well, he would have disappeared from her life had Admiral Mantiquez not put her right back in the middle of it.

Perfectly aware that she was too restless to sleep, she logged onto her computer and started reading through the latest intelligence reports. When she failed to find anything of significant interest there, she then pulled up the previous mission files.

She was surprised to see that the report she did when in training at the CIA was now part of the file on her unit's previous mission. Skipping over her own report, she opened the summary of the last assignment, the same one that had called Brent away so unexpectedly.

She thought of the boy who had been killed during that mission, and something pushed her to find out just how he had died. She started scanning the detailed reports and then, suddenly, there it was before her. The moment that Brent had been stolen from her, the moment he had been a second too late to save the little boy's life. She couldn't even begin to comprehend what that must have done to him, seeing an innocent life taken.

Could that be why Brent hadn't called her when he had returned to the United States? Was it too painful a thought now to start a family of his own? She thought of his words on deck. He seemed to think that she should have some normal guy in her life. Maybe it wasn't her that he was running away from, but rather relationships in general.

None of the other guys in the unit were married except for Kel, and it hadn't taken long for Amy to appreciate how much effort he made to spend time with his wife when he was in town. She sensed after meeting Kel's wife that she didn't like her husband's long absences, but Kel appeared to spend a lot of time with her when he wasn't on assignment. Maybe Brent didn't think it was worth it, the sacrifices needed to balance his work with a serious relationship.

Amy closed the file and shut down her computer. There wasn't anything else she could do before morning besides sleep. She stood to leave just as the door opened and Brent walked in. He studied her for a moment, then took a deep breath.

"I owe you an apology," he said slowly, closing the door behind him.

"What are you apologizing for this time?" Amy asked, bracing herself. If he was going to apologize for kissing her, she might just have to haul off and hit him.

"For a lot of things." Brent took a couple of steps into the room. "For not calling you when I got back, for not explaining why I thought it was a bad idea for us to keep seeing each other."

Amy's voice held understanding when she spoke softly. "It was the little boy, wasn't it?"

Brent shut his eyes. "I can still see it, the moment the life just drained out of him. His mother screamed, and she held him, and all I could do was tell her that he was dead."

"I'm so sorry." She wanted to reach for him but was afraid to offer anything more than her words.

"When I saw the little boy's mother . . ." He broke off and shook his head. "She was completely devastated. Her world just stopped and there was nothing anyone could do to bring her son back to her."

"Brent, what happened was a tragedy, but I still don't understand what that has to do with me," Amy admitted softly.

"I was afraid of your feelings for me," Brent explained. "I knew you cared for me. I even hoped that someday you might love me, but . . ." He sighed and struggled to find the right words. "My job isn't exactly the safest in the world. I mean, fatalities are rare in the teams, but that possibility exists. I couldn't stand the thought of starting a life with you and then leaving you behind to finish it by yourself."

Amy just stared. Was it possible that he really loved her too? She forced herself to take a deep breath, and then another. "Can you stand the thought of me being alone for the rest of my life knowing that all I want is to be with you?"

Brent blinked hard, as though trying to bring her into focus. His eyes narrowed, and then he let out a short laugh. "You're serious, aren't you?"

Suddenly uneasy, Amy just shrugged.

Then Brent closed the distance between them. He reached out and touched her hair, tucking a stray lock behind her ear. "Maybe I should start over again. What I should have said up on deck was that I love you and I'm sorry I've wasted so much time being an idiot."

Slowly, Amy smiled. "That would have been a good start."

"And then I should have said that I've been miserable without you and then asked you to marry me."

"Even better."

"Well?" Brent's eyes widened in anticipation.

The smile turned to a grin. "Well what?"

Brent sighed in exasperation. "Will you marry me?"

"Yes, I'll marry you." Amy slid her arms around his neck. "Just promise me you'll always be careful."

"Believe me, if there's anything that can make life worth living, it's knowing that you'll be waiting for me when I get home." And then he kissed his bride-to-be.

EPILOGUE

For once in his life, Brent seriously considered tossing out everything his parents had taught him. He approached the senator's house and took a deep breath. He had to do this, but he didn't have to like it. How would he feel, he wondered, if a soldier showed up on his doorstep and asked for his daughter's hand in marriage? He'd probably grab the closest gun and scare him off. A corner of Brent's mouth quirked up as he considered the fact that the senator probably didn't own a gun.

Amy had returned home just three days before, when she and the rest of the squad had taken a Navy transport plane to Norfolk after being away for over two months. They had stopped at the naval base in Key West a week earlier, and Amy had made a point of making sure Brent could meet her brother Matt and his family. Though they had only managed to spend an hour together, Brent thought that he could easily be friends with Matt and CJ given the time and opportunity. They were both so genuine and down to earth.

Despite the progress he had made with Amy's father before they were deployed, Brent still wasn't sure what to expect from the senator. He had overheard enough of Amy's conversations with her father during their time together at sea to know that the senator was less than thrilled that she had been allowed to go along on their training mission. The one upside of Amy being on board was that she was present when they received the news that Namir Dagan was among those confirmed dead after their strike on the weapons plant, leaving her free to live a normal life once again.

In an effort to placate her father after her time away, Amy had spent the weekend at home and once again tried to fill her role as a dutiful daughter. Besides spending time with her family, she had also attended some political dinner on Friday night, just hours after she arrived home. Brent had gotten that little tidbit of information out of the society pages of *The Washington Post* rather than from their dozen or so phone calls over the past few days.

Now here he was on a Sunday morning preparing to fight an uphill battle. The engagement ring he had bought just the day before weighed heavily in his pocket, and he prayed he would have the opportunity to see it on Amy's finger by the end of the day. In a true act of bravery, he knocked on the door and braced himself for what would certainly be an unforgettable meeting. The door swung open, and Brent watched surprise register on the senator's face.

"Good morning, sir." Brent extended his hand, pleased that the older man shook it without too much hesitation.

"Lieutenant." Jim glanced over his shoulder momentarily and then turned back to Brent. "I'm sorry, but if you're looking for Amy, you missed her. She went with her mother to choir practice."

"Actually, I came to see you," Brent said.

"I see," Jim responded, his eyes narrowing. With a sigh, he moved back and motioned Brent inside. "Would you like to sit down?"

Though he would have preferred to stand, Brent took the seat offered him and forced himself to look the senator in the eye. "I'm sure you are aware that Amy and I have spent a lot of time together recently."

"I know that you were on assignment together," Jim stated simply.

Brent nodded and caught a glimmer of something in Jim's eyes. That something told him that he knew exactly why Brent was here and there was no way he was going to make this easy for him. That glint of challenge pushed Brent to get straight to the point of his visit. "I came here today to ask for your daughter's hand in marriage."

Jim was silent for a moment as he studied Brent intently. Finally he shifted in his chair and asked the obvious. "Have you already discussed this with my daughter?"

"Yes, sir."

"Am I to assume that she has already said yes?"

Brent nodded.

"Heaven forbid that I try to tell her what she can and can't do." Jim shook his head, partly in frustration and partly in admiration. "Exactly how long have you two been engaged?"

"Two months."

Jim's voice rose. "Two months?"

"Yes, sir." Brent nodded, rushing on before Jim could comment further. "Amy wanted to tell you and your wife right away, but I felt it wasn't appropriate until I could discuss it with you first."

Then, to Brent's surprise, his future father-in-law was grinning at him. "Well, you've got guts. I'll give you that." He paused for a moment. "Have you given any thought to when you want to get married?"

"As soon as we can arrange it," Brent told him honestly. "What do you think, Senator? Can you support our decision?"

"You're a good man, Brent." Jim stood up and extended his hand. "You have my blessing."

"Thank you, sir." Brent stood as well and managed a smile. "There's one more thing I have to ask you," he started, waiting for Jim to look at him before he continued. He didn't want to say the words, but he forced them out. "I need your promise that if anything ever does happen to me, you'll make sure Amy is okay."

Brent paused, not daring to even look into Jim's eyes. "I don't mean the money. I'll make sure she'll be provided for. I just need to know that she'll still have someone to rely on, someone to love."

The muscle jumped in Jim's jaw and for a moment Brent thought he had just undermined all of his dreams by pointing out once again what a high risk he was in the husband category. When he saw tears glistening in Jim's eyes he didn't know what to think.

Jim took a deep breath and finally spoke. "Both of you can count on my family to be there for you for whatever you need," he said, his voice hoarse. "Just remember that you have a lot more prayers now every day asking the Lord to keep you safe."

Brent felt tears sting his own eyes, and all he could do was nod.

* * *

"What did you do to my father?" Amy whispered as she led Brent out her front door. She had returned with her mother to find Brent and Jim chatting like best friends.

Brent grinned, waiting for the front door to close behind her before answering. "I just showed him what impeccable taste I have by wanting to marry his daughter."

"Are you really sure you want to go to church with my folks?" Amy asked hesitantly. "You'll probably be asked about a hundred times how you survived falling out of a helicopter."

Brent's grin widened. "You know, falling out of that helicopter was probably the best decision I ever made."

"Oh, really?" Amy's eyebrows lifted.

"It gave me the chance to get to know you, didn't it?" Brent reached for her hand and pulled her closer. "By the way, I got you something."

Amy's eyes widened when Brent pulled a ring box from his pocket and settled it in the palm of his hand. "If you don't like it, we can pick out something else." Then he flipped open the top, revealing a gold band with a single tear-shaped diamond.

"It's perfect," Amy managed, watching as he pulled it from the box and slipped it onto her finger.

"So are you." Brent kissed her hand and then slipped an arm around her waist. "I love you."

"I love you, too." Amy smiled, reaching up to kiss him.

They both ignored the sound of the front door swinging open. Neither of them could miss the humor in Jim's voice when he called out to Brent.

"Kiss my daughter later, Lieutenant. We're going to be late for church."

Brent just grinned. "Yes, sir."

ABOUT THE AUTHOR

Traci Hunter Abramson is originially from Phoenix, Arizona. After graduating from BYU, she worked for the Central Intelligence Agency for six years before resigning to become a stay-at-home mom.

Traci currently resides in Stafford, Virginia, with her husband and four children, where she serves as the stake Young Women's sports director. She spends much of her free time writing, reading, and transporting kids to sporting events (usually three at the same time on opposite ends of the county). She also coaches the North Stafford High School swim team. *Freefall* is her fourth novel.